Jake Edwards
&
The Gentle Phenomenon

Intro:

The 1960/70s, is a particularly potent time for us teenagers to spend our growing up years in, and although we would never admit it, very frightening.

All this freedom of choice is something previous generations of young men didn't have to concern themselves with.

Decisions about their futures were generally taken out of their hands by parents and others who had authority over them.

Decisions for some however, through no fault of their own, are thrust upon them by forces way beyond their control.

Is this the case for me, a young Jake Edwards???

Author's notes: -

[A]   I have used double inverted commas to denote when my two main characters are communicating aloud, but when they're communicating solely by thought transfer; I have used single inverted commas.

[B]   For non-British readers 'The Archers' is a very long running Radio Soap Opera about farming, and farming folk.

[C]   Other than some place names, this is a work entirely of fiction.

© Douglas C James 2012: This is the first Novel in the series. I hope you enjoy it.

My special thanks go to my son Brett, for his cover design, but mainly for his expertise and patience in guiding me around the intricacies of my Computer.

Jake Edwards
&
The Gentle Phenomenon.

Contents:-

Jake Edwards
&
The Gentle Phenomenon

1

Jake Meets Phen

Early 1970s.

One fine spring morning, I'm riding my bike, which I've named "The Don", and this morning, like every workday morning, is soon to be marred by two minor irritations.

The first is my ride over Gasworks Bridge, which is going to require an enormous breath that has to last till I reach the other side.

By the way, let me introduce myself, I'm Jake Edwards.

The second niggle is, I'm riding to Coburn's Ltd; the company at which, for the past four and a half dreary years I've been striving to become a furniture maker and restorer.

Thankfully, the end of my tedious apprenticeship is fast approaching. I know it's not going to run to term. They never do with this company. The management always finds some way to get rid of its apprentices before they start demanding full wages.

This morning there's nothing strange about my ride round to the rear of the factory. I intend, as usual, to park in my number one spot in the bike rack; there being this hierarchy thing going on; whereby you move further up the rack the longer into your apprenticeship you happen to be. Only this morning I find my spot being usurped by some tyke of a first year.

I stretch to my full six foot plus height; emphasise my rippling weight trained muscles, and give him a scathing look, hoping that's enough to make him change his mind. BUT NO! He's standing his ground, and saying, "It's not your rack, you can't make me move to the other end," and seeing my muscles tense, as though I'm about to spring on him; he adds defiantly, "I'm not afraid of you."

I think; this kid is deliberately testing his bravado on me. So, I surprise him by smiling and saying, "I'm pleased you're not afraid of me. I'd hate it if you were, and you're right I don't own the rack, so if it's that important to you to park in my spot; fine! Leave it there.

With that he slinks of to his work place, looking somewhat puzzled.

Next morning, I arrive to find that my spot is free and the tyke's bike is back at the bottom end of the rack where it should be. He's about to disappear into the factory when he turns, smiles and waves at me. I smile and think, cheeky whatsit, but problem solved.

After work, my mate Dave and I'll be going to our weight training club. We've known each other since school. He's a handsome chap, so he's useful for attracting girls. Not that I'm bad looking myself, but compared to Dave, no-contest! However, in the charm department, I've got the upper hand!

Arriving home after my ride through heavy traffic, a gruelling ride from one side of the city to the other, I'm feeling ravenous. It's made me doubly pleased to be sitting down to one of Mom's sumptuous dinners. I say to her, "Turn the Radio on for "The Archers" please Mom. I have to say please, if I don't, even at my age and size, my Dad'll fetch me one across the back of my head with the back of his hand.

I try never to miss an episode of "The Archers." It's sad for a young man I know, but there you are, that's me.

After dinner, I get back on my bike, turn on its lights, and head out for our Wednesday night workout.

I'm cycling along, thinking of nothing more than what I'd heard in tonight's Archer's episode, when I notice a strange, narrow, triangular light in the sky. It seems to be following me. It's not the first time I've seen it either. I've spotted it several times this past month but paid it no mind as I've not felt it's had any particular interest in me.

3

But tonight --- God!! It's coming in close! If it's not careful it'll have me off my bike! Now it's somewhere behind me! Wham!!! What the hell!!! I've been flung through the air onto a grass verge on the opposite side of the road; all of thirty feet away. Something has hit me in the back, and doesn't appear to have come out the other side. Strangely enough no part of me is hurting. You'd expect that something would, wouldn't you, after me being flung ten yards through the air?

I fearfully double check that I am in one piece, but apart from a feeling of strangeness inside, I'm fine. I'm remarkably intact.

Oh no! I think, how's "The Don"? I look across the road, and see that he's, neatly parked against a lamp post.

How can that be? The last sight of my bike, as I was flying through the air, was of it spread-eagled, with wheels spinning, in the road.

Shaking a little, I think, that's bloody puzzling? I wander if my path through the air had deviated long enough for me to right my bike. If it did, I have no memory of it.

I quell my fears by thinking to myself, me being ever an optimist, don't worry about it for now; I'm sure there's an explanation lying around somewhere.

Having thought that, I hop back on my bike and carry on to the weight training club.

The next two days are strange. It might be that my weight training and the extra food, I separately buy from what Mom feeds me, are beginning to pay off. I don't know how, but I somehow feel stronger, healthier and more invigorated. The time it usually takes me to ride to and from work seems to have shortened and my concentrations better than usual.

I still have this feeling of strangeness as I'm riding to work the following day, but I'm determined not to let it trouble the optimistic me.

Sucking in huge lungsful of air having just got past Gasworks Bridge, and coming up to the crossroads that I have to go over; I stop, check both ways, and start to cross. Out of the blue, this car cuts right in front of me! I'm going to hit it for an absolute certainty!!! My hands go up to shield my face, I close my eyes and prepare for the impact. It hasn't happened??? "The Don" and I are flying through the air for the second time in two days, but this time together, and further!

We've landed and I instinctively brake to a halt. "OK!" I cry out, more from shock than anything else, and to no one in particular, "What's going on??"

I can feel my vocal cords vibrating but I'm not speaking. I hear this voice saying, "Jake, I am so sorry, this is not the way I wanted to introduce myself, and certainly not this soon, but if I had not intervened you would have, most certainly, been badly injured; if not killed."

It's a very strange feeling; talking to someone who isn't there, but I pluck up courage and say, "Well thanks for that; who or whatever you are, but that doesn't explain what's happening to me and how you know my name?"

I'm thinking to myself, have I become schizophrenic all of a sudden, and started hearing voices?

"No Jake, there is nothing wrong with you. In fact, of the thousands of young people I have observed over the past two of your years, I have chosen you as my number one choice. Not to invade you, but to partner you, and I know your name because I have heard other people referring to you as Jake," he pauses, and then continues "You must have many more questions to ask, but may I suggest that now is not the time and place for it. You have your work to get to, and you must not let me delay you."

As I get back on my bike, I ask, "Are you the thing that crashed into me a few days ago?"

To the casual observer, it must look as though I'm talking to thin air, and probably appear off my trolley.

"Yes, I am, but I prefer to call it merging with you."

"Well did you have to merge so bloody hard," I nearly shout.

This thing, which I'm now thinking of as some kind of phenomenon, says, "I can explain that, but can you get going, I will explain on the way to your work place?"

"OK, but sooner or later, you're going to have to tell me why you're inside me in the first place; not to mention listening to all my private thoughts."

As I continue my journey, my mind is racing, trying to make sense of it all.

Jake, do not do that! As we get to know each other, all will be revealed. Let me first explain what happened the other day".

"See what I mean? You're reading my every thought."

"Please Jake, the other day, the rest later," he says patiently.

"In the form that you saw me before our merging I was unable to communicate; it was necessary for me to merge with you before I could speak with you. I know I did not straight away, but as I have said, I sincerely wanted to introduce myself to you slowly. By the way, it is not necessary for us to communicate out loud. We can communicate with each other by thought transfer, would you like to try it? It may prove less embarrassing for you, as you will no longer seem to be talking to yourself."

I say, "If we must. Is it going to hurt?"

"Not in the slightest. I do think it will be a lot easier and more private if we do."

'OK,' I think, 'let's give it a try.'

'Good', he thinks back, 'you are a quick learner, as I knew you would be.'

'So why,' I think, 'did you strike me so hard and send me flying?'

'I will come to that, but first let me say, very good, those thought transfers did not hurt, did they?'

'No.'

'Now let me answer your question,' thinks the phenomenon, 'you see as yet, I am unaware of how much power I need to use in the performance of certain tasks, especially when merging with a human being; this being the first time I have ever done it. So, I am afraid I rather over did it, but at least I made sure that you and your bicycle, "The Don" I think you call it, were unharmed.'

With my journey completed and "The Don" safely in the bike rack, I make my way to the somewhat depleted polishing shop, in which I've been working for the last two years of my apprenticeship.

I say depleted because the amount of interesting work we used to do has dwindled; likewise, the staff. Jim, the foreman, is still with us but barely. Sadly, his wife died a month ago, which was a hell of a blow to him, as he and his wife were inseparable. The kind, rotund man, that I've come to know and like, seems to be shrinking daily.

Today, I'm French polishing a gentleman's small wardrobe. The Phenomenon seems to be fascinated by this process. This is a job I'm finding a little more interesting, but it seems the Phenomenon's enjoying it more than me.

Hello? Jim's calling me. "Yes Jim," I say.

"Jake, Mr Glum (*he's the works manager, and suits his name to a tee)* has just been in, he wants you to get your outwork kit together and go to the address written here." He hands me a card.   Apparently, there's been some delivery damage made to a dining set.

As I walk out the factory I think, 'Okay Phen, we've

8

got a twenty-minute bus ride before we get to the customer's house. So, let's take the time to get a few of my questions answered.'

'Phen?' questions the Phenomenon, 'why Phen?'

'You know very well my thinking on that; you being able to read my mind. So, stop messing about and get down to business,' I answer.

'As you said, there are lots of questions I need answers to, but for now I have selected the four most urgent ones: Why are you here? Why inside me? Is there a way that I can get you out of me? and lastly, is there a way that I can stop you from being privy to my every thought?'

'Mmmm,' thinks Phen, 'let me see. Mmmm, if it is alright with you, may I answer the first and second questions later, as the answers to those could be more complex.'

'As you see fit,' I think as we board the bus. Oh! Oh! Watch out, I'm already starting to think of this Phenomenon and me, as WE.

'Fine by me' thinks Phen.

'See! I can't think anything privately, can I?'

'I am sorry about that, but let me answer your third question. The answer is YES, but before I tell you how to get rid of me, I need to extract a promise from you. Will you agree to delay any decision of whether to rid yourself of me, for one of your weeks?'

I think, 'what's all this one of your weeks – two of your years - all about?'

'That's another question,' thinks Phen.

'Oh, alright I agree to one week from this morning, happy now?'

'Yes Jake. Thank you very much.'

I think, 'For God's sake, will you get on with it.'

'That's another thing we will have to talk about,' thinks Phen.

'WHAT?' think I, impatiently.

'GOD,' thinks Phen.

That's another question,' I retort.

'Touché,' thinks Phen. 'The answer as to how you can rid yourself of me is really very simple. If you really and most sincerely mean it, and it is not said as a reactionary thought......'

'I'm losing patience here, will you please, please, get on with it, we're nearly at our destination and you haven't answered one question yet.'

'I see,' thinks Phen, 'time for you has immediacy about it, but for me, it is infinity, but as time is important to you, I will answer your question directly. You simply say, or think: Will you leave and never return.'

While he's thinking that, I have this vision of him, assuming he has form, of holding his hands palms upward to the sky and giving a little shrug of the shoulders; a bit like a Jewish gent.

'The answer to your fourth question, is going to seem simple, but it is not. As you complain, I am able to read your every thought, and you may have noticed, you are unable to read mine.'

'That's obvious!' Think I. 'Or I wouldn't need to ask questions.'

'Quite! The powers that I have that enable me to prevent you being privy to thoughts, that I believe you are not ready to hear yet, can be given to you. Then you will be able to block my intrusions into your thoughts in the same way that I block yours, but it is not that simple. There is the question of emergencies, like this morning for example, there will be times when you will need to drop your defences against my intrusions very rapidly, so that I can prevent any harm coming to you, and far faster than you can conceive of at present.'

I think, 'That's all very well, but why only me? Will you be prepared to drop your defences; so that I can prevent any harm coming to you?'

'Jake, if I may say so, that will not be necessary. There are no emergencies on your world that can possibly harm me.'

I get off the bus and start walking toward the customers house, thinking to Phen as I go, 'OK, let's say for a trial period, that we can review at a later date, that I continue to allow you to be privy to my thoughts; unless I specifically tell you, or think to you, BUTT OUT! In other words, you give me the power to block any very private thoughts I particularly don't what you, sticky-beaking into.'

'Sticky-beaking?' questions Phen.

'It's rhyming slang for peeking.'

11

'Why did you not think that then? And while I am in my questioning mode, what is "off your trolley"?'

'It's nice to discover, even though I don't yet have the power to block you, I can, by thinking in a way you're not familiar with. By the way, this is the house that we've come to work in, so the remaining questions will have to wait till later.'

With another satisfied customer behind me. Me and Phen make our way back to the bus. He thinks, 'I had an interesting time back there, watching you at your work.'

'I'm glad you enjoyed it! The only good thing for me was the cup of tea and biscuits, the lady gave me, and I only got them because I was whistling "I like a Nice Cup of Tea in the Morning".'

While we're waiting for the bus, Phen thinks, 'Now Jake, you want to know why I am here, and why I have chosen you. I have already partly answered why you. You remember that I had observed many candidates before settling on you?'

'Yes.'

'Well my final decision was made when I saw how you handled the situation when that young man usurped your place in the factory bike rack. I was so impressed by the way you handled that. As to why I am here? To be honest, I am not entirely sure myself.

Perhaps the better question would be how I am here? I will try and explain it as simply as I can. Some of my fellow beings and I where passing your planet on

12

our way to another galaxy when I thought to them, that planet we are approaching looks interesting. Can we slow down so that I can take a look? They thought to me: that is not a planet that we could survive on, at least not in our normal form, we would have to find hosts and that is not the way for a proud people like ours to live; but I thought that I would like to explore your planet for a while, so they slowed right down and kindly dropped me off; so to speak. It was not that simple of course, but I think you know what I mean, and as you now know, after two of your years of searching, you are the host I have chosen to spend my time on your planet with.'

'Yes, I suppose I should be flattered, but I wasn't given a choice. Not until we agreed to a week's trial, that is. Now we'll find out by the end of the week if this merger, as you call it, is to continue?'

2

The First Adventures

We've arrived back at Coburns Ltd. later than I wanted to be. It's been a cloudy, overcast day, so it's getting dark earlier than usual for the time of year. I collect "The Don" and turn on his head and tail lights. I know I shan't be home in time for "The Archers" so I take my time.

Again, I've got past Gasworks Bridge, hopefully with lungs intact. I'm approaching the Park, which is on my right. Normally I glance at the Park as I pass; it cheers me up to see a bit of greenery after being stuck in a workshop all day, but on this occasion, it's too dark. I still take a glance however, probably more from habit than anything else, and think to the Phen thing, 'You've been very quiet since we last communicated?'

'Yes, I have had a lot to think about and … HALLO! What was that?'

'What?'

'In the Park,' thinks Phen, 'a young lady is screaming for help.'

'I'll get over there and see what I can do.'

'Not so fast; you may need some help.'

'Like what?'

'You know that I have powers. Well, I am able to bestow my powers upon you, but at this stage in our relationship, I am only prepared to lend you some. To help you with this situation across the road, I am going to lend you the power to move very rapidly; faster than the human eye can conceive. That will go hand in hand with a tenfold increase in strength. I could increase your strength one hundred or even a thousand-fold, but tenfold will be enough for this circumstance.

The extra strength will enable you to leap great heights. Now stop looking so startled, and leap over the road and help that distressed poor young lady, and do not forget to take your bicycle with you; if you leave it here, it may be stolen.'

I'm too bewildered to think a reply, so I put my trust in him and try a little on the spot leap. "WOW!" I say out loud, "that was great."

'Yes,' thinks Phen, 'but you have only leaped us twenty feet in the air. That is not going to get you across the road and into the Park, put some vigour into it, and do not forget to aim forward as well as up, or you will only go straight up and come back down again.'

'What if I over-shoot?'

'You will not, with only a ten-fold increase in your strength you will just about make it. By the way, I am also lending you the power to repel firearm and knife attacks, and do not worry that you may hurt yourself when you land; you will not be able to, hurt yourself that is, not that you will not be able to land. One final thing, you are not allowed to use your powers to

15

physically harm another human being. Now get going, the poor girl is getting distressed; she is screaming the word, RAPE!'

With that I grab "The Don" and take a flying leap into the air. I've landed about thirty feet away from two perpetrators. Leaning my bike on the nearest tree, I shout, "Ay! You two, any chance you could leave that young lady alone?"

They look startled. The one guy is kneeling on the girl's shoulders and holding down her hands and arms, while the other guy is attempting to rape her.
He says, "Where did you come from?"

"Please help me!" The girl cries out piteously.

With that, I make use of Phen's rapid movement power, and from entirely the opposite side that I was a millisecond ago, I say, "Never mind where I came from, I'm asking the questions, are you going to let her be or not?"

Their heads swing round as if they're Owls, but by now I've moved back again to the other side, this time closer to them and say, "Well?"

"Bugger off," the kneeling guy says, "or you'll get this in yer," taking an ugly looking knife out of his jacket pocket and brandishing it toward the place that I was, he says, "Now where've you gone?"

"Here," having made another lightning move, I add, "right behind you." Before he can swivel his head round again I've grabbed the hilt of his knife and snapped the blade off.

He glares at it stupefied, looks at his mate and

says, "Come on, we're out of here, this bloke's weird".

But, too late, I've lifted the kneeler off his feet and hung him by his clothes from the branch of a nearby tree, about twenty plus feet from the ground, and rapidly follow up with the same treatment for his mate. (*Well I'm nothing, if not democratic!*).

"Are you okay?" I ask the girl.

"Yes, I am now, thanks to you," she says while straightening her clothes.

I think, I can't take all the credit, but think also, that Phen won't want me telling her about him so I just say, "That's okay, no thanks needed."

"I don't know why you're bothering with her for, she's only a half cast bitch" says the kneeler's mate.

"She deserves to be treated the same as anyone else," I say, and add, "When I've seen her safely home, I'll be back to continue this conversation, so don't go away."

I say to the girl "What's your name?"

"Jenny," she replies.

"Come on Jenny, let's get you home." We start walking; she tells me that she's taken this same route home dozens of times before, with never any bother.

"That's partly the trouble, these two," I say pointing, with my thumb, over my shoulder, "have obviously clocked you. You should vary your route, so that no one can predict when you'll be passing."

"I'll bear that in mind and thank you. My place is only around the corner from here, I'm sure that I'll be okay now," says Jenny.

17

"Before you go Jenny, can I ask you not to mention the stranger parts of our encounter to anyone, and as for those lout's; I think I can deal with them more effectively than the cops, but it's up to you, what would you like me to do?"

"I'll leave them to you, and I won't tell anybody about your super speed and strength," says Jenny, smiling, "who would believe me anyway, right! If I do tell anyone about my ordeal, I'll just say that some nice man came to my rescue in the nick of time." That said, she stands on tip-toe, gives me a peck on the cheek and whispers, "I'll never forget you," and disappears around the corner.

I note Jenny's house number and with a few more leaps I'm back at the lout's hanging tree and find that they've managed to struggle out of their top cloths, and have reduced the height they would have to drop by hanging from their jackets etc. As they land, I'm just behind them. I clap my hands and say, "Well done gentlemen."

'Gentlemen? That's a laugh.' I think to Phen.

'I agree,' thinks Phen, 'the word does not seem appropriate to these two, but otherwise you are handling the situation well, so far.'

"Gentlemen, you are brighter than I would have given you credit for," I say flatteringly, "so I can't help wondering why you're wasting your youthful energy by trying to perform such foul acts. Can't you find a better use for your lives?"

"Like what," says the kneeler?"

"I don't know, let me think, --- what about starting a football team? Or better still? Start a "Good Deeds Club?" if you don't want to call it that you could call it a, "Let Us Help Club", L.U.H.C. for short. Sounds like luck, if you say it quick, don't it?

Whatever you choose, you mustn't allow yourselves to become confused with do-gooders, they are a different breed altogether."

"Aren't you going to give us up to the Cops?" asks the kneeler's mate.

I say, while retrieving their jackets and stuff from the tree. "What good would that do? They'll only drag you in front of some magistrate. He'll give you a slap on the wrists, and send you packing.

Tell me, what're your names? You needn't tell me your full names; your first names will do."

They look at each other, wondering whether to trust me with this information. The kneeler says, "If he's not giving us up to the Cops, I can't see that it'll do any harm."

His mate nods and says, "My names John and he's Ken." then adds, "What's the difference between someone who does good deeds, and a do-gooder?"

"Good question. If you start a L.U.H.C; you will only be helping those who want to be helped, were as do-gooders stick their noses into matters, whether those concerned want them to, or not."

"Like you did with us?" asks Ken.

"No, the girl wanted me to help."

"How would we go about starting one of these

L.U.H.C.'s, and what would be in it for us?"

"You could start slowly by putting a card into a local shop window, saying for example: **Do you need help with odd jobs but can't afford to employ a tradesman? If so, contact John & Ken on --------.**

As to what's in it for you, just imagine going for a job interview, and when the interviewers ask: Have you got any interests outside the job description? And you tell them about your "Let Us Help Club," I guarantee that it will make a big difference as to whether you get the job; I can't say you will get it, but you will most certainly stand a better chance than telling them your hobby is raping young girls."

"Now you're being funny!" says Ken.

"Perhaps, but why not give the idea a try? I'll stop by now and again to see how you're getting on."

"How can you; you don't know where we live."

"That won't be a problem. I shall be able to look for your cards in local shop windows, and if I see one or two, I'll know you're up and running. If, on the other hand, I hear of anymore rapes in this area, I'll come looking for you, and make no mistake, I will find you. When I do, what you've experienced today won't come close. Now get gone, and remember I'll be watching."

'That should do it,' thinks Phen, 'but are you happy about not knowing where they live?'

'Of course not, I plan to follow them, but so that I can do it without being detected, how can you help?'

'Mmmm, I could lend you some hovering power. I will probably have to increase your strength further to achieve it, but it is a power that you will need anyway, if you are to learn to fly.'

After I pick my chin up of the ground, I think 'Go for it, and preferably before they reach their destinations and disappear into their respective houses.'

With Phen's help I've hovered over John's & Ken's addresses and noted them. Now, Phen me and the Don are heading home; with for me, if not for Phen, a feeling of satisfaction of a job well done.

It's dawned on me, as I'm riding home from work after another happy Friday at the pit face, that I didn't tell John and Ken not to talk about their encounter with me. I can only hope that they would be too embarrassed to do so.

Soon after our park adventure Phen relieved me of the powers that he'd lent me. I must say that it has left me feeling vulnerable; although why it should I don't know. I don't remember feeling vulnerable before Phen, came along. Perhaps it was nearly getting killed by that car that's making me feel this way; after all, as he said, I could have been seriously injured.

I've asked Phen to keep out of my thoughts for a while. I need to think seriously about what my decision is going to be next Thursday when I have to decide if I want to keep him with me. On the one hand, without him, I could be lying in some hospital and I certainly wouldn't have been able to help Jenny; not without

21

doing physical harm. To be honest, I would have ridden past, as it was only Phen's superior hearing that drew my attention to Jenny's plight. On the other hand, do I need all the upheaval that my association with him is likely to bring? My life before Phen, had a modicum of tranquillity about it, with him, my life will never be the same again!!

My decision, as I arrive home, is for the present, to ask Phen, a few more questions. Like what his intentions are. My god! It sounds as though I'm about to consider marrying him!

Seriously though, it is that serious a decision, but for now, Mom's telling me my teas ready. I'll open up negotiations with Phen again later.

After tea I go up to my bedroom, lie on my bed and think, 'Phen, are you there?'

'Yes, Jake.'

'Thanks for letting me shut you out; I wanted to think about the decision I have to make next Thursday.'

'What have you decided?'

'I haven't decided anything yet, I need to ask you a few more questions.'

'Go ahead,' he thinks.

'You've told me how you came to be here, but what are your intentions now that you are here? Also, how can I be sure that you are the only one of your people to have come here?'

'Jake, at this point, I honestly do not know what my intentions are, other than to become good friends with you, learn through you, as much as I can about this planets people, and without drawing attention to myself; be of as much use as I can be.'

'Why do you need to gather this information? Is it in readiness for a future invasion?'

'Ha! Ha! Jake, I think you have been reading too much science fiction. I think you already know the answer to that one. My species have no interest in living on this planet. They are very happy with the planets they currently live on, and see no need, now or in the future to live anywhere else.'

'So why do YOU want to live here?'

'Well in spite of what you may think, apart from being telepathic, we are much like yourselves, individuals. I am the only one who was curious enough about your planet to want to explore it, and its inhabitants. Can I say, by way of further reassurance, that so far, I am delighted that I gave in to my curiosity, and that I chose you as my companion for my stay here; however long that may be. If that last comment concerns you, for you may think that I would leave at any moment, let me answer one of your earlier questions. You asked, what is this one of your hours, one of your weeks all about?

Well, when I tell you that one of your years is the equivalent to only four weeks on my planet. In other words, my planets revolve around their Sun, on average, about twelve times faster than yours. Therefore, we age much slower than you do; so, if I am with you, say for twelve years, I shall have only been with you in my terms for one of your years. BUT, as time has no meaning to us, this whole discussion about time is irrelevant. I have mentioned to you before, time for me is infinity. Have I answered all your questions to your satisfaction Jake?'

'For now, thanks Phen, it's a lot to take in. There may be more, when I have had the chance to absorb all of your answers. --- Now you come to mention it,
-- there is one thing that's been puzzling me?'

'I am intrigued! Do ask.

'Well, you told me your species can't survive on this planet without occupying hosts. Yet you were here for two of our years before you merged with me. How, during that time, did you survive?'

'Mmmm, I see, tricky one! The answer is that I descended with a reserve of survival powers, knowing it may be a while before I found the right host. However, that reserve was fast running out; I only had, in your terms, about a month of survival supply left. Thankfully I found you before that time ran out. If I had not, I would have had to contact my colleagues and ask them to return for me.'

'Thanks Phen, that clears it up, --- I think!

Anyway Phen, I shall be meeting Dave shortly. We're off to the club for our Friday night workout, so if you don't mind, please let me block you out for a while. I don't want to appear distracted and have Dave wondering if there is something the matter with me. I'm not ready to take anyone into my confidence about you yet, not even my best mate.'

'Very wise Jake. May I ask, before I let you shut me out; what are you doing tomorrow night? Because if you are available, I think we should find some remote spot and practice the powers that I have, so far, introduced you to.'

'That's a date Phen, but for now, adieu.' I bet Phen didn't know I knew a word of French. I'm now wondering what he meant by: So Far? Can it be there are other powers up his sleeve that he hasn't seen fit to mention yet?

'Is this, remote enough for you Phen?' I ask. I've, cycled to a large open park north of the city; this park covers some two thousand four hundred acres of scrubland, lakes and woodland.

'Yes Jake, this is ideal and as it is dark we should be unobserved. Did you and Dave enjoy your workout last night?'

'Yes thanks, Phen. '

'I am pleased that you are looking after your physique. It makes it so much easier for me to pass on powers to an already powerful body. A weak and unhealthy body would find it harder to cope with the sudden increases in strength etcetera, and it would mean that I would have to work so much harder in caring for such a person's well-being. I may be an advanced being, but I do share one other trait with you humans. I can be a bit lazy at times; I do not like working harder than I have to. Let us get started on your practice. You may feel a slight tingling sensation

25

as I increase the intensity of your powers. For the small amount I lent you before you wouldn't have felt anything.'

'Yes Phen, I can feel it, but it's not at all an unpleasant sensation.'

'Good, now take a gentle straight-up-in-the-air jump which should take us up to about fifty, to one hundred of your feet, then hover.

Good, this is excellent, now just hang here for a few minutes until you get used to this feeling of being suspended in the air.

Now, using a very small amount of your hovering power, slowly turn yourself until you are lying horizontal. Okay, slowly increase the hovering power and you should gently move forward.'

Whoosh! 'O my God! I'm about six miles away from where I was!' I exclaim.

Phen says, 'I said gently! Please turn around and gently, and I mean gently, go back to where we were, and this time, will you please do so face down instead of on your back!'

After a few more goes I think, 'This is great, Phen, I'm actually flying.'

'You are indeed, Jake. Now, I would like you to make about ten circuits of the park, and as you do, gradually increase your speed with each pass.'

The exhilaration that I'm feeling, especially with this last pass, which has happened in what seems like a blink of an eye; I can't find words to describe.

'Why did I ever doubt you Phen? Let's not wait till Thursday. Let's agree to stay together now.'

'As much as I am tempted to accept that honour, I do not think you should make the decision while you are in your present heightened state. No pun intended. Let us continue with your practice for now, and then see how you feel after you have slept on it.'

'You're right Phen. I'm also, at last finding out how wise you are. What is the next thing I need to practice?' I think to him as I land us.

'Do you see that log of fallen tree over there?'

I say 'yes'.

He then asks, 'Do you think that you could have lifted it before I lent you your increased strength?'

'No chance!'

'Try now.'

Going over to the log, which is about twelve-footlong by about three-foot diameter at the blunt end, I grab it underneath, and to my amazement lift it of the ground, almost with ease.

'Now Jake; lift it over your head and then throw it.'

To my further amazement, having followed Phen's instructions, the log soars through the air and finally comes down some five hundred yards away.

'My God Phen, did I actually do that???'

'You most surely did, and that is as nothing, compared to what you will eventually be able to achieve.

The next thing I want you to try is to take that large thick stick over there and crack yourself over the head

27

with it.'

'What! Are you kidding?'

'No, I am not Jake; you must trust me, but if you wish to build up the trust, first give yourself a light crack.'

'Mmmm alright,' I think warily. With that I smack myself a gentle one. Nothing! I didn't even feel it. I whack myself again and again, ever harder, not only on my head but on other parts of my body. I'm dancing around, laughing hilariously and hitting myself over and over again.'

'That is enough,' thinks Phen sharply. 'Calm down, and let us finish for today. We will resume tomorrow. In the meantime, I think you should hang on to your powers for now. Please do not give in to any temptations to misuse them, or use them for personal gain. I am sure that I need not have thought that to you, but I feel that if I had not warned you; I might have been neglectful of my duties. Now collect your bike, and let us fly home.'

I'm awake early, this lovely sunny Sunday morning, but to be honest, I've hardly slept a wink. The thoughts that have been going through my mind would fill a book. 'So Phen, where do we go from here?'

'You may or may not agree Jake but today, I believe is going to be the hardest day of your training, because the whole project that we have embarked on is going to hinge on whether you are able to act, and if you can, how well?'

I'm scratching my head in bewilderment, then I think, 'How come Phen? Surely last night's training had to have been harder than a bit of acting?'

'That was just the beginning Jake, the powers that I have given you, and yes, I meant given, including the power to block me without having to ask, you can now keep. I have decided they are no longer on loan. The powers are the part of our partnership that you can rely on me for, but your ability to act totally convincingly, is down to you. It is not something that I can help you with. Take this morning for example, how are you going to appear to your family when you go down for breakfast? Another example could be, how will you behave at your next weight training session?'

'I see what you mean Phen, it could well be tricky; I don't want to be going down stairs looking like the cat that's got the cream.'

'Cat that has the cream?' thinks Phen.

'Yes, you know; grinning all over my face like a cat that's got cream instead of plain old water to drink.'

'Oh, I see,' thinks Phen, 'but at the same time you do not want to appear as though you have been up all night; which you do by the way.'

'Thanks Phen, love you too, and before you ask, that is known as sarcasm.'

'Yes Jake, I do know what sarcasm is.'

"Morning Mom-Dad. What's for breakfast Mom?"

"The usual cornflakes, porridge, I do have a bit of bacon left from last night, I could make you a bacon sandwich."

"Yes please Mom, that'll do me. Dad, can I have a quick squiz at Saturday's local paper after you've finished with it?" I've just noticed the head-lines, something about a gang terrorising the "Sharp's End" area of the city.

"You don't normally bother with the paper," says Dad, looking at me over the top of his glasses.

'Be careful Jake,' thinks Phen.

To my Dad, I say, "I know, it's just that things aren't going to well at work. I may have to start looking for another job soon."

'Not bad,' thinks Phen, 'you got out of that reasonably well, but don't bother to read the front page of the paper; I have already scanned it. I will fill you in later. Go straight to the jobs page. That will be more believable.'

'Thanks Phen, but I had already worked that out. I'll ask you about it on my way to work on Monday. I'll block you out for the rest of today; if you don't mind; I've got things I need to do.'

3

There's crispness to the air this Monday morning as The Don and I, are on our way to my work place. With nothing better to do, I think, 'Okay, Phen tell me the details of that front page you scanned?'

'Apparently,' thinks Phen, 'there is a gang of around twelve, fifteen to twenty-year-old youths causing mayhem in the "Sharp's End" area. Old people particularly, are afraid to leave their homes. Not only that, children are also afraid of them. They get jeered at on their way to and from school. The police seem powerless as the youths, as yet; have not done any physical harm to anyone. Although the Police are aware of them and have issued warnings, they say they cannot arrest them for the mental damage they are causing; as that is much more of an intangible thing to prove in Court.'

'Is this something I should get involved in, do you think, Phen?'

'It is up to you Jake, whatever you decide, do remember, you must not physically harm these youths, but seeing as they do not seem over bothered about the mental anguish they are causing??? My other reservation would be, harking back to your principal of only helping when someone has asked for help; I suggest we tread carefully.'

'Yea, I'm going to have to give some thought to this. Thanks, Phen.'

I'm half way through my morning's work and it looks like matters have reached a peak. I arrived this morning to the terrible news that Jim had died in the night. Since then, there has been much toing and froing by the management; discussions taking place in dark corners, and finally here comes Mr Glum or Gloomy as I call him. Not to his face of course.

"Edwards, will you please come with me."

I assume that is not a question, but just about the most pleasant demand that Gloomy's ever come out with, and because I'm in shock at Jim's passing, I can't think of any defensive retort. So, I follow meekly behind him. He leads me into what was the Brady Box making department, and is now the Spray Department for the mass production of Cots, which the company went into production on a few months back.

There waiting for us is Mr Harry, one of the Directors. "Young Edwards we are all deeply saddened by Jim Harvey's demise," says Mr Harry, "but I am sure you will appreciate, that we as a company, cannot justify keeping Mr Harvey's department going now that he is no longer with us. Mr Glum has therefore bought you down here to give you the chance to complete your apprenticeship in this department, spraying Cots."

Here it comes, the policy that I have seen so often, but I'm in no mood at present to put up a fight, so I simply say, "Mr Harry, I appreciate you're making an effort to keep me on, but as Mr Glum knows full well, I have a medical note saying that I must not do any spraying. Regrettably, and to save any unpleasantness in the light of this morning's news, (*this I'm saying with a lump in my throat,*) I'd like to tender my resignation and give you one week's notice."

Gloomy, looks at Mr Harry, they nod to each other and Mr Harry, says, "In that case we can only accept." (*I bet you can, think I. I bet you're secretly rubbing your hands together.*)

"We, definitely need someone in here to do the spraying, and would have liked it to have been you," Gloomy adds.

(Pull the other one! I think privately.)

The look on my face tells him I'm not going to budge, so he says, "You needn't work your notice. If you come to the office, I will give you your cards and a week's wages in lieu of notice. That way, you can use the week to search for further employment, which I'm sure you'll find fairly easily with your skills."

All I can think of saying is, "Thanks" and follow Gloomy into the Office.

I'm outside the factory, leaning on the handlebars of my bike, when Phen thinks, 'What are you going to do now Jake?'

'I've only got one option at the moment Phen. When I was reading the job adds in Dad's Paper on Sunday, I noticed that "Bumbles" the big Department Store in the city centre are looking for a French Polisher to do maintenance work. I'll probably try there. I'll drop in tomorrow morning, and if they agree to employ me, I'll tell them I can't start till next Monday. That will give us a bit of time to see what we can do about this gang terrorising the folks on the "Sharps End" estate.'

I've managed to secure the job at 'Bumbles' and Phil, the foreman of the maintenance department has agreed that I can start next Monday, at nine o'clock, and to report to him in the maintenance sheds; which are on the roof of the building some six storeys up. What a luxury, not starting till nine. I needn't start out now till eight, instead of seven o'clock. Plus, the fact that "Bumbles" is a fair bit nearer to where I live.

'Phen, this gang of twelve problem? I think what we should do is target some of the victims first and get one or two of them to trust me, and ask me for my help.'

'How do you propose to manage that, Jake?'

'Well, I think I'm going to have to perform a couple of feats of strength; something that will convince them that I can handle this gang.'

'Do you propose to do that as yourself?'

'Who else can I do it as? Are you suggesting I disguise myself?'

'No,' thinks Phen, 'I feel that if your disguise is penetrated you will lose all credibility. Better to go as an entirely different person, at least outwardly. You will still be you on the inside of course.'

'Hang on, you've lost me, or if I'm hearing you right, is this one of those powers that you haven't, so far, seen fit to mention?'

'You suspected then, that I have a few powers, as you say up my sleeve,' thinks Phen.

'I did wonder, after you'd used the words; So far.'

'Ah yes, I remember now, I shall have to be more careful of what I think. Not really, it was, I believe, what you would call a slip of the tongue, or in my case, a slip of the thought.'

If I could see him, I'm sure I'd see him having a little laugh at his own joke.

'Explain please Phen? Why you obviously believe that I should go to great lengths to conceal my powers from everyone; even from those nearest and dearest to me? Hence, all this talk yesterday, about the importance of my acting skills.'

'Jake, how can I put this? If it gets out that you have all these alien powers, you will be hounded by the media and they will not rest until they have extracted every ounce of information out of you; not only about yourself but about me also. I, for one would find that intolerable, but much more importantly, it would render the work of helping people much more difficult, if not impossible, and as you know, I do not like working harder than I have to.'

'I understand and agree Phen but let's get back to this talk of disguise.'

'The way that I see it, you will have more freedom when using your powers if you do not look like you. If it does eventually get out that there is someone running around with super powers, no one is going to know it is you. You will have the media etcetera, running around in circles looking for someone who does not exist.'

'Do you know Phen, that you have a very devious mind!'

'Or is it wisdom? Anyway Jake let us not digress. Concentrate on how you would like to appear in order to achieve your goal of gaining the confidence of "Sharp Ends" harassed people.'

'I think, I would have to look like someone who could inspire confidence, say about six feet four inches tall, big in the sense broad, not fat, have a tough looking face but with a kind of gentle look to the eyes, which can however appear cold to those who get on the wrong side of him. He could claim that he is an ex SAS soldier, or something like that.'

'Yes Jake, I think that should do it, I do not claim to know what an ex SAS man looks like, but I assume he would look like the person you describe. When you are ready, I will pass on the powers that will enable you to alter your appearance, not only your head and body, but your footwear and clothing as well. I am sure a six feet four-inch man would look silly in your clothes, and I am doubly sure he would not fit his feet into your shoes. You may once again feel a slight tingling sensation.'

'So! I've now got another power to worry about.'

'Why should it be a worry?' Phen muses.

'Because, it's super having these powers, but with the restrictions that you have placed on them, it's going to be a constant worry of how I can use them without infringing your rules.'

'I am sorry Jake, but my restrictions are necessary for now. Later on, when you have got used to living within the rules, it will not seem so much of a burden. It will feel no different, than say, a Christian, trying to lead his or her life by Christ's, teachings.'

'Are you now, comparing yourself to Jesus?'

'Of course not!' exclaims Phen, 'I would never think such a thing. The point that I am trying to make, is that eventually I shall be able to lift the restrictions, because by then I shall be able to rely entirely on your own judgement as to when, and when not to use your powers; plus, others that I have not introduced you to, yet.'

'I'm sorry Phen, I keep on doubting your intentions. From now on I'm going to show more faith in you, and hope that I may soon be able to convince you that my judgement can be trusted.'

'I am sure that day is not far off. Now, while we seem to be alone, why not give your power to change your appearance a try. Not the full thing. First try a hand; try making it bigger.'

I'm looking at my left hand but nothing seems to be happening. 'Nothing's happening Phen, why?'

'That is because you are not concentrating enough. If it was as easy as you are trying to make it, you would find yourself changing shape all over the place. Every time you fancied some other persons hairstyle for instance. No, you must really concentrate in order to make these changes. Now try again, really focus!'

I'm trying, really trying this time, and YES! I'm standing here, watching my hand slowly change shape. 'Phen that is absolutely amazing!'

'Change it back quickly, there is someone coming.'

'Right, I'll tell you what then Phen, there's a "Lyons" café around the corner from here. I'll get something to eat, and then we'll get a bus directly to the "Sharp's End" estate.'

'Why go on the bus? Because you are on your way to try and help some people, you will not be abusing your powers. So, fly; it is a dull day so there should be plenty of cloud cover. Do you happen to know, at what size and height, an object becomes visible on Radar, as it may be an idea to keep under it?'

'Those sorts of things, I would never have thought of, Phen but I think I would have to be made of something inorganic for that to be a problem; otherwise radar would pick up large birds.'

'Let us not worry about it then. All these changes to your previous way of life are going to take time to get used to. While we are on the subject, with Thursday's dead line looming, can I safely assume that the answer is yes, to my staying with you?'

'I don't think you need to ask, but if it makes you feel better the answer is a resounding YES! I'm very excited at the thought of how much we can achieve together.'

'Okay Jake, do not wear yourself out. Please, if you have finished eating, will you find a spot where you are unobserved and take off? By the way, you do not have to wait until you are at our destination before you make the changes to your appearance. You can start them during the flight, providing you fly slowly.'

I've lost height a few times during my journey with trying so hard to concentrate on changing, I'm not too hot at this multitasking, but Phen assures me I'll get better at it.

'That wooded copse there, looks a good place to land,' thinks Phen.

'I agree,' and go down with only the finishing touches left to complete my disguise. That done, I take off again, and slowly scout the area to see if I can spot any evidence of the gang. After half an hour I've not spotted them. 'This is probably not the right time for them to be about Phen. I think I'll stand a better chance at school chucking out time.

In the meantime, I think I'll pop by some buildings that I spotted earlier, they looked like the sort of properties that the elderly might occupy.'

'Tread carefully though Jake, the way you look now could scare them; even more than the gang of twelve do already.'

'Point taken, Phen.'

I'm now approaching the first of the little bungalows, and ring the bell. There's a wait that for me seems endless.

I'm about to go and try the one next door, when the door opens a small crack; the door is obviously secured by at least two chains. "Hello" I say giving the lady behind the door, who must be at the very least seventy, my most gentle eyed look, "My name is Gordon."

'Gordon?' thinks Phen.

'Well, it's no good changing my appearance and keeping my own name, is it?'

'Carry on then; I will keep quiet.'

"Please don't be frightened, I'm not here to sell you anything, I'm here to try and help you and your neighbours. Can you tell me if either you, or your neighbours have been having trouble with a gang of youths?"

'Oh! Very good Jake,' thinks Phen.

'I thought you were going to keep quiet.'

"Who are you? Are you from the press?" The old lady says.

"No, nothing like that; I'm just a concerned citizen who's able to help rid you and other people on the Estate, of the youth menace."

"What makes you think you can do what the Police and others can't?"

"Well if you could open your door a little wider, I don't want you to take your chains off though; just enough to see me properly. You will see that I'm a hefty lad, and on top of that, my job in the SAS was to train the troops in close quarter combat. Sorting out this bunch of hoodlums that are bothering you will not be a problem for me."

"Why don't you just go and sort them out then?"

I think, there's nothing wrong with this old girls' brain, she's as sharp as a razor. (*I wonder, are they all like this in "Sharps End"?*)

"I'm afraid it's not that simple, I'm honour bound only to act if my help has been specifically requested".

She is looking deep into my eyes, and I can almost feel hers boring into my brain.

Then, as though she has suddenly made up her mind, she says, "You'd better come in." The chains are released. I step into a pleasant little hallway and follow her into a back lounge where there's a gas fire on, and a television program in progress. She leans over and supported on her walking stick, she turns the telly off. "Would you like a cup of tea?" she asks.

"Yes please, that would be lovely, just a weak one, with milk and one sugar thanks".

'Going well so far,' thinks Phen while the old girl's out of the room, 'you would think that you had been doing this sort of thing all your life.'

'Yes, and what's more amazing, I'm doing it without any help from you!'

'The acting IS your province,' thinks Phen as the lady returns with a tea tray, on which there are biscuits as well as tea.

"May I ask your name, dear?" I say.

"Doris," she says.

"Well I'm pleased to meet you, Doris."

"And I might be pleased to meet you, if you can help with this blight that's affecting the estate, but there's

41

one thing that's bothering me: what will happen once you have gone? Things could just revert to the status quo. So, except for a small respite, we will be no better off than we are now."

"Doris, I can't tell you how I intend to go about clearing up, as you say this blight, but however I do it, my aim will always be to strive towards a permanent solution. Now, are you willing to help me, to help you?"

"Yes Gordon."

"Wow! You remembered my name."

"An occupational hazard I'm afraid. I was a school head mistress for many years, it was very important to remember pupil's names. It's a skill that, touch wood, has never left me."

"You know, I thought that there was something about you from the beginning, I thought this lady is sharp.

Anyway, I'm digressing again, it's a bad habit I have. Doris, what I would like you to do is talk to as many of your neighbours as you can, and get them to come to a meeting here this evening. If you could manage to get one or two Moms to come along, that would be even better. With you having a foot in both camps, I think you might manage that. Good cup of tea by the way."

"Flatterer! You know, I'm having difficulty imagining a nice man like you taking on a bunch of hooligans."

"Now who's flattering? I'll go now and I'll see you around seven if that's all right?"

"Fine, can you see yourself out," she concludes.

It now being time for the schools to turn out, Phen and I fly high above and hover, observing all the time for signs of the twelve youths.

We don't have to wait long, we spot them making their way towards the school; jeering at passing school children and their mothers as they go.

They have now arrived outside the school gates, and are standing in a group, hurling abuse at the kids coming out of school. There're making obscene gestures and comments toward their mothers. Shouting and making horrible faces at the children, trying everything they can to frighten them, and their mothers; short of any physical attack.

'What is your plan, Jake?' asks Phen. It's an internal question, of course, as we, as you know, don't actually speak openly. (*Phen, is unaware of what my plan is, as I haven't thought it yet.)*

'I think what I'll try to do Phen is identify the ring leader or leaders, that way when we approach them, we'll know who to target first. We'll observe them here, and when they disperse, follow as many as we can to their lairs, so to speak. The more we can learn about them before my seven o'clock meeting at Doris's the better. I'm going to move in closer, perhaps hide behind a chimney or around the corner of a building, anywhere out of sight, but can hear what they are saying.'

'Would you like me to enhance your hearing? That way you will not have to risk being spotted as you will not have to get so close.'

'Thanks Phen, if you can, that would be useful, but not too much, I don't want these guys bursting my ear drums. While you're at it, is it possible you can give my eyesight a boost also? I'd like to get a closer look at the features of these guys, and with the extra hearing; try to pick up some names, particularly the leaders, also the lad holding the Pit Bull Terrier.'

Phen thinks, 'Consider it done,'

I've done observing and as none of them seem to be in a hurry to go home at the moment, and as I'm feeling hungry, I land behind a tree in the rear grounds of a local pub that's advertising all day home cooked food.

I go in, thinking that it looks cosy enough, order a meal of steak and kidney pie, chips and peas, and while I'm waiting, order a pint of mild beer shandy.

Having selected a corner seat, which wasn't difficult, as there are not many customers in as yet; I settle down with my pint and think to Phen, 'Let's recap what we've learnt so far. The lad with the dog is about sixteen, his name is Freddy. The coloured lad, with the dreadlocks and the white lad, with short curly dark hair, seem to be the ring leaders. Their names are Winston and Joel, respectively. They'd both be about nineteen years old. I didn't get much else, did you Phen?'

'Not really Jake, I heard a few other names bandied about, such as Fin, Billy, Ron, Syd, but could not say for certain which ones they belonged to.'

With the meal out of the way and feeling refreshed, Phen and I head for Doris's place. I ring Doris's bell and the door is opened by a young woman carrying a baby. "Hello, my names Gordon, I'm pleased to see that we have at least one Mom," I say.

"I know who you are; Doris's description was pretty accurate," she says smilingly and adds, "Please come in"

I enter and see Doris in the kitchen. "Doris, before we start, may I use your toilet?"

"Of course, it's on the right; you passed it on your way in."

"Thanks" I slip into the toilet, use it, and think, 'Phen, will you please tone down the enhanced hearing. It nearly blasted my ears off when the ladies spoke and the toilet flushed.'

'I've given you, those ear and sight powers. You must tone them down yourself. Do it the same way you adjusted your appearance. Concentrate, you know what normal sound and sight is, so make the alterations.'

'But there are no sounds in here for me to adjust to.'

'Well, hum like singers do, you know Mmee, Mmee,' suggests Phen.

I concentrate and Mmee—Mmee—Mmee, 'Yea that's better Phen; let's go and address the meeting.'

I tap on the lounge door and Doris's, voice says cheerily, "Come on in, you sounded happy in the Loo."

I say with a quirky grin, "Well you have to make an effort don't yea. My Doris, you've gathered a good crowd haven't you. Mind you, I knew you would."

Doris makes the introductions. There are four elderly fellers, six ladies of a certain age, including Doris and three Moms. "This is Gordon, the man I've been telling you about."

I say, "Hello and good evening everyone, I'm so pleased that you felt able to attend this little meeting. Doris must have done a pretty good sales job. I think I'd make her my agent if I was in show business.

The purpose of this gathering is to see if there is a consensus among you that would like my help clearing up the scourge that is blighting your estate. Without you asking for help, I'm afraid I wouldn't be able to do anything; any questions?"

"Yes, I'm Bill," says one of the men, "you have obviously convinced Doris that you can work this miracle, but I have some doubt, you look a tough strapping feller but you will be taking on at least twelve of them. I know that we would dearly like you to do this thing for us, but not at the risk of getting you seriously injured."

"That's very thoughtful of you Bill but you needn't worry on that score."

'Phen, I think I'm going to have to do a little demo here. What do you think?'

'I think you are doing splendidly and if you think a demonstration would clinch it, go ahead. Do not forget you are in disguise; no one knows it is you.'

"First of all," I say to the group, "before I show you one or two minor things that may help you all to ask for my help, I must beg you all not to tell a soul what you are going to witness, not even your nearest and dearest. Do I have your assurances?"

Doris takes charge again. "Let's see a show of hands to Gordon's request." Every hand goes up.
Some I'm sure, only through curiosity.

"Good! Doris, have you got a "Rolling Pin"? If you have, can you go and get it please?" Doris gets up to go to the kitchen. While she's out of the room I say to the rest of the group, "While Doris's not using her chair for a moment, will you three Moms hand your babies to someone and pile yourselves upon it?" The Moms oblige.

Doris comes back and is gob smacked at what's going on?

"Bear with me Doris," I say, "can the rest of you create a path down the centre of the room? Good, now stand well back."

I now go to Doris's, chair, haunch down and lift the chair, complete with the three women, and make four trips up and down the centre of the room, finally resting them back where they were. "Now, Doris will you please give me a crack on the head with your Rolling Pin?"

"Oh! Oh no, I couldn't."

"Would anyone else like to give it a go?" With the shaking of heads all round, I give myself a hefty blow on the head and say, "I would like you all to come forward now and tell me if you see any damage to my scalp also inspect the Rolling Pin; which you will find is almost broken in two." They all come forward, and go back to their seats, looking a lot paler. I assure Doris I will buy her a new rolling pin.

Doris seizes the moment and says, "Let me see a show of hands for asking Gordon's help."

Every hand goes up as though someone is conducting them, with added cries of, "Please help us!" And, "your secret is safe with us!"

'Well Phen, that's the first hurdle over. I think we'll call it a day now and go home for some relaxation.'

'Why do you call it a day?'

'It's just an expression Phen, meaning that's enough for today.'

'Oh, I see, I will remember that for the next time you say it.'

A few days later we are in a sports shop and Phen, asks, 'Jake, what are we doing here in this sports shop?'

'We're going to buy a football.'

'Why?'

'You'll see!'

It's a busy Saturday morning, so I'll have to be extra careful not to be seen taking off.

I manage to find a quiet spot behind the shops, and after a quick glance around, fly off to "Sharps End Estate"; changing into Gordon as I go.

Now that I've had some experience at this changing, I'm able to achieve it a lot quicker, so that by the time we arrive in the target area, I'm ready to go.

I slow down, and start searching, once again, for the gang; known to us now as the gang of twelve.

It's five minutes before I spot them. They seem to be making their way towards the shopping centre, no doubt intent on causing mayhem when they get there.

The wait appears too much for one of them; I have just seen him hurl a stone through the window of a house that's just past a piece of open ground. They all stand around laughing for a moment then run off, but now find me blocking their way as they try to use a narrow walk through that leads to the estate's bus station and shops. I'm standing there clutching the purchased football, smiling and leaning on a lamp post.

"Ay! You, if you know what's good for yer, get out of our way," says dreadlocks.

"Anyone for a game of football," I say, while bouncing the ball.

Dreadlocks takes a truncheon like stick from a long thigh pocket of his Jeans and says, "Do you want to get your head caved in."

"No, I just want a game of football. I work all week, and on my time off I like to kick a ball around, but it's so boring on my own."

"Are you going to move or not?"

"Let me think, mmm. Not."

"OK lads" says Dreadlocks, with that they all take out their truncheon sticks, "get him." They start to charge,

49

but by then they are charging at fresh air, I'm now the other side of them. (*Well the tactic worked before right, it can't hurt to give it another airing.*)

I say, "You're going in the wrong direction boys." With that, they whip round and start charging again; not realising, in their frenzy, they could have carried on to the shops, but too late, once again I've reverted to the other side of them, but this time I put the ball down and wait for their next charge, saying, "Wrong again boys," they're now even more in a frenzy and blindly charge again.

I move like greased lightning and remove all of their truncheons. They gasp with astonishment as I ask, "Now what boys?"

"Are you some kind of freak," says the lad who I know to be Joel.

"No, I'm an ordinary guy, who would appreciate a game of football; so how about it Joel?" The shocked look on his face is a sight to behold.

"You know my name?"

"I just said it, didn't I? What's the name of your dog, Freddy? And Winston, I like your hair style, you should keep it like that."

"Don't answer him, Freddy," says Joel. "Look, I don't know who or what you are, and you may be able to stop us going through to the shops, but you can't make us play football, if we don't want to."

"True, we could just stay here and chat all day," I say nonchalantly.

"What the Hell, let's give the freak his game of football, then perhaps he'll leave us alone," Says Winston.

They turn around and head for the common ground, which they passed earlier.

"Freddy, what is the name of your dog?" No answer. "Which one of you is Ron?" Still no one answers, but I notice that one of them blushed and looked more nervous than the others; a ginger haired spotty youth of about seventeen. That seemed to work, so I try the same tactic on Fin, Billy and Syd.

Great! Now I've got faces to go with the names of seven of them, only five to get. Fin is a coloured lad, around fifteen going on sixteen, Billy, a burly lump of about seventeen, and Syd, a slim six-footer, possibly aged eighteen.

"Listen mate, or whatever your name is, we're going to give you a game of Football, but that doesn't mean we have to talk to you," says Joel.

"Fine" I say as we arrive at the open ground, "just listen then, we are thirteen, so if we are going to have two teams of six, one of us needs to stand down, and by the way, my name's Gordon."

"Freddy, can stand down, he's got to mind his dog," says Winston, "and so yea know, we're only go-in ter play half hour each end."

"That'll suit me, I tire easily," I respond.

The game is part way through the second half, with the score at two apiece, and I say, "I'm dropping out, let Freddy, have a go, and I'll look after his dog."

Freddy, who could see his mates beginning to enjoy themselves, was looking glum at being left out.

"Thanks, but "Crusher" won't be looked after by anybody but me."

"Ah! So that's his name, is it?"

Freddy, looks embarrassed as he glances toward Winston, knowing he's slipped up.

"Go on Freddy, I'll take my chances with "Crusher". Great name by the way." Freddy, passes me "Crusher's" lead, and runs on to the make-do pitch.

"Crusher" starts growling at me, so I stoop down on my haunches and say, "What's the matter with you then?" and give him my knuckled hand to sniff.

He gingerly sniffs it and looking into my eyes, seems to decide that I'm alright, so I stand up to watch the remainder of the game, only to find that all of the players are staring at me in absolute wonder! I'm sure they all expected me to be mauled to death.

What they didn't know, is that I have always had a way with dogs. I can remember that there was, what many people called a vicious dog, living at the first house that, when I was a Paperboy, I had to deliver a newspaper to. This particular road was one that I had to double back on before proceeding to the next. The dog, wouldn't you know it, was named "Brute," I used to roll up the newspaper for each house and put the paper for each house into "Brute's" mouth, and he would help me deliver that road's papers.

"What are you all staring at? Get on with the game; it'll be final whistle time soon." They come out of their open-mouthed stupor and complete the game, with Winston's side winning three/two. I clap heartily and say, "Well done boys, there are some good players among you; you should consider forming a team, and entering a league."

"Look Gordon, you've had your game, now clear off and leave us alone," says Winston.

"That's a pity I was hoping to treat you all to a drink at "Mollies Café" (*I'd spotted it earlier*) by way of a thank you for the game, and I promise this time to let you down the bus station passage," I say with a smile.

"You didn't give us much choice about that, and you know you didn't. By the way where's our sticks?" asks Winston.

"Oh those, you'll find them in the copse, about two miles away."

"Great, so what do we defend ourselves with now?" says Joel.

"You don't need defending, guys. It's the people of this estate that need the defending."

"So, now we come to the real reason you're here. I thought it was too good to be true; someone who might possibly care about us," continues Joel.

"I care a lot more than you think. I hate to see young people like us, throwing our lives away; as you're doing. Why don't we go for that drink and talk about it?"

"Get stuffed" says Joel.

Winston jumps in with, "Hang on, why pass up the chance of a free drink? We were going to the shops anyway. We can always have our usual fun afterwards."

As we all pile into "Mollies café." Molly, the proprietress says, "You lot get out of here, you're not welcome in here."

I say, "I'm sorry, it's my fault; Molly, is it?" I know it is, she has a name tag on her blouse. "Only these youngsters have just done me a good turn and I would like to buy them a drink. I will make sure they behave while they're in here, is that alright?"

"This lot, doing a good turn, wonders will never cease, but I suppose there's a first time for everything. What are they having?"

"I'm sure they can speak for themselves, Molly, in fact, I find them quite intelligent. Come and tell Molly what you would like to drink lads."

I've asked Molly if it's alright if we put a couple of tables together; if we re-site them afterwards. She gives the go ahead and serves the drinks, which I've paid up front for, plus tip, "Thanks Molly," I say, and look at the boys and nod towards Molly. One or two catch on, and finally they all say. "Yes, thanks Molly."

Molly smiles and says, looking at me, "Perhaps they're not so bad after all."

"OK lads, let's get down to business. I meant what I said to Molly. You lads, on the whole, are bright; not in the educated sense because it's obvious that you have wagged school more than you have attended, and you have been lacking parental guidance, but in the raw intelligence sense. I would sincerely like you all to think very seriously about the idea of starting a football team, if not that, perhaps some sort of youth club with Winston and Joel as the club leaders."

"Why not you as the club leader," says Freddy.

"Because, Freddy, I wouldn't be able to devote enough time to it. Besides I would like it to be your club not mine."

'My goodness Jake,' thinks Phen; 'that was a good one!'

'Thanks, Phen, I was beginning to think you had gone to sleep.' 'No, just observing.'
'Well don't let me disturb you,' I think, slightly irritably.

"Winston, I would like to take you and Joel on a little trip to meet a couple of friends of mine."

'Where are you thinking of taking them Jake,' thinks Phen?

'To John and Ken's, as you know we've dropped by to see them a couple of times and each time found that they are doing better and better. In fact, they have now found some small premises to operate from and two more lads have joined their LUHC. I think it would do Winston and Joel some good to meet them.'

Phen thinks, 'do you think John and Ken will recognise you when you get there?'

'Good question Phen; I'll try and work it out on the way there.'

"What about us?" asks Syd?

"You can either hang around here in Mollies or have a wander around the shops, but keep out of trouble. We shouldn't be too long."

I lead Winston and Joel round the side of the café and say, "What's going to happen now, is that I'm going to lift you both up and fly you to see two friends of mine; please don't be afraid, just trust me." With that and before they have a chance to protest, I wrap an arm around each of their waists and take off. Seconds later, I've landed behind John and Ken's little premises.

"You must be from another planet," says Joel; just before Winston can say the same thing.

"No, but that's a long story, that I may tell you one day, but for now, let's go and see my friends. Actually, that part's a bit of a fib."

"You mean a lie?" says Joel.

"Well, yes but only a small one; they are really friends of a friend."

Luckily, John and Ken are in, "Hello" I say. "My pal, you know the guy that got you started on your project, has asked me to ask you, if you wouldn't mind having a chat with Winston, here and his pal Joel. They've got themselves into a spot of bother, so I would appreciate your telling them, roughly, if you know what I mean, about how you got started, what it is you do, and where you feel your project is going to take you?"

Half an hour later as John and Ken wind up their talk, I say, "Thanks John, Ken, I really appreciated that, and I'm sure the boys did. It's, been nice meeting you."

"You too, what is your name by the way, so that I can tell our friend we have met you," says John.

"It's Gordon."

"Well it's been great meeting you Gordon," and with a glint in his eye adds, "You know your voice sounds very familiar??"

'Get us out of here quick!' thinks Phen.

I needed no prompting, and have the lads in the air and back behind the shops before you could say Jack Robinson. 'Before you ask Phen it's just an old saying. Don't ask me to explain it; I've no idea who Jack Robinson is or was.

"Why do you choose places to take off and land where you can't be seen, are you ashamed of your powers?" asks Winston.

"No, I just don't crave publicity, so I would appreciate it if you didn't tell anybody about our little trip. Now, before you re-join the others, I would like to know if you found the meeting with John and Ken useful."

"Yyyes-- but it doesn't relate to our situation does it, because those two lads are obviously decent lads from good backgrounds to start with."

"Winston, Joel, I'm going to tell you something now, that you must never repeat. Those two lads are both from broken homes, and where a lot worse off than you, also they were a more evil than all you lads put together. When my pal and I first came across them they were in the throes of raping a young girl."

"God how sick!" says Joel.

"Yes, but as you saw, they have turned their lives around, and you can do the same.

You all have a lot to think about, so I'm going to leave you now, but I will be back in a few days to see how you're getting along."

With that, I take off for home, but drop by on the way to give Doris a progress report. Then leave by saying, "Fingers crossed".

4

Funding and Stuff

Phen I've been thinking about the name I gave you at our first meeting. It doesn't seem appropriate anymore. If you remember, I referred to you as the Phenomenon, which I shortened to Phen. Well, I no longer think of you as a phenomenon, more like, as you say, a partner, but more accurately, as a brother. I could start calling you Brother or Bro, for short.'

Phen thinks, 'I understand your thinking, and I too feel that we have become more like brothers than partners, but I do not like the name Bro. So, if it is alright with you, I would prefer to keep the name that I have become used to. Even though, as only you and I know, it is short for phenomenon.'

'Suit yourself, Bro!'

'Ha! Ha! Very funny!'

We've been back twice to see the gang of twelve, and Phen and I are pleased with the efforts they're making. We know that it isn't easy for them to make such big adjustments to their way of life. Phen and I are trying to give them as much support as we can.

What they are doing, which I feel is very ambitious, is to combine the two ideas of starting a youth club and a football team at the same time. They plan to have a youth club with a football team attached, and possibly take on other youth club teams, if such things exist. On this visit I say to them, "Have you any idea of how you are going to fund it?"

"Not really, as yet," says Winston. "We did think of asking local shops to help us, if we don't cause them anymore trouble."

I responded to that with, "That sounds too much like a protection racket," I say with a hint of a smile. "However, if you tell them what you're doing, and what your plans are; they may volunteer some help, plus I know some people in the area who may also be able to help."

Phen thinks, 'Who do you have in mind for that, Jake?'

'Why! Doris and her cronies, of course.'

My final words to the gang are, "Hang in there; I'll see you soon."

On my way back I call on Doris, not only to see how she is, but also to ask her to rally her troops, and ask them if there is any way they could do a bit of fund raising for the boys.

Another Monday morning, and it's back to work. It's my first day on the new job. I report to Phil in the maintenance sheds.

He provides me with a French polishing kit in the shape of a wooden box with sloping sides. It has a raised partition in the centre, out of which a slot has been cut, so that it can be gripped. Phil tells me to go down to the cosmetic section. One of the counters there has been damaged on one of its corners, but adds, "Be sure to be back up here for tea break at 10 o'clock."

I'm off to the lifts, one floor down, and meet with a lift attendant who tells me his name is Ted. I say, "Pleased to meet you Ted, my name is Jake. I've just started this morning as maintenance polisher."

"What floor do you want, Jake?"

"I don't know, I was told to go to the cosmetic section."

"First floor," says Ted.

Ted is a guy with one arm, and looks as if he could keel over any minute.

I say, "Are you sure you're feeling alright?"

"Oh, you know, Jake." He says, with a sigh, "Up & Down."

I can't help wondering, how many times during his time working the lifts, that he's made that response.

I arrive at the cosmetic section, see the problem, and begin to rectify it. In what seems like only ten minutes, I glance at the clock on the wall between the lifts; it's nearly 10 O'clock.

I think to Phen, 'Where's that time gone?' I quickly stash my kit away behind the counter and dash to the lifts. I've, only got two minutes to get up to the workshops for tea break.

It's great, for the first time I'm not the one having to make the teas. I sit down for fifteen minutes, and then begin to get up to resume my work.

Phil looks up from his newspaper and says, "Where are you going?"

"To get on with my work," I say.

"Sit down," Phil and the rest of the work force say in unison, "are you trying to ruin it for the rest of us!"

Another half hour later, I'm allowed up. The other guys slowly raise themselves, fold their newspapers, have a bit of a stretch and wander off to their respective tasks.

Again, in what seems no time at all, we're back for the lunch break, which takes up another hour and a half of the day. A bit more work and we are up for afternoon tea, which takes up another three quarters of an hour.

Before I know it, I'm on the way home, and think to Phen, 'Well that was easy enough; I didn't even have to break breath. If every day is the same, I'm going to rot in that place. It's a job that would be more suited to an old chap. A job he could use to finish up his career.

Let's pop in and see John and Ken, I need at least one thing of interest in my day.'

"John," Ken says, "is out on a job."

I say, "How're things going?"

"Not so good Jake. I don't know how much longer we can hold out. Some people donate a little for what we do for them, but not enough. We have to pay rent on our premises, and find that we, more and more, have to dig into our own earnings to subsidise the project."

"I see, I'm sorry to hear that Ken. All I can ask is that you hold on. Rest assured, I'm going to do my very best to find you and John, some funding."

We chat awhile longer, then we shake hands and I say, "I'll see you soon, Okay?"

Phen and I continue home. There is no contact between us for a while. Its weight training night and I have to say, I'm getting this acting thing down to a fine art. The strain that Dave sees on my face as I try to beat my latest Bench Press record, is worthy of an Oscar.

One of the Body Builders, a guy with muscles on his muscles, has seemed unlike himself for some time now. His speech is slurred and I know for sure he doesn't touch alcohol. His eyes seem glazed over at times, and he gets agitated more often, also what is strange, he locks himself in the loo, and when he comes out; within a short time, he seems like his old self.

I re-establish contact with Phen and describe this strange behaviour to him.

He does one of his Mmmm's, and thinks to me, 'Jake I think your Body Builder friend is probably on some sort of drugs. I have seen this sort of thing before; mainly in some of the poorer parts of America.'

'Really…You know more than me then, but from what little I do know, the symptoms do seem to fit his strange behaviour'

I go and have a word with Harry, our coach, and ask him what he thinks. He confirms Phen's suspicions, that

Stewart, he fears is hooked on some sort of drug, perhaps some kind of muscle enhancer, or whatever.

'Phen, I'm going to follow him for a few nights to see if we can find out from where he's getting these drugs.'

'What has happened to your principal of only helping after you have been asked? No one has asked you to help them.'

'I'm sorry Phen, it looks like I'll have to bend the rule in this case. This is too important to ignore.'

Dave makes his own way home, and I dog Stew's footsteps.

I've struck out tonight, Stewart has gone straight home. It's not to say he is getting his drugs at night, but like me, he has to go to work during the day. So, logic dictates he's probably getting his supplies after dark; when these sorts of transactions are less visible.

After work for the next three nights, we keep an eye on Stewart.

It's on the fourth night, a Friday club night that we strike gold. Soon, after he left home, he dodged down by the side of the "Globe" pub, where he met a slimy sort of a guy who sold him something wrapped in a small packet.

Phen and I watch as Stewart continues on his way to the club, but instead of following him, we follow, who for want of a better name, I'll suitably call Slimy.

He goes into the "Globe" where he sits with a pint, obviously waiting for more clients. During the evening, a few come and sit with him and surreptitiously pass money to him, and he drugs to them.

We follow him the rest of the night, hoping he'll lead us to the guy, above him. No luck so far.

We manage to pick up Slimy's trail again the next day, and follow him to the red-light area of the city. We watch him meet up with a grubby looking character in an abandoned warehouse.

There is no dialogue between Slimy and Gruby, also for want of a better name, but Slimy, hands over what looks like a goodly sized wad of notes, and receives a largish package, about the size of a bag of flour, in exchange.

'What's your rule Phen about using some of my powers to steal from guys like these two?'

'Just apply the guidelines that you have come to accept.'

'I see, so, what you're thinking is: providing I don't physically hurt them when relieving them of their ill-gotten gains, and don't keep the proceeds for myself, I'm within the guidelines.'

'I knew I could leave you to work it out for yourself,' he thinks, with mild use of my sarcasm.

We've followed Gruby and as he walks down an alley running between some houses, I land, right in front of him, disguised as Gordon.

"Where did you come from!!!" exclaims Gruby.

"You don't want to know. What, you need to do, is hand over the money you received a while ago, for supplying drugs."

"Get lost, and get out of my way." At which he produces a gun from behind his back, and he's about to aim it at me when I reach out and bend the barrel skywards.

He stares down in bewilderment. Before he can recover, I reach into the pocket, that I had earlier seen him put the money, and relieved him of it.

A little fifty-foot leap, plus hover, puts me where I can observe him. He is standing there, or more accurately, staggering there, completely and unbelievingly stunned. He keeps looking around searching for me, and finally drops down in despair, with one hand wiping his brow and the other feeling his empty money pocket. He screams out, "NO! What the hell just happened???"

He finally calms down and heads for a house across the road from the passage. I linger awhile, until I see a light go on, in an upper floor window.

I'm hovering outside the window, and see him go to a wardrobe and take down a large box. On one side of the box's interior, are packages of drugs, and on the other, bundles of banknotes. He peers at the contents, with a look of relief. I wait for him to replace the box and leave the room.

I enhance my hearing, so that I can hear where he is in the house, hear the kettle being put on in the kitchen, break the lock on his window as quietly as I can, and enter the room. I creep over to the wardrobe, and relieve him of his stash of drugs, leaving his cash untouched.

'Why have you not stolen his money?' thinks Phen, 'I thought that was the idea, to provide funds, for John, Ken and the gang of twelve.'

'That certainly was the idea Phen but events have now exceeded the original idea. I think we have the opportunity here to do some lasting good and on a bigger scale. There is enough money in Slimy & Gruby's original wad to ease the pressure on the lads for now.

What I'm interested in now Phen, is what is going to happen when Gruby finds that his stock of drugs has gone missing. I reckon that, if he wants to stay in business, his only recourse will be to take his money and go and restock. I hope to follow him to the drug dealers even higher up the chain.'

'Now who has the devious mind,' thinks Phen. 'I take it that you have thought what you are going to do with the stolen drugs?'

'I'm going to throw them into the lobby of the West Midlands Police HQ, with a note attached saying, ... Drugs relieved from a drugs peddler, please dispose of them as you see fit ... I shall of course, like all good thieves, wear gloves and wipe any finger prints that I might have already left on the packaging.

I shall make my pass at speed, so that no one will see me. After that I shall inform "The Post & Mail" newspaper. That will act as a safeguard should the enterprising policeman who picks up the drugs, takes it into his head to make a few bob, or should I say bobby, on the side.'

67

'Jake, I think there is a bit of devilment to your nature that I had not noticed before.'

After popping home for some snap, 'food and drink, to you Phen, if you're thinking what's snap?' I fly off and resume my vigil over Gruby's house.

It's nearly midnight and there has been no sign of Gruby going anywhere. I think, 'Home to bed, gets my vote, Phen.'

'Very wise Jake, I know I do not need sleep but I am sensing that mentally, if not physically, you are tiring.'

I've spent a week of evenings keeping an eye on Gruby but so far, he's gone nowhere. He must have some emergency supplies stashed somewhere, and talking about supplies I'd tracked down Slimy, relieved him of his bag of drugs and added it to those I'd delivered to the police.

The rest of the dreary week I'd spent at the new job, including Saturday.

The only thing to relieve the weeks boredom, was noticing, through my peripheral vision, several young lady assistants, leaning over their counters and ogling my posterior as I've passed. I still can't stop smiling about it, and to be honest, I'll admit to a feeling of pride. After all, not every young man has a bum worthy of being ogled by the store's girls!

Come Sunday morning I head for the weights club and on the way think to Phen, 'I feel we should give ourselves a pleasant day for a change, Pal. After my workout, why don't we go and divvy out the money we relieved Gruby of.'

Afterwards though, it's important that Phen and I pick up Gruby's trail, as we want to make sure that he's got no drugs to sell to Slimy and through him to Stewart. It's not going to be easy for Stewart to go cold turkey, but in the long run I'm hoping he'll benefit. If I can find the time, I'll see if there is any way that I can either comfort him, or get him some comfort. Perhaps Harry can help, there's a chance I'll see him at the club, shortly.

Dave and I make our separate ways to the club these days. There has been no falling out; it's just that our priorities have changed. We still, make our way home together, well mostly anyway.

At the club, Stewart is looking a bit grey; I go over to him and ask him if he's alright.

"Yes!" he snaps "why wouldn't I be?"

"No reason, it's just that you haven't been looking your usual healthy self these past few weeks."

He softens, his head goes down and he says, "Jake, I'm in trouble, I've allowed myself to get hooked on drugs, thinking it would help my training for the Mr England Physique contest but I'm afraid it's having the opposite effect; I don't know what to do."

"No names - No pack drill, Stewart but the problem may shortly be resolved. It will probably mean you going cold turkey, but at least you've got this early warning, so you've some time to prepare yourself."

69

With that I give him a pat on one of his massive shoulders, and leave before he can ask me what I mean.

I go over to Harry. "Harry, I've been talking to Stewart and now know for certain that he has a drug problem. Don't ask me how, but I know that his supplies are going to be cut off. This means, he is going to have a tough time. I do believe though that he genuinely wants to quit. Is there any chance you could keep an eye on him; say for the next two weeks?"

"That'll be alright Jake, Stew's worth the bother."

Me and Dave say a general, "See you soon" to the guys, and this time, leave together.

Dave says "Are you alright Jake? Only I've known you for years and I have to say, there is something very different about you."

"Thanks for caring mate, but it's nothing to worry about, I think it's called growing up."

"Good," says Dave, "because I've done some growing up too. I've met a smashing girl and we are going to get married and emigrate to Australia."

"My God, Dave! You don't make changes in small steps do you, but congratulations mate, I suppose it had to happen to one of us sometime, I hope you and your girlfriend will be very happy.

Who would believe it? The great philanderer getting married; she must be quite a girl?" We get off our bikes at the spot we normally go our separate ways, and I give him a man hug and say, "Don't forget the invitation."

I grab a sandwich at home, use the loo and leaving "The Don" behind, fly off and head for John's. I know he and Ken usually get together most Sundays, and it's usually at John's. Phen and I have discussed the money on the way and have decided to give the larger half to John & Ken. They will receive two thousand, two hundred & five pounds, which should keep them going nicely for a while.

Phen and I arrive, and I say, "John, Ken, I thought I'd find you here; how are you both?"

"Fine," Ken replies. "Apart from what I told you the last time I saw you; we've just been talking about those matters."

"I thought you were looking a bit gloomy," I say with a beaming smile all over my face.

"It's not funny Jake! Ken and I have worked really hard for this project," says John, somewhat agitated by my seemingly flippant behaviour.

"You will think it funny; when you get a hold of this." As I speak, I dump the bundle of cash into John's hands.

They both look at it with gaping mouths, and in chorus say, "Bloody hell! Where did you get that?"

"As I said to Ken the other day, ask no questions hear no lies. All you need to know is that you can use it without worry. The only thing I would say to you both is don't rest on it. You both need to be a little more business-like. I suspect that a fair number of the people that you have done jobs for have been taking advantage of your kindness.

71

They could, I'm sure, have afforded to be a little more generous with their donations. After all you're saving them the cost of hiring expensive professionals. If you have any problems with any of them, don't hesitate to ask for my help."

I stop with them for a while longer while I drink the cuppa that John's made, and then depart.

Phen, on the way back thinks, 'What's going to happen with the other two thousand? Are you going to give it all to the gang in cash or …?'

'You're jumping ahead of me again, Phen. I think the best thing to do is go and see them, and see how the land lies.'

I've spotted them playing football, on the open ground that we'd had our previous game on. I land behind a big tree, change back to Gordon and walk forward as though I was just passing.

I stand watching the game and to my delight there are a few other spectators, one of whom I recognise immediately, it's Doris. Going over to her, I say. "Hello Doris, I didn't expect to see you here."

"I don't see why not, you did ask me to see what I could do for the boys"

"Yes, but I didn't mean for you to have to traipse around like this, especially with you having to use a walking stick."

"Gordon it's given me a new lease on life, I'm so grateful to you. There's Bill over there by the way, and the others watching are parents of some of the boys, isn't that great!"

"It certainly is," I reply. "How's it going otherwise? Has there been any progress on the fund-raising front?"

"Some Gordon but it's slow, one or two shop keepers have helped a bit, including Molly at the cafe, but we will keep trying. I have told the boys that I'm a friend of yours, and that I have formed a committee to help raise funds for their projects. I can't believe how grateful they are. Two weeks ago, they would have spat in my face."

"That's progress for you," I reply, smiling.

'Are you thinking, what I'm thinking Phen?'

'I think so Jake, instead of handing the cash over to the boys, you are thinking that at this early stage of their development, it would be more prudent to leave it in Doris's hands, so that she and her committee can use it as they see fit. For example, football boots etcetera.'

'Precisely my thoughts Phen. That way it'll build a stronger bond between Doris's mates and the boys. The boys will think they are really going out on a limb for them.'

"Doris, please open your handbag for a moment will you." She looks at me quizzically, obviously thinking that's a strange request, but as she now trusts me, she complies.

I drop the bundle of money in her bag and say, "Buy them some football boots and kit. Anything left over

73

use it as you and your pals see fit. The boys must believe that the money's a result of your fundraising, so introduce it to them slowly. Although, I don't know why I'm saying this to a wise old bird like you," I say smiling, then add, "Don't tell the boys that I've been here on this occasion, unless they ask. If they do, just say that I was just passing through, and that I will see them again for a longer stay, shortly."

5

It's time to get back on Gruby's trail. I fly to his house, this now being late Sunday afternoon and see no sign of him. I enhance my hearing again and listen at his back door, but hear no movement inside, no radio, no television on, so apart from a bit of scratching; possibly from a few house mice, the house is deserted. I fly up, hover and notice that the green car that had been on his front drive the last time I was here, is missing. It's a pity we had to delay making this trip till now, Phen. It looks like the pigeon has flown.'

'I am, gradually, getting used to these sayings of yours Jake. I have not asked you about them lately, as like this one; I have been able to work them out. Me being a modest super intelligent entity, you understand.'

'Well, try using some of that super intelligence to think, what to do now?'

'Whatever it is Jake, we will have to do it before your bedtime. You have work tomorrow.

'Don't remind me Phen. I don't think I'm going to last too long in that job.'

'Let us concentrate on the matter in hand Jake. We could try asking one or two of Gruby's neighbours if they know where he has gone,'

'I suppose it's worth a try.'

'Do you think you should change your appearance, before you do?'

'Phen, that's a good idea,' I say as I change.

Phen, thinks, 'You do not look a bit like Gordon!'

'That!' as I stand here dressed in a black suit and shirt, with a white "Dog Collar", 'is because I'm not Gordon. Just call me Father Smith.' I now have a more angular face with slicked back brown hair, a parting on the left, and standing a slim six foot tall.

I ring the bell on the house to the left of Gruby's as you look at it. There's no answer, but I see the curtains twitch.

The resident's probably saw my "Dog Collar" and thought that I'm collecting for the church fete or something, and decided not to answer the door.

I'm now ringing the bell on the house to the right. I'm hoping to have more luck here. There's a chance that this lady & gent; who I also saw peeking through their curtains, are more your stereotypical busy bodies.

As the door is opened, I say, "Good evening, I am so sorry to disturb you. I'm Father Smith. I have been told that the gentleman next door is a troubled soul, and seeks the solace of a priest. Would you happen to know where he is?"

"I can't be sure Father. George might know. Would you like a cup of tea?" before I can answer she calls out, "George, go and make the Father, a cup of tea. Milk and sugar?" she asks.

"Yes please, one sugar. You were saying about your neighbour?"

"Oh yes, as I was saying, I can't be sure, but he does go off to Liverpool about once a month. I asked him about it once; he said that his mother lives there, and

76

that he has to go and see her on a regular basis; else she gets worried. I also asked him, if he was brought up in Liverpool. He said yes, but do you know it's strange; he doesn't have any trace of a Liverpudlian accent at all?? In fact, I'd say he's more Brummie than I am.

"Did you, by any chance, notice when you last saw him?"

George, who had just finished pouring the tea, says, "I spoke to him this morning. He told me his Mother wanted to see him earlier in the week, but he couldn't get away. He said he would be going today. I think it was about three o'clock when I noticed his car had gone off his drive."

I finish my tea; thank them very much indeed for their help, and say goodbye with a heartfelt, "God bless."

'There we are then Phen, we're in luck…. Liverpool. …. Do we go now or ….?

'If we don't go now, he may well be on the way back before we find out who he is meeting,' interjects Phen.

'Yes, and if he left here at three o'clock, he's had a good head start, so we'd better get a move on.'

I lift off, and after a quick stop off at home to throw a few things into a Holdall, I head for Liverpool at near top speed, enhancing my eyesight as we go. In three minutes, we reach the junction between the Motorway & the East Lanc's Road that leads to Liverpool.

'I'm slowing down, Phen. I think I spotted something a few miles back.' I retrace my route. Yes, what had caught my eye was a traffic accident.

'That would have slowed him down Phen and I'm fairly sure that I didn't spot Gruby's green "Austin Princess" up till that point. Let's press on and take a look along the East Lanc's Road, I'll go a little slower to make sure I don't miss him.'

It's not until I've passed the sign saying, "Welcome to Liverpool," that I spot a green "Austin Princess", that's pulled on to the forecourt of a petrol station.

I fly down, conceal myself, and wait to see who gets into the car after paying the petrol bill. Dam!! It's not Gruby!

'What are the chances Phen, of there being two green "Austin Princess's" on this stretch of road?'

'Slim I would say Jake.'

Quickly, I'm back in the air, and further enhance my eyesight and scan nearly every street and road in the city.

It's not, wouldn't you know it, until I'm almost on the point of giving up, that I spot another "Princess," partially hidden by a canopy. The car is parked down the side of a store house that's by the docks. I tone down the eyesight and look across the wide road hoping to see a café opposite. One in which I can eat, hide and observe. No café! That's not fair! There's always a café opposite the observation site, in any of the books that I've read, and the detective films I've seen.

I'm hungry, so I have a quick fly around, and clock a café two roads away, with a sign saying, "We never close."

I order a bacon and egg sandwich, a lidded carton of tea to take away, and use their loo. That's another thing, in all the brave, bold hero books I've read, or films I've seen, none of them seem to eat or go to the toilet. I suppose if they don't eat, they won't need the toilet, but they must have bladders like steel!

I hurry back to the site, clutching my comestibles, see that the car is still there, look around for a vantage point from where I can observe comings and goings, and see that there's a high-rise block of flats, one row of houses back.

'That should do it, Phen. It has a flat roof. I'll pop up there and eat while I watch.'

Not until I've finished eating, and taken my last sip of tea, do I notice any activity. There is someone emerging from the store house. Blast it! A bus and tall lorry have just obscured my view.

'If I can jump in here for a second Jake, it might have been a good idea to ask me to lend you some X-ray vision. Then the inconvenience, of the bus and lorry, would have made no difference.'

'Now he tells me! But fortunately, Phen, it's alright. Gruby hasn't left yet.' Hello! Things are hotting up, time to enhance the hearing. Gruby's arguing with someone outside. He's telling this guy about his recent experiences, and trying to warn him, but the guys having none of it.

He's saying, "Stop wasting my time with these feeble fantasies, Scarface."

"I'm telling you it's true, and if he or it, can find me, he/it can find you. So be warned."

At this point, six evil looking types come out of the building and stand in a half circle around whom, from their body language, must be the boss man. He's saying, "Now, get lost Scarface before I have the boys sort you. You've got what you came for, so on yer bike, and if you come again, don't bring me anymore sob stories."

'I've not noticed any scars on Gruby's face. Have you Phen?'

'Not before it was just mentioned, but using your enhanced eyesight to look more closely, I can see he has a scar down his left jawline, from his ear to his chin.'

In the meantime, Gruby/Scarface has made his way round to his car. He opens the door, gets in and starts the engine. He winds down his window, slowly backs the car out and drives passed the boss man; making, through his open widow, the parting comment, "Don't say I didn't warn you!" and drives off with a screech of tyres.

'We've got a dilemma Phen, should we go back with Scarface and relieve him of his new supply? Or, stay here and investigate this gang of drug dealers? They must be on a different scale to Scarface entirely; otherwise they wouldn't need at least seven of them.'

'A tricky one,' thinks Phen. 'On the one hand, if you do not go after Scarface, his new supply will get back to Slimy, and so to Stewart, whom you are trying to help quit. That is the scenario on a personal level; whereas going after this Liverpool gang will deprive so many more drug dependent people, and help them to kick the habit also. Not that they will appreciate it initially of course, but as they will not know that it is you who is starving them of their drugs; they are more likely to blame their suppliers.

Staying here to do that, will of course, mean that you will not be available for work tomorrow.'

'I'm afraid, Phen, a tricky one doesn't cut it, I'm tempted to let my new job slide, because, as you know, I don't see anything long term about it, but it would be irresponsible of me to quit the job after only one week.'

'On the other hand, what you are doing is too important to let that bother you much.'

'You have a point there Phen but I do have to earn a living.'

'As I see it Jake, there are two solutions to our problem: One, we are planning to steal the ill-gotten gains away from this gang of drug peddlers and use the money for the benefit of, not only those you are currently helping, but possibly many others.

It is likely that the cash from this gang will be a substantial amount, so you may well need to devote a lot more time to overseeing things. You will not be able to leave it all to the likes of the good Doris etcetera.'

'What are you trying to say, Phen? Will you please get to it?'

'What I am saying, Jake, is that I am prepared to bend the rules a little and allow you to keep some of the stolen money for your upkeep. In other words, pay yourself a living wage so that you need not seek employment in the conventional sense.

The second solution may be the best short-term answer, and that is to become self-employed. That way, you can work, but are not restricted to the standard hours and days of working.'

'Phen, I think you've cracked it, you've put the whole thing in a nut shell.'

'Oh no! Not more of your weird sayings!'

'I've decided Phen, I'll follow Scarface to prevent any of his drugs, as you say, getting back to Stewart. Hand in my notice to Phil, then get back here as soon as I can. After all this Liverpool lot aren't going anywhere soon.'

I change into Gordon. Then clutching my Holdall, I fly off to try and pick up Scarface's trail.'

'There he is,' thinks Phen as we are following the Motorway.

'Good, let's wait and see if he stops.'

With fifty or so miles to go, Scarface turns into the car park of an off-road Service Station. I hide until he has gone in, sneak behind his car and wrench open his boot, or trunk as the Americans might say, where earlier we'd seen him load his drug supply. I quickly stuff the drugs under my bits and bobs in the Holdall and close his boot as best I can. Then hang around for a while until we see him get back into his car. Thankfully he's not checked his boot, so as yet, he's not aware of what's happened to him.

'The temptation, to follow him all the way to his home to see his reaction when he opens his boot, is almost overwhelming Phen. I'm sure the display that he gave in the passage leading to his house, will be nothing in comparison, but I'm also certain, that as soon as he gets a grip, he will be on the telephone to his cronies in Liverpool, and saying, I told you so!

What this means for us, is that the Liverpool lot will now take Scarface more seriously, and be on their guard.'

'On that last point, I think you are right Jake.'

After writing another note for the police as before, and depositing these other drugs at their H.Q. I fly home for a good Sunday night's sleep. Hopefully, I will be able to sleep; the thoughts of what I'm going to say to Phil when I hand in my notice, are hanging over me and making me restless.

I'm not looking forward to this one bit. I've arrived at work early for once. Phil hasn't come in yet. I make some tea, as this could come as a slight shock to him. Here he comes. "Good morning Phil, I've made you a cuppa."

"Hello! That's ominous" says Phil.

I say nervously, "I'm afraid it is Phil. I'm very sorry, but I've come in this morning to tell you that I'm leaving."

Phil looks genuinely taken aback, and finally gets out, "Well you haven't lasted long have you? Why on earth would you want to leave a cushy number like this? Plus, the fact that I'd marked you down as the man to take over from me when I retire."

"The cushiness, Phil is one off the problems for me. It's not challenging enough, but that's not the whole story. In fact, the main reason is that over the weekend, something has cropped up which will mean I'm going to be extremely busy, and would need a lot of time off work. I don't think that would be fair to you and "Bumbles." If you and the store manager would like me to work my notice that would be no problem," (*although privately, I'm thinking, it would.*) "I see," says Phil, "I'll go and see what he says."

Fifteen minutes later Phil's back and says, "The manager is extremely disappointed. He feels that you have wasted his time setting you on. He told me to tell you to leave now, and has given me your cards to give you."

"Is that how you feel also, Phil?"

"No, but yes, I am disappointed, but wish you well. I can see that it hasn't come easy for you to quit your job." So, we shake hands, and I leave, but not directly.

Before I leave the store, I go into the store's café and sit down because I'm feeling shaky. I order a pot of tea from the waitress to steady my nerves.

Phen thinks, in his most comforting way, which I have to say is quite endearing. 'It had to be done Jake. It was never going to be easy, but if it is any comfort to you; I am very proud of you.'

I think humbly, 'Thanks Phen, that's nice to know.'

'While you are here, you may as well get something to eat as well. Because if we are going to Liverpool, it may be some time before you get the chance to eat again in comfort.'

'Back down to business ay Phen, like the old adage: If you fall of your bike, get right back on. Okay, so be it, let's talk strategy. When we were doing our observing yesterday you mentioned X-Ray vision. This mission we are going on is likely to be the most dangerous so far. If there are any remaining powers that you haven't told me about, this is the time to tell me. I'm not saying you should pass them all to me now, but it would be helpful to know what is available, should I need any particular help.'

'I take your point Jake and the short answer is: almost any power you think you need in any circumstance; short of some of the powers that your comic book Superman displays. For example, sucking up huge amounts of flood water, huge amounts of poisonous gases and then there's the blowing out of huge amounts of icy breath to quell fires etc. or blowing things and people around.

All very far-fetched do you not think, even for a superman? I mean take the sucking up of huge amounts of water for instance, it defies the laws of physics. Where in the frame of even a giant, is all that water going to? Come on!!!'

'What about lasers, coming from the eyes, to say, melt off locks, or cut through steel bars?' I ask.

'Do you not think that your eyes have enough to do? What with having to change shape and colour when you change your appearance. Then there is sight enhancement, also X-Ray vision? No Jake! If you MUST have lasers you will need special training, so that you can produce them from under your finger nails! But I do not know when you would need that particular power? After all, if you are confronted by steel bars etc. you can simply break them with your great strength.'

'Yes Phen, but that could be very noisy.'

'Okay Jake I will give you that. Perhaps, it would be better to do the training, before we depart for Liverpool, and that applies to X-Rays as well.

While we are at it, we might as well throw in the enhancement of all the remainder of the six senses, and I mean six. What humans call the sixth sense is a highly developed sense in my species.'

After a week of Phen's training, which basically requires different but targeted levels of concentration and focus, I think I'm ready to take on whatever the Liverpool gang can throw at me.

Armed with my packed Holdall and final savings from my bank account, which isn't a fat lot, Phen and I set off.

We take up our position on the roof of the Liverpool tower block we'd used before, and prepare to wait. After an hour, a white van arrives and drives down the side of the store house where Scarface had parked, but this time drives round the back.

'I don't think X-Rays are going to do it, Phen. We are going to have to change our observation site.'

I see an old almost derelict dockside crane. Its cabin is fortunately intact, so settle down in there to watch what happens with the white van.

One of Boss Man's henchmen, comes out of the back door, and greets the van driver, but at the same time is looking around, trying to spot anything unusual.

'It looks as though Scarface managed to spook them after all, Phen.'

'Yes, it does look that way.'

Half an hour later, four of them come out. Three of them start loading the van with boxes labelled flour, but we are sure that with the possible exception of the top layer, they are filled   with drugs. The forth, who is the Boss Man, is now doing the looking around.

On completion of the deal, the van man and the Boss do a kind of handshake cum-hug, and part company.

I enhance my hearing and hear Boss Man say, "Well, that's another deal done without incident. I don't know what Scarface, has been fretting about!"

I think to myself and Phen, 'You will! You will!'

'What, do we do now Phen? Shall we follow that van and destroy the guy's stock of drugs, or shall we wait here in case any more vans turn up?'

'I think we should wait here Jake. We need to see the extent of their operation. We will find the white van later. I see that you have made a note of the number plate.'

So, we wait, and wait, until late into the afternoon, by which time only two more vans had turned up, one dark blue one, and a black one, and I've taken the numbers of both.

What is more interesting, is that, as we're thinking of calling it a day, a beautiful chauffer driven "Rolls Royce" pulls up to the rear door, and a huge man levers himself out of the rear of the car, aided by his chauffeur, as he is not only huge in height, but has the girth of a small moon!

'Well what do you make of that Jake?' thinks Phen.

'I think we have just seen Mr Big and, in more ways, than one. This is becoming more complicated by the hour.'

'I beg to disagree, Jake; I think that our way ahead has just become clearer. We must follow this man. He is probably the top man, and from our perspective, he is the one that we have been trying to get at. "Top Man" has handed himself on a plate to us, to use one of your sayings.'

'Once again Phen, you've hit the nail on the head!'

'Oh dear! Please spare me,' thinks Phen.

We carry on our surveillance, until "Top Man" decides to grace us with his departure. We follow him into the countryside, where his Rolls takes winding lane, after winding lane.

Finally, it turns down a narrow one that ends at a pair of very grand wrought iron gates.

They're opened, on the car's approach, by a gate man. The gate man shoulders his firearm and waves to the chauffer as the car passes.

It continues along a gravel drive for about two hundred yards. The Rolls has now pulled up outside a magnificent Victorian manor house, probably of around twelve bedrooms.

"Top Man" unfolds himself, once again with the help of his chauffeur. The chauffeur reaches into the car and brings out a large doubly thick briefcase.

'What do you think Phen, is that briefcase full of money?'

'If you hurry up Jake, and X-Ray it before they get indoors, you may find out!'

'Sarky!' think I, as I apply my X-Ray vision to the briefcase. 'Yes, it's cash alright and a lot of it. It's no wonder he can afford a place like this.'

'Do you feel, Jake that we should steal that now?

'Not yet Phen, I believe that a lot of these top men have a legitimate face that they present to the general public, and particularly the tax man.

What we need to do is find out what that is? In the meantime, we can at least pinpoint where "Top Man" keeps his cash; ready for lifting later on'

I look for and find a cheap B & B in which to spend the night. I book in as Father Smith and pay up front. "Excuse me Mrs Clegg," she's the landlady, "do you have a telephone I could use?"

"Yes, a pay phone. You passed it in the hall as you came in."

I rake my pockets for loose change and ring the Cole's; they are the only ones in our street with the telephone installed.

I hear the voice of Barbara, a girl who used to take me to school when I was a nipper.

"Hello Barbara," I say barely above a whisper, "it's Jake, I'm not going to be able to make it home tonight. I wonder if you would mind letting my Mom know, to save her worrying?"

"That is Jake from number fifteen, isn't it?"

"Yes Barb."

"Why are you whispering?"

"I'll tell you that when I see you next. If you would kindly pass on my message, I would appreciate it."

"Consider it done," Barbara, replies, and hangs up.

Next day I'm up early, as I want to make sure I don't miss "Top Man" going off to wherever he goes.

It's ten a.m., "Top Man" squeezes into the driving seat of an old "Land Rover". I wonder why he is not using, either his "Rolls Royce," or his chauffeur? I suppose we'll have to wait and see.

We, follow him into Liverpool city centre, and watch him park at the back of a shop.

The shop sign at the front reads, "Big Fred's, Turf Accountants."

'So that's it Phen, that's how he gets away with having so much cash lying about, and why he drives that old "Land Rover." He doesn't want his punters to realise that he's making so much money out of them.'

There's nothing to do here for now, so I take a walk, (*no I haven't forgotten how,*) to Old Hill Street, and after changing into what I think a typical journalist would look like, I go into the nearest newspaper office, and say to a bespectacled, but attractive lady, "Hello, I'm doing some research for a book that I'm writing about betting shops. I wonder if you can help me. Apart from the big ones like "Ladbrokes", are there any others in Liverpool?"

"Oh yes." and she goes on to mention three others.

"I did notice on my way here one called Big Fred's, you haven't mentioned that one."

She smiles at me, and says, "That's because you didn't want the names of the big ones."

"Big Fred's is big, is it?"

"Big Fred's is not only big, but he is big as well, in the physical sense I mean. He must have dozens of shops, up as far as Blackpool and down as far as Chester."

"Well thank you very much for your time, you have been a big help." It's my turn to smile now!

'Well Phen, that eases my conscience. If we steal Big Fred's drugs related cash, he's hardly going to miss it!'

6

Big Fred

It's Wednesday, late afternoon, I've timed it so that I can get in and steal Big Fred's drugs cash before he gets home. I change into Gordon, bypass the front gate, and land outside Fred's study window. There is a large safe in the left-hand corner from where I'm standing. The door to the room, a solid Mahogany beast, is on the right. I look around the window and notice security metal strips crossing from frame to window, in several places. The window is of the sash type. If any of the strips get severed, alarms go off.

'We need a plan B, Phen.'

I glance around and in the nick of time, manage to hide as I can see the chauffer coming out of the four-car garage and going into the Manor's back door.

I sneak into the garage, and there, in the far-left hand corner, is a work bench and a variety of tools.

I strike lucky; stored in the rafters, with a bunch of other stuff is a bundle of thin metal strips. I take two four footish lengths and head back to Fred's study window. I hold one of the strips down the length of the bottom half of the window frame, and using lightning speed and laser power. I weld all the security strips down the left-hand side of the window frame together. Then repeat the process on the right. I'm now able to melt the window lock and lift the window. Whoever might be monitoring the alarm signals, would probably have only heard a couple of tiny bleeps or pings, and fingers crossed, have ignored them.

I climb in, go to the safe, and using my lasers again, start burning around the lock. It's taking forever! It finally gives way and with me enhanced hearing, I hear the drive gates opening.

'Phen I can't believe my eyes! There's cash in here alright, but not nearly as much as I thought there would be. Fred must have taken a lot of it with him.'

Not looking a gift horse in the mouth, I quickly scoop up what cash there is into my empty Holdall. I've left my gear at my digs, as I expect to be back soon for a longer stay. I take the time to wipe away any finger prints, and fly out through the window; just before Big Fred's Land Rover pulls up in front of his garages.

I think to Phen, 'Fred's probably brought some more money home with him, but we can't stop for that now.'

I fly to a quiet spot and count the cash, all ten thousand-four hundred and twenty pound of it.

Phen thinks, 'Jake, you should keep the four hundred & twenty pounds and put the rest in the projects fund.'

'I don't need that much for wages Phen.'

'It is not only for wages, but also for expenses while we are on project business. We don't know how long we are going to be here. There is another thing; where are we going to hide the ten thousand?'

'I'm going to hide it where no one'll think f looking

93

for ten thousand pounds in cash, Phen.'

'Where is that Jake?'

'You'll see.'

With some of Fred's cash in my pocket, I visit a department store and purchase a large briefcase like Fred's, with a catch on it that can be locked, and go into a stall of the stores loo's; fill the briefcase with the ten-grand from my Holdall, and then, still as Gordon, fly at top speed to Doris's.

'Do, you think this is fair on Doris?' thinks Phen.

'Perhaps not, but I can't think of a less likely place that anyone would think of looking, and we're a long way from where we stole it.'

'Yes, Jake but Scarface doesn't live far away.'

'I hadn't thought of that Phen but go with it for now. Perhaps later we'll be able to think of a better place for it.'

With that, and Phen not coming up with any further objections, I ring Doris's door bell and wait the usual length of time for her to answer. She has obviously had a peek through her curtains, because there is no hesitation about removing her door chains. She flings wide the door, and gives me a big hug. I'm sure it would have been a kiss if she could reach. I go in, and she makes me a cup of tea. It's not possible to visit Doris without having a cup of tea.

We settle down and she brings me up to date about the gang, which thankfully is all good.

When I finally get a word in edge ways I say,

"Doris, is there any chance you could find a safe place in your house for this briefcase. You can share the location with Bill if you wish, but with no one else?"

I leave Doris with Mrs Clegg's number, and say, "If you need to contact me, ask for Father Smith. Please don't ask me why.

Before flying back to Liverpool, I pop home and tell Mom I've been invited to stay with a friend for a few days. I go upstairs, pack a few other things into my Holdall, then go down and say to Mom, "Mom there is something I want you and Dad to do for me while I'm away; that is, to get the telephone installed. I'll pay for it when I get back, and for the quarterly bills."

I take some of the money stored in my pocket and say, "Here's my next week's housekeeping Mom, just because I'm away is no reason for you to go short, and by the way if you decide to test the phone, by ringing me, please ask for my friend Father Smith."

"You're a strange one at times Jake but you're a good lad, we'll see you when we see you."

'Will your Mother not worry about your being away,' thinks Phen.

'No, not now I've said I'm going to be away. She's used to my being away, from when Dave and I used to go on bike holidays.'

Carrying my Holdall, I walk until I'm out of site of the house, and of anyone else; then take off for our return trip to Liverpool.

I'm booked in as Father Smith again at Mrs Clegg's

B & B, and this time for a week; which she is pleased about as she has no other guests at the moment.

It's Thursday morning. I'm back spying on Big Fred's mansion and the puzzling thing is: there's a police car on the drive.

I land in a spot just short of the study window, and with my hearing turned up a notch, try to pick up on any conversation that may shed some light on the puzzle. I hear Fred say, "Yes Chief Inspector there is much that is strange about this theft, as you and Roger have pointed out, and yes, Roger did say that the metal strips that are welded to the alarm strips are identical to some he has stored in the garage, but what I must stress is: whatever investigations you make, must be done quietly. I what no publicity about this; do I make myself clear?

"I'll do my best Fred but you know how these things have a habit of getting out."

"I would appreciate it if you would do better than your best or I may start wondering what I'm paying you for. Now I must leave you, if you need to contact me, I shall be at the Blackpool shop."

'That seems to answer your puzzlement Jake,' thinks Phen.

Twenty minutes later, I follow Fred and his Land Rover as they exit his estate.

After two very brief stopovers, at two more of his betting shops, he arrives in Blackpool, and parks his Land Rover in front of what I can't help thinking is his number one shop; judging by its size, and how palatial it looks.

He remains there all morning and into the afternoon. By four o'clock he leaves the shop and drives to Blackpool's "Pleasure Park", goes past the "Big Dipper", and comes to a halt beside a large mobile home. Apart from Fred's, there are four more vehicles parked in front of the trailer. Fred's greeted by a dark feller, possibly West Indian, and a Chinese looking chap. They both stand aside to let Fred squeeze passed into the caravan. I creep up behind the caravan and X-Ray it.

There are six skeletal frames including Fred's and if you want me to be technical, there are, apart from Fred, two other endomorphs, who are probably the enforcers of the group. Two mesomorphs and one ectomorph, who is most likely the Chinaman, (*I got this stuff about body types from Harry, my weight training coach.)*

I now tune in my ears and easily make out Fred's voice, who's saying, "How's business been?"

The man with a West Indian accent answers, "No bad, we may need fresh stock in abou a month."

"That won't be a problem," says Fred and adds, "I'll say to you what I have already said to the Liverpool cell: we need to make more effort to expand our markets. At the moment we're selling to the pop industry and sports, but we need to get to places like prisons and also twelve to eighteen-year-old adolescents, as they are our future business."

'Did you hear that Phen? This man's got no conscience; it's profits at any human cost. We've arrived none too soon …. Targeting twelve-year old's!! The man's a sicko!'

"Here you are Frederick, your usual tipple," says an unaccented voice.

"Thanks Joe. Cheers all."

The meeting winds down by Fred saying, "Wang, if you'll load this month's takings into my car; I'll leave you all with a warning to be on your guard. There have been some very strange occurrences lately." He tells them what Scarface had told the Liverpool cell, to use Fred's terminology, and about the strange robbery at the mansion. He then heads back to Liverpool.

'If I get the chance Phen I'm going to lighten Fred's load. We need to make him a lot jumpier, so that he starts making mistakes.'

'He doesn't strike me as the type to get jumpy,' says Phen, 'he is clearly in charge of a vast network of these cells, not to mention his betting shops and goodness knows what other pies he has his fingers in.'

'Your sayings are getting as bad as mine Phen! But you may be right, I may be taking on more than I can chew at this stage, but it seems to me, until we can find a way to put a really big dent into his operation, we'll just have to keep nibbling away at him.'

'I think we should review the idea of lifting Fred's cash for now. I do not know if you noticed but he has his briefcase chained to his not insubstantial wrist. You cannot wrench it from his wrist, as that may physically harm him, but you can take whatever's in the briefcase, and the money from the locked boot of his car, but I think at this stage we do not want to make your presence too obvious; it is best to keep Fred thinking of you as an enigma. There may be a better way to get to him in the short term.'

'How's that Phen?'

'You remember when he was with the police inspector, he was very insistent about keeping the robbery out of the public eye. Well, I think we should give him the publicity he does not crave.'

I take Phen up on his suggestion, and fly to the newspaper office, I had previously visited.

Hoping I've remembered the details of my previous appearance, I walk into the office where thankfully the same lady is seated at her typewriter.

"Hello again," I say.

"Oh Hello; how's your research going?"

"Very well thanks, but that's not what I'm here about this time. I was wondering if it's possible for me, as a freelance journalist, to get a news item that I've come across in the course of my research, printed in your newspaper?"

"I suppose, it may be possible. I would have to run it by the Editor first, of course. What is the news item?"

"Well, I see that there's a typewriter not being used on that desk over there. With your permission, I'll type it up for you, then you can read it and decide if you can help, or not."

'I did not know you could type?' thinks Phen.

'I can't, I'm just going to wing it, and hopefully with my super speed etc. I can manage to look authentic.'

On completion of the document, I give it to the lady.

She takes about five minutes to read and re-read it, then looks up and says, "this is explosive stuff, are you sure of your facts?" "Positive," I say.

"Wait there a moment," she gets up and goes and taps on the Editor's glazed door.

"Come in Jane." She goes in. I enhance my hearing and hear her explain what's happening. She then passes my document across his desk for him to read. He reads it, and says to Jane, "you had better leave this with me. Ask the young man to come back in an hour. I will let him know then, if I'm prepared to run it or not."

Jane comes back and tells me what the Editor has said. I make to leave, but stand just out of sight of the doorway, and giving my hearing an extra boost, focus it on the Editor's office.

I hear the telephone being lifted and dialled. "Oh, Hello Sir, this is Harold from the Liverpool Gazette. Yes, I'm fine, and you… good. What I'm ringing about is…."

He finishes the story, and reads my document to whoever is on the other end. After listening for a while, he puts down the phone, and comes out to Jane and says, "I've been on to the Proprietor. He's going to ring Big Fred and try to confirm the young man's story. As you know, he and Fred are members of the same businessman's club. He says he will ring me back in twenty minutes."

I go back after the hour is up but I already know the answer. Jane tells me, "No, we can't use it," but I detect a slight tone of regret in her voice. I don't want to embarrass her, so I write a note on her pad saying, would you meet me for a drink after your work, to discuss this further? She rips the note off, destroys it, and writes a note to me simply saying five thirty, "Kate's Café". I'm Jane.

"Thanks ever so much for agreeing to meet with me Jane. My name is Sean. I could sense that you were not happy with your Editors decision back there, and your agreeing to talk with me confirms it. You don't have to tell me, but what is the name of the Paper's Proprietor?"

"Information comes with a price Sean," she says with a smile, "you haven't bought me a drink yet."
"How could I forget, what would you like?"

"A pot of tea and a slice of carrot cake, please."

"I'll have the same." I say to Kate, who's hovering for our order, and add to Jane, "Decadence just oozes out of us, don't it?"

"His name is Reginald Martin-Smyth; he owns a chain of local newspapers up and down the coast. Now, it's my turn: is it really true that the Chief Inspector's on Fred's, pay roll?"

"I'm sorry Jane, but every word in my news report is the gospel truth. The worst thing for you is that your Proprietor's at least covering for himself and Fred. Plus, the thought that there is probably very little we can do about it."

"Don't be so sure Sean, it mustn't come from me, you must go and see him yourself, but there's only one independent local newspaper left. It's owned and edited by a friend of mine. His name is David Jones and the newspaper is "The Inquirer." I'll ring him on Kate's phone, and ask him to see you. After that you're on your own, I can't get involved any further; it's more than my job's worth, but good luck."

"Thanks Jane, you've been a Godsend."

With that she goes and makes the call, comes back and says, "David will see you now. So, turn right out of here and go to the very end of this same street, but be careful, it's only a tiny place. You could easily miss it."

Ten minutes later, I'm sitting in a tiny office with David Jones, a pleasant man no more than ten years my true senior. I say true senior, because my Sean character is older than I truly am. We've shaken hands, talked a little about Jane and I'm now laying out, verbally, what I had typed for her. David, using shorthand, takes it down and reads it. He then says, "Jane tells me, that you swear that every word of this is true."

"That's exactly right David."

"There is only one problem Sean. You are the only witness to this. It probably wouldn't stand up in court. It would be thrown out on the grounds of it being your word against theirs."

"David, I have no intention of it coming to Court, for

me or for you. I will take sole responsibility for the article. Only my name must be attached to it, my surname is Brooks by the way. The whole idea is to stir things up for those slime bags. Do you know that Fred is the number one man in a huge nationwide drugs trafficking operation?"

"No, I didn't know, you don't mention it in your article. Can I ask if you have any proof of all this?"

"None, other than my solemn word, that it's all true."

"If you don't see all this going to Court, what are you asking me to do?"

"I would like you to run my document, but not the drugs bit. Should you get any heavies asking where you got the information, perhaps you could reluctantly drop it out that it was from the Chief Inspector. That should stir things up even more.

If you're worried that any heavies may do you harm, don't! I am going to recruit a good friend of mine to keep an eye on you and your business for the next two weeks, or more, if necessary. This friend was a top close order combat instructor in the SAS."

"Don't ask me why Sean but I somehow trust you. Just answer me one thing. Why do you so passionately what to stir things up for Big Fred?"

"The main reason is that I believe Fred is going to expand his drugs operation to include the targeting of twelve to eighteen-year-old young people. If there anything I can do to throw a spanner in his works, I'm determined to. Where you are concerned, I don't want to put you in any more danger than necessary. I'm hoping this is the only time that I shall have to ask you to do anything for me."

"OK, we have a deal. The article will appear in tomorrow's edition."

We shake hands and I say, "I don't suppose you would let me treat you to a meal out, as a thank you."

"Perhaps when this is all over, but until then, I don't think it would be wise to be seen in your company."

I nod in understanding, shake his hand, and leave.

At breakfast the following morning, I think to Phen, 'What did you think of the film last night Phen?'

With nothing else to do last night until, if you'll excuse the expression, the shit hits the fan, I went to the pictures. I had thought of inviting Jane but thought that the same thing applies to her, as to David.

'Do not be offended Jake, but it was very dull.'

'No offence taken Phen, the important thing is: what do we do now? For one thing, I would like to be there when, or if Fred reads "The Inquirer".'

'We could go and see if things are going alright at home, but you really need to be here to protect David should Fred retaliate.'

'Yes Phen, that's our number one priority.'

Breakfast is half over, when Mrs Clegg comes in and says, "Father there is a telephone call for you in the hall."

'That's puzzling Phen, who would be calling me here?'

I don't wait for Phen's thoughts but go and answer it. "Mom!" I'd forgotten that I'd left this number with Mom. My first thought had been that it might be Doris, remembering I'd given her the number also.

How's things …. Yes, I'm pleased you've got it installed but you wouldn't be ringing me if you hadn't. … no Mom I'm not being sarky," … I note the number, and say, "Yes Mom, love you too…. yes, goodbye, thanks for the news, bye."

'What time did David say this Friday's paper will be on the streets?' thinks Phen.

'He didn't but if it's like the local at home; it will be about mid-day. Which means, we have time to go and relieve Fred of some more money, before the fun starts.'

'Or,' Phen thinks, 'we could chase up the three vans that you have the numbers of?'

'I think you're right as usual Phen and as you said before, best not to stray too far from here. Let's go to the local Vehicle Licensing Office and see if they will let us know who the vans belong to?'

'Mmmm, (*here we go again with the Mmmm's,*) I was thinking Jake, would they give out that sort of information to just anybody or would it have to be some kind of official person, such as a police constable or a detective?'

'I don't know but it might be an idea to be prepared, as the "Scouts" say.'

I'm here in this photographer's studio having my

105

passport style picture taken as Sean.

"They will be ready in one hour," says the photographer.

"Thank you. Please let me pay you now."

Next stop is a stationery shop to buy some card; followed by another call at David's.

"I'm sorry David, I know I said I wouldn't bother you again, but is there any chance I could use one of your typewriters for five minutes."

"Go ahead but excuse me if I go on werkin; I have a deadline ter meet."

Ten minutes later I have half a dozen cards saying, Sean Brooks Private Detective Agency. Ring ------ This is Mrs Clegg's pay phone number. On the right-hand side, I've left a space for the pics.

I've collected the photos, attached them to my cards and am now on my way to the licensing office.

"Good morning, I represent the Sean Brooks Detective Agency. I wonder if you could run some numbers for me," I say, as I hand over one of my cards, and a note of the numbers.

From those, serving at the counters, I've picked out this man because by the look of his badly worn suit he has the look of a man who could possibly appreciate a few extra quid.

"I'm, not sure whether I can give out that information to an unofficial detective."

I say, "Perhaps you can help me with this other problem then," and hand him a folded sheet of paper in which there's fifty pound in notes. The man glances quickly at the contents and even more quickly pockets it, with more glances left and right, to be sure he hasn't been seen.

"I'll see what I can do, please take a seat over there." Fifteen minutes later he gives me a nod and passes my folded sheet of paper back to me. "I'm sorry; I am not able to help you on this occasion."

But, the merest hint of a wink is enough for me to respond, "Well thank you for your time anyway." I get outside and unfold the paper and there are the addresses that Phen and I, wanted.

When I get back to the city centre the time is twelve thirty. I notice that more than the usual amount of people are standing or sitting reading newspapers. The papers are all "The Inquirer."

One man, who has finished reading his, drops it into a waste bin. I wait until he's walked away and retrieve it.

The Headline reads: -

HEADLINE

A reliable source has informed this newspaper that our Police Chief Inspector is in the pay of Big Fred, the well-known proprietor of the Big Fred betting chain. The inspector who is looking into a strange robbery at Big Fred's Mansion, which has armed guards, cannot understand how the thief could have achieved it without extraordinary abilities. The source maintains that Big Fred told the inspector to keep the robbery quiet, or he would start wondering why he is paying him.

Is this Hoax or Truth?

'Well Phen, the news is out. I'm not sure about the hoax or truth bit but I suppose because of the libel laws; David had to cover his back.

Let's get over to David's, I don't suppose anything will happen yet, but we can't take the chance. Before that though, I may find time to drop by Kate's Caf and grab a takeaway sandwich.'

I find a hiding place from which to change into Gordon and because I'm able to increase or decrease any of my six senses; I can feel the warmth of my hot sandwich through my inside coat pocket.

I then walk along to "The Inquirer" office. I've done an unusual amount of walking today, up until now I hadn't realised how slow it now feels, and enter by ducking under the doorway. Poor David, the look on his face as he sees me, I'm sure he's thinking: it hasn't taken Fred long to send around one of his heavies.

"Hello David, I'm a good friend of Sean's, he may have mentioned me. I'm Gordon."

David calms his heartbeat sufficiently to respond, "Pleased to meet you, please call me Dave. Sean has told me some things about you. How do you propose to look after me? You're only one man. I'm sure that Fred has dozens of men at his disposal."

"Rest easy Dave, you can get on with your work in the knowledge that you are entirely safe."

"Is that arrogance or confidence?"

"Confidence, now the first thing to say, is that this is a very small space, which is to our advantage, as no matter how many men Fred or the PCI send, there is a limit to how many can get in here at one time. The second thing is; do you have a back room?" I take my sandwich out of my jacket pocket, "with a chair in which I can sit and eat my sandwich? And thirdly do you have a loo I can use? I've been busting to go all day."

Nobody comes, apart from Dave's normal customers etc. but come locking up time; Dave looks out before opening his front door.

Dave has worked late, as he often does. That's information I gleaned from the potted biography that he has regaled me with during the afternoon. It's dark outside, and Dave has spotted two unsavoury looking characters lurking across the road.

"What do I do?"

"Dave, if there is one thing that I have learned about you in the short time that I've known you, is that you're a man of courage." Before he can respond I ask, "Which way do you normally turn, when you leave your premises?"

"Right, towards the car park," Dave replies.

"Go out there and do what you normally do. If they only want to engage you in conversation; don't forget to seem reluctant when you drop the PCI into the mire. If they want you to go with them to Fred's or whatever,

109

refuse and don't worry I shall be right with you. You may not see me but I will be there."

'Phen, I have a question before I send Dave out there. I know that I'm not allowed to harm those guys, but are there any rules preventing me from causing them to hurt each other?'

'We will see. I shall be interested to see how you will achieve that.'

"OK Dave, out you go."

Dave opens his door and feels a draught go by him as he turns to lock up, puts his keys in his pocket, and walks toward the car park, just like any other day.

Phen thinks, 'David is playing his part well so far, Jake.'

'Yes, he's doing great.'

Dave has almost reached the car park, when the heavies catch up with him. "Mr Jones, we would like you to come with us, Big Fred would like a word with you."

"What about?" Dave asks, as he continues walking. "You will find out when we get there."

"I'm afraid I have a prior engagement this evening, tell Big Fred that if he needs to talk to me; to come and see me tomorrow."

"You don't understand Mr Jones, when Big Fred wants someone to come and see him, he means now!"

"Well, that is unfortunate, but never mind as I can guess what Big Fred wants to see me about, and that is: who is my source? So, far be it from me to deny Fred what he wants.

Tell him to look closer at his bunch of friends, especially at someone who he has asked to investigate his robbery, and now gentlemen, I bid you goodnight."

Dave starts to walk away, but one of them makes a grab for him, but finds me blocking his way.

I say, "Tut-Tut! That is no way to show respect for one of Liverpool's finest." Out the side of me mouth I say to Dave, "move out of the way Dave" and give him a gentle shove to help him on his way.

Now I have one heavy in front of me and one behind, with Dave looking on.

"You shouldn't have interfered Mr! Now you are going to find out what pain is," says heavy number one.

With that, the one behind tries to grab me round the torso and pin my arms to my sides. The one in front takes an almighty swing at my jaw.

The only contact that he makes is on the jaw of his mate, who goes down like a sack of potatoes.

I re-land after my leap in the air and back up so that I'm standing with my back to the car park wall.

Heavy number one comes after me in a rage, and because he has hurt his hand on his mate's jaw, he takes a vicious kick at my shins, and yes, you've guessed it, I'm no longer there; he only makes contact with the wall. He screams out in agony, swearing, "You've broken my bloody toes."

"No, you did that yourself. Tell Fred when you get back to him, to sleep soundly. If he wakes up, he may find me standing over him. Now, to mimic my friend, we bid you goodnight, and if you try harming Mr Jones

111

again, it's you who will find out what pain is. What you have experienced tonight, won't come close."

'Very impressive,' thinks Phen, 'but I am not sure that I can agree to you causing a lot more pain to those two.'

'Phen you have always said that I must not use my powers to harm another human. Well, in the case of those two, I did them no physical harm, and apart from a bit of speed to leap out of their way, I didn't use my powers. Who knows, I might have been able to move that fast anyway. The other thing is, you didn't say I couldn't threaten harm, only that, I mustn't do harm.'

'I think you are splitting hairs, but we will let it go for now.'

'I'm sorry Phen; I was just having a laugh. I do know, and understand the rules. Just call it a mental exercise, and I like the splitting hairs saying by the way.'

7

I suggest to Phen that we leave Fred to stew for a few hours. Even though I would have loved to have been there when his heavies get back, and listen to the reception they get; I thought it more important to look after David. He's been a stalwart, but at the same time, he was clearly shaken.

Phen agrees by thinking, 'Yes Jake, it probably is a good idea to let Fred mull over what is happening to him.

After seeing Dave safely home and wishing him a goodnights sleep, I get back to my digs for my own goodnights sleep.

The following morning, I enter the dining room to find Mrs Clegg has cooked me a sumptuous breakfast, probably because I've paid her over the odds for my accommodation.

Phen thinks, 'I assume, or more accurately I know, because I have read your mind; that we are going to have some fun this fine Saturday morning chasing van loads of flour!!!'

As we, hover over the first address on the list supplied by our friend at the Vehicle Licensing Office. I notice that the dark blue van is parked outside a three storey Victorian looking place, all brick and no garage.

'That's awkward Phen, I was hoping for a nice easy garage break in, and a quick away. In this edifice the drugs could be stored anywhere. Let's take a look round the back.'

On landing on the patio, I sneak a look through a "French Window", into what appears to be his lounge. There is a shed in the garden but I'm fairly sure he wouldn't keep the drugs in there. Nevertheless, I give it a quick scan. Then turn around and look back at the house and notice that there is a small window open on the top floor.

'Time for another change Phen, neither Gordon, Sean or Father Smith are going to get through there. So, what do you think, a slim young lady or a small thin young teenage lad?'

'The latter, Jake.'

'You've got it Phen.'

A look in a mirror would now reflect a sallow faced dark-haired lad, who looks as though he hasn't seen food for a month. He/me fly up, open the window wider, and slip in. The room entered doesn't appear to have been used for quite some time, apart from some footprints in the dust from the door to the window.

'I don't think we are up against a big chap, Jake; judging by the size of the footprints.'

With heightened hearing, I make my way through the door, search every attic room and scan every eve space. Nothing! So, I move to the staircase, where I pick up sounds of two voices on the ground floor, one male and one female.

I start a search of the rooms on this first floor, looking inside "Wardrobes," and "Blanket Chests".

Nothing again!!

Then BINGO! In a small box room hidden under a blanket and loaded into two large suitcases are the flour bag size packets of drugs. Without hesitation, I refasten the cases and fly up the stairs, cross the attic room and squeeze the cases through the small window. Let them drop, exit the window, and catch them before they hit the ground.

Until I've collected the stock from the other two dealers, I need to find a temporary hiding place for this lot.

The second property is easy; it's the garage one I was hoping for previously. So, it'll be a quick in and out job. In fact, the stuff is still in the back of the black van.

I see a dustbin in the corner of the garage, and after taking the boxes of drugs out of the van; I empty the contents of the dustbin into it, then load the bin with the drugs.

Back at the hiding place, I tip the contents of the suitcases into the dustbin also and hide it. Then I'm off with the cases, to find number three, changing back to Sean as I go.

Number three is our white van driver. I hover high above his house, and think to Phen, 'This could be the most difficult.' This is a large detached house on an exclusive estate that's concealed by a high hedge right across the front of the property; except for the in-and-out drive.

The van driver is standing outside of his front door, with the van's rear doors open. He's talking to two younger men, both of whom I recognise as two of the men that were with Boss Man when he was arguing with Scarface.

I listen and hear white van man saying, "Ray, Sanga wants four packets. You have a walk round to his pad with those, but before you do that, put the remainder of the stock back in the safe."

"OK, Dad."

"Dan, you take the van and deliver these three packs to Sid Jackson and make sure you come back with the money this time, no going into Big Freddie's and blowing the lot on the Gi-Gi's."

"I'll do me best Dad," says Dan.

"Try harder than that," replies the white van driver. Who we now know is the Father of the other two.

Ray unloads what's left of the boxes. Only two remain to be put back in their safe; the rest must have already been distributed.

'Phen I feel sorry for the end users of all those drugs, but we can't steal them now, as it's more important to get back to look after Dave. I think, reluctantly, we'll have to give this one a miss, at least for now. Before I fly off though Phen, I'll take a little time to see where Ray goes.'

He only goes to the bottom, of the unmade-up road; rounds the corner to a house at the end of that road.

He has the drugs in a carrier bag, which as he's about to knock the door, I fly by and snatch. Thinking to Phen, 'It's not much, but every little helps the cause, right?'

Back at the hiding place, I empty the dustbin, break all the packets open and let the contents fall into the bin.

I then bury the wrappers & suitcases, and fly off at high speed to Big Fred's; clutching the dustbin in front of me as I go.

I arrive at the Mansion, and scatter the drugs at high speed along Fred's drive, then drop the bin into one of his many bushes. One of the guard dogs, now part of Fred's extra security, barks but other than that, I go unnoticed.

'What was the idea of that Jake?' thinks Phen.

'A bit of irony, when Fred finds out that some of his profits have come home to roost, he's going to be even angrier.'

'How will he find out?'

'That's part of my dastardly plan. He will find out, because as you can see, the dogs are sniffing the gravel. Very soon now they will be useless as guard dogs.

My plan is to enter the mansion via the door that we saw the chauffer using the last time we were here.

We will first confirm my suspicions that Fred will have had a stronger safe installed and increased the security of the study window.'

I confirm the window security part of the plan using my invisibility speed. Then stop at the garages and X-Ray them. Inside, there is only one being, and he's got his head under the bonnet of a car. I creep up to the Mansion's back door and try the handle. Locked! I thought it might be. The chauffeur's obviously been warned to lock it every time he goes in or out.'

'Not to worry Phen,' I locate the spot where the lock bolt enters the door jam and apply a little laser power. The door gives and I quietly enter, making sure that no bits of the door drop noisily on to the tiled floor.

Listening with my heightened senses, I move to the door leading to the kitchen, and hear the movement of someone approaching.

As the door opens, I oscillate to invisibility. The aproned lady, who is coming through, probably feels a draught as I pass by her, into the kitchen. I go through it and out the other side and find myself in the dining room. I leave that, and still unhindered, head for the study. Oh! Oh! Someone's going in there; looks like a workman. I change into what I think approximates the look of the chauffeur and say, "Sorry to bother you but could you come and give me a lift with something in the garage?"

He looks at me quizzically but shrugs and says, "Sure" he puts his tool bag down and I say, "Go ahead I'll be with you in a moment."

As soon as the workman is out of sight, I'm in the study and studying what he's been doing. It becomes clear as soon as I look at the new, much bigger safe, that he's preparing to erect a steel cage around it and bolting the cage to the wall.

'Oh Fred! You still don't understand do you,' I think to myself, and of course to Phen, who is always in my thoughts when we are doing anything dangerous.

Without more ado, I change into Gordon and think to Phen, 'Do you think that I have enough power to lift and fly with that safe?'

'You would be near the maximum, but I could manage a little more to be on the safe side, if you will excuse the pun. I am only kidding Jake, the answer is yes, you have more than enough, in fact if you had a few more arms you could carry four safes.'

With that I shove the steel cage aside and wrench the safe of the floor and hurl it through the window. The alarms start wailing, and I can hear running feet on the gravel path, but they are too late, I'm already out of the window and away with the safe before they are anywhere near.

I've flown up the coast and found a nice little cove that could only be reached by a mountaineer. I think to Phen as I put down the safe, 'What a nice spot for a leisurely swim and sunbathe.'

Time to test my strength again, I grab the safes handle, and wrench at it in an attempt to rip open the safe's door.

Phen quips, 'That has made a start Jake!! You have managed to get the handle off!'

'Thanks Phen, you're a big help! Nothing for it now, I shall have to use the laser again. I don't think throwing the safe against the rocks will do it.'

It's a slow process but it eventually yields. Phen and I stare with my gapping mouth at the contents.

'That's more like it Phen!' Apart from two packets

of drugs, which I sling far out into the sea, 'there must be over a million pounds in here. This has got to hurt Fred financially this time.'

I write a note for Boss Man, put it in the safe, close the door, and quickly fly off to collect the dustbin from Fred's. Which fortunately is still in the bush. Then on to unbury the suitcases. I fly back to my cove and load the money into all three items; then survey the cliff face for a good size crevice that's above the tide line.

I spot one that I think will do the trick, so unless we have a tidal wave, that's my hiding place for the stash.

After a leisurely stroll along the sea shore, and a nap on the beach, I grab the safe and fly off.

Dusk has descended. It's fairly certain that Boss Man and his crew will have left work for the day but to be sure I check that there are no vehicles in the car park. A quick fly past the windows, reveals, along with my X-Ray vision that there's no one inside. I fly up to about a hundred feet and drop the now empty safe, apart from the note, through the roof of Boss Mans building.

'That will be a nice surprise for them, the next time they open up!' I think to Phen.

Time at last to fulfil my desire to eavesdrop on Fred and maybe pick up some of his reactions.

I spot several armed guards but no dogs. There are six vehicles on the drive of all grades. No police cars but that doesn't mean the Chief Inspector isn't here, he may have been suspended and using his own private car. There is only one car with a chauffeur. He's sitting in the car reading a newspaper. My guess would be its Reginald Martin-Smyth's car.

There are no lights on in the study or the dining room. That leaves one of the lounges as the most likely place for their meeting.

I can see that Fred has finally caught on, that it's no use locking every door and widow, as those things aren't going to stop me. Which is why, one of the upper floor windows is open. I change into sallow face. I suppose I should give sallow face a name, 'Phen why don't you pick one?'

'Mmmm,' (*not More Mmmm's*) 'I am thinking "Windy" as he keeps getting through windows.' Phen replies.

"Windy" it is, then Phen.'

I/Windy, fly up and enter the mansion for the second time today. We wind up the hearing, and listen at every bedroom door for signs of movement or breathing. Where there is none; enter, until we find the one that is over the lounge from where the voices can be most clearly heard. This lounge would, in the old days, have been known as "The Family Room."

We hear Fred saying, "Right gentlemen, what can we do about this thing that is attacking us?"

"The problem, Fred," says the PCI. "Is that we have no leads or evidence. What is happening is beyond belief. How can anyone lift a two-ton safe, hurl it through a window and make off with it?"

"One of my guards said that he just saw, as he came around the study corner, a blur, but swears that the blur was a man flying off carrying the safe."

We hear the telephone ring and Fred, say, "Excuse me …. Hello …. Yes Carl, …. You what! Hell, what next? …. OK Carl, thanks for letting me know. Bye." *Click* "Carl said he had to go back to the warehouse for something he forgot, and found my safe on the floor and a hole in the roof where it had been dropped through. The only thing left in the safe was a note that read: There will be no more drugs coming to your premises, I suggest that you all seek alternative employment."

Reginald, who up till now hasn't spoken, is saying, "This thing is becoming weirder by the minute. I'm sorry Fred but I can no longer be associated with it."

"Deserting the sinking ship ay Reg?"

"Whatever Fred. I'm sure you will understand when you have the time to think about it."

"What did Carl, have to go back for, Fred?"

"He didn't say, Jack."

Jack, who Phen and I, take to be the one we call Boss Man, says, "I'll give him a ring later and find out. What's bothering me is what we do now? None of us has enough supplies to keep going for much longer, and who knows if this thing won't take what little we do have?"

"There's one thing I do know, and that is; we're not going to let whatever it is beat us," asserts Fred.

"Well it's beaten me Fred," the PCI's saying. "I'm also out of here."

"Fine, but you can forget any more hand-outs, and don't think of blabbering, or you'll regret it!" threatens Fred.

'Well Phen, that leaves four, Fred, Jack, Wang and I think the other one is the West Indian who is speaking now. "How we a gon stop dis ting from beaten us den, Fred?"

"I've got a shipment coming in, from Singapore this time. It's due to dock at eight o'clock Monday night. The Ship is a cruise liner called the "Coastal Queen". We'll give her two hours to unload the passengers, meet with my contact, and unload our new stock. This stock, we are going to hide with much greater effect, and guard it in shifts, day and night. I've noticed that the thing does have one weakness."

"I haven't noticed any weaknesses yet," Jack says.

"That, if you don't mind my saying Jack, is why I'm the brains of this operation and you're not. This thing's weakness is: he's done no physical harm to anyone of us, at least not as yet."

"How about the two lads you sent to fetch that newspaper ass-hole?"

"They hurt each other or themselves. He merely stepped aside while they did it. I'm thinking that the guards can guard the stock without fear for their lives."

Jack's now saying, "It's possible they could, Fred." Then changing the subject, continues, "What time do you want me and the lads at the docks?"

"Be there for ten and go to pier four. You'll find

me waiting at the stern. There has been a hatch built into the hull well above the water line. Although the captain gets a nice, turn a blind eye hand-out, he won't be there. The hatch will be opened by my contact and the stock lowered down to us."

"How a come a stock no a bin a noticed lying about by crew?" asks Wang.

"That," Fred, is saying, "is because cabin 118 is not as deep as it should be. The back wall is false. The space behind it is full of our stock, and as cabin 118 is my contact's cabin, no questions have been asked."

"So, after Mundy, we's back in business ay Fred," says our West Indian, rubbing his hands together.

"You can bet your house on it Josh."

'So, Jake, the West Indians name is Josh.'

'Yes, Phen, and our way ahead's now clear. We've got all the information we need to knock the final nail into Fred's coffin.'

'It had better be a big one!'

'Phen, I do believe you've just cracked a joke!!! Come on let's get out of here, there's nothing more we can achieve tonight.'

8

Sunday, after a leisurely breakfast Phen and I discuss tactics. I think to Phen, 'What we need to know is when the "Coastal Queen" left Singapore.'

'I do not think that matters Jake, what matters is, how many knots per hour the ship makes. If the ship averages say twenty-five knots, then two hours from docking at eight O'clock the ship is roughly sixty miles away. What we really need to know is the ships itinerary.'

'You're applying your super intellect to good effect today Phen. Where do we get that information from on a Sunday? Travel Agents are closed on a Sunday.'

'We could try the Maritime Museum, they are probably open, but I think you are right Jake, our best chance is to find a Travel Agent. Perhaps David Jones can help us; he may know a local agent?'

'Good idea Phen. Although I hate to disturb him again after saying I wouldn't. Let's get round to his place anyway; before he decides to go out.'

A short time later I knock on David's door. There's no response. I give it another go and hear an, "Alright I'm coming; hold your horses." As he starts to open the door he says, "Who is it?"

"Sorry Dave, It's Sean Brooks. Is it possible that you've got, among your friends, a Travel Agent?"

"Come in; don't start questioning me on the door step." Dave, is still in his pyjamas and his hair looks as though he's been pulled through a hedge.

"I'm sorry to get you up Dave. Especially as it's only eleven O'clock!" I say with a modicum of sarcasm.

"Don't be so dam cheeky, you're lucky I answered the door at all after the night I've had."

"Should I ask?"

"No, but I'll tell you anyway, my press broke down as I was trying to prepare some advertising for Monday's paper."

"Bad luck mate, if there is anything I can do, you've only got to say."

"Thanks, but it's sorted now. Speaking of luck; it so happens that my best pal is a Travel Agent here in Liverpool. If you go through to the kitchen and make us a cuppa, I'll give him a ring and see if he can come round."

"That would be great, Dave. Could you ask him to bring anything he has on the itinerary of the "Coastal Queen" cruise Ship?"

Dave makes the call and puts down the phone saying, "Greg, will be round in thirty minutes. He'll have to pop by his shop first, to pick up a "Coastal Queen" brochure. So, Sean, what's the story?"

"I can't tell you yet, but if there is anything you can print at the end of this, without jeopardising anything, it's yours exclusively."

"Fair enough, but you can tell me the whole story. You have my werd that I will only print what you've approved."

"That's a deal Dave but I'll still wait if you don't mind. Drink your tea before it goes cold."

Gregg arrives and after an hour's chat between the three of us, I come away with the knowledge of the ship's itinerary, especially the last sixty miles of it.

Having nothing else to do the rest of the day, I fly up the coast to the cove where the moneys hidden and have me a leisurely swim and sunbathe.

With the advent of Monday morning, and feeling rejuvenated after my lazy Sunday afternoon, and pub grub in the evening; I want to get stuck into bringing the Fred saga to its conclusion. It's frustrating to have to wait until this evening.

'Why not fill the time with a visit to see John and Ken?' Phen, thinks.

I act on Phen's suggestion, and after a leisurely flight, I land in John's garden. Luckily, he's in, but not Ken. After the usual warm greeting, John says, "Ken's, at work and I'm on a late shift today; which is why I'm here; having said that, I haven't got long. I've promised an elderly lady that I would give her garden a good going over this morning."

"Can I come with you; I've got a few hours to burn?" I plead.

"Yes, but none of your super power stuff."

"I promise. It's going to be a nice change to be ordinary for a while, feeling myself, so to speak." John looks at me a bit quizzically and smiles but says nothing. I'm sure he suspects that I can change my appearance, but knowing him he won't raise the subject unless I do.

During the morning John and I talk about old times, and he brings me up to date with what has happened lately. He's been telling me that the project is now up to a dozen helpers, two of whom are girls, and one of them, Suzie, has become his girlfriend. I wouldn't say this to John, but I can't help thinking: I hope he's treating her right.

Whether it is the look on my face that has given me away, I don't know, but John says, "In case you're wondering. The past is so far behind me that I have to pinch myself to believe that was me."

"I'm sorry John; I have no right to judge you based on the past. It's what you've done since, that matters, and I have to say, that you and Ken have done yourselves proud. On top of that, I feel that we have become more than mates, more like brothers."

"Thanks Jake, I couldn't in my dreams, have wished for better."

"Let's move on before I start blubbering, tell me how are things on the financial front?"

"Much better. We have hardly touched the money you left us with. It's sitting there as a kind of insurance policy. The people that we've helped lately have been a lot more generous with their donations to the cause; as Ken and I now phrase it."

"That's great John, but please if you need to spend the money don't worry about it, as soon, there maybe some more coming your way."

I've taken John for a pub lunch and after leaving him with Mom's telephone number, in case he needs to contact me, I leave him and pop briefly in on Mom.

She was pleased to see me, but now, I'm on me way back to Liverpool.

On route, I stop off and do a bit of sightseeing, arriving in Liverpool at five thirty.

I change back to Sean and after a visit to Kate's caf for a snack and a drink; I take off in search of the "Coastal Queen". I start my search grid about sixty miles out. Either the liner is late or I need to widen the angle of my vision.

Ten minutes later it's Phen who's first to spot the very faint dot on the horizon. I fly towards it and YES! It's the beautiful "Coastal Queen" alright. I hover over her, taking in as much detail as possible, including trying to spot the position of the hatch Fred spoke about.

My endeavours are not being helped by my wide-angle vision, so I narrow it and that's done the trick. I must say who ever installed this hatch has made a super job of it. It's hardly visible, even with my enhanced sight.

'The next thing Phen, is how to get into cabin 118?'

'Why bother, Jake? Why not, now that we know where the hatch is, use your laser to cut your way through that part of the hull; we know the drugs are behind it.'

'It could take a while to do that, Phen. The sparks may be seen from the lower decks. Besides, I hate the thought of marring this beautiful ship. I think we should wing it. I should try disguising myself as a passenger, the sort of person that all but the very observant would walk by without noticing.'

'Such as?' thinks Phen.

'I don't know, perhaps an elderly, plain looking, spinster lady?'

'For someone who does not know, that sounds pretty much it to me Jake.'

I land behind a lifeboat, check that no one is watching and change into what, for our purpose, I think an elderly spinster lady would look like. Plain looking, plainly dressed, slightly forgetful and wearing sensible heels. Which is just as well as I don't trust myself in high heels.

I wander around a bit to test my disguise and to my delight; I have never been more pleased to be ignored. Several other passengers and two stewards passed by me without even a glance. I spot a young inexperienced looking steward whose name tag reads Philip and say, "Excuse me young man, I'm lost, I was supposed to meet up with the steward from cabin 118 but I have forgotten his name. If you could tell me how to get to his cabin, I would be eternally grateful."

"I'm afraid madam that cabin 118 is in the staff quarters; you would not be allowed in there."

"Oh dear, and I so wanted to speak to him further about an important matter. You know young man; it is awful when you get to the forgetful stage in life. You of course, are far too young to understand yet."

"Well, I know that I shouldn't, but I can see that you are distressed. The steward's name is Colin, who is in fact, the chief steward. Just ask around; all the staff know Colin."

"Thank you, young man, please accept this pound note, as a token of my gratitude."

'You know Jake, if you could go public, you would get a knighthood for acting, without doubt.'

'Phen, you just concentrate on the details of that young man's appearance and on the details of his name tag.'

'Why do you need that, Jake?'

As I have, since Phen made my powers permanent, had the power to block him from my thoughts, I reply, 'All will be revealed, Phen.'

'You know Jake, I sometimes regret giving you the power to block me.'

'You will just have to get used to it. I had to with you,' I think, with an inner smile.

With much cajoling and tipping, I finally locate the staff quarters.

'Now then Phen, stir your memory,' as from a hiding place I change into what I remembered Philip looked like. 'What do you think Phen?'

'The border of the nametag needs to be a darker red.'

'Like this?'

'Yes, that is right, and your chin needs to be a little more pointed.'

'Say when.'

'That is it, stop. Perfect!'

I hang about just around the corner of cabin 118 and wait in hope that another steward comes along.

My prayers are answered, there is a steward turning into the bottom end of the long corridor. I come out of hiding and stand outside Colin's cabin pretending to have lost my pass key. With my super vision, I read the oncoming stewards name before he gets to me.

"Hi Sid, could you do me a favour? Colin's asked me to get something out of his cabin; only I've left my pass key in my other uniform and he's in a hurry. Could you use your key for me?"

Sid is obviously the silent type, as he, without saying a word, opens Colin's, door and walks on. Lucky or what!

A look round the cabin soon reveals that there is something wrong with it, the proportions aren't right. Even if I didn't already know that it had a false back, I would have thought, there's something odd about this room.

'What are your plans now Jake? Are you going to smash the back wall down and kick the hatch open?'

'No Phen, partly because of the restrictions on the use of my powers, I want to do as much as possible as myself. I suppose I'm a little bit afraid of losing who I am but mainly I'm enjoying using a power that you don't know you've given me.'

'I am intrigued.'

'Yes Phen, it's the power of thought and the use of my intellect. Before we met, I didn't do a lot of thinking or fathoming out. In trying to understand you and in a way attempting to compete with you on an intellectual level, my powers of reasoning have increased beyond belief. So, as I say it's a power you've given me without knowing it.'

'I appreciate what you are thinking Jake, and I am glad for you. It cannot be easy competing with a super intelligent being!!!'

Oh, let's get on with it; your humour is getting worse than mine.'

'Perhaps Jake, that is a power you have passed on to me?'

'My intention, Phen, is to sit here in Colin's chair and change my appearance into, …… wait for it, ……
Big Fred!'

'You are joking, are you not?'

'No, I'm perfectly serious Phen. Who do you think the most likely person Colin would show how to open the back wall and hatch?'

'Yes, your intellect has increased. I shall have to watch myself.' Quip's Phen.

We hear a key in the door and the room is entered by a burly man of around forty years, who is nearly bald, and dressed in a well starched steward's uniform.

I'd taken a rapid glance, and now sitting with the chair facing away from him, I say, "Good evening Colin." (*I've seen this idea used to great effect in films.*)

"Who's there? How did you get in here?"

"How is not important. Who, you will find out when you come round here."

"BIG FRED!! What brings you here?" Colin exclaims.

"I'm afraid, Colin we have been having some trouble ashore. I must admit it's been making me nervous, and you know me; that's not an easy thing to do.

This shipment is vital and my last chance to recover from the problems we've been having, so I've come to make sure everything is going well your end."

"Everything's fine Fred. We're all set."

"Just to humour me, I wonder if you could open the back wall so that I can see for myself."

"No problem Fred. There you are, all shipshape." The drugs, in their brown paper packets, are neatly stacked to the ceiling either side of a narrow passage leading to the hull.

"Wonderful Colin, I knew I could at least, rely on you."

"I'm sorry to say this Fred, but you don't seem like your usual self. In all the years I've known you; that's the first time you have dished out praise. It's usually the other way around."

"Yes, you're right Col, but things have changed, and they have changed me."

"That's better! I've been a bit suspicious while you've been calling me Colin, instead of Col, which you've always done."

"You know Col, while you have been speaking. I've been looking at your hatch. It's a marvellous piece of engineering. I'm unable to work out how it opens?"

"It's easy when you know, Fred. Do you see the row of rivets above the hatch?"

"Yes."

"Well the one to the right of the hatch, is the one that operates the hydraulics that open and close the hatch. If you turn it to the right the hatch is raised up to the ceiling, and closes when you do the opposite."

"Fascinating Col. I wonder Col, if you would do me another favour, I haven't eaten since breakfast and I'm starving. What are the chances of a fry up and a mug of tea or coffee?"

'I thought I'd mention both Phen, in case he happens to know if Fred, has a preference.'

"No trouble Fred, it shouldn't be more than fifteen minutes. Make yourself at home, and would you mind closing the back wall. See you soon."

As soon as Col's, out of earshot I've got the hatch up and in a blur of speed, emptied the whole cargo of drugs into the sea.

'That should give the fishes a high old time,' quips Phen.

'It's now official, your humour, is worse than mine.' I say in response.

They say that curiosity killed the cat, but I can't resist it. I fly out through the hatch, change back into Philip, and position myself, as near as possible to the communications room, but try to remain out of sight, in case the real Philip, comes by.

I haven't had to wait long, here comes Colin, with a face like a beetroot, racing up the stairway and diving breathlessly into the comms room.

"Quick Bill, I've got to make an urgent ship to shore call."

"No panic Col. What's the number?

Colin gets through to Fred and I eavesdrop.
Although Fred is on the other end of the line, there is no way I can avoid hearing a thunderous, "WHAT!!!" as Colin is relating to him what has happened. Colin eventually puts down the phone, with, I'm sure, his ears ringing and burning from the power of Fred's wrath.

'I think Phen, that Fred has finally cracked!' I'm taking a slow smooth flight back to dry land, totally undisguised. In fact, I'm just flying around for the sheer pleasure of it, and the freedom of being myself, not having to act at being someone else.

The cool wind blowing past me, and the breathing in of salty air, are reviving my spirits.

Oh well, all good things must come to an end, so they say, but who they are, I have no idea. I change into Gordon and go into an Army & Navy store with the hope of buying a white flag. Success, I manage to get their only one; plus, four canvas kit bags.

'I assume this is another one of your weird ideas,' thinks Phen.

'Yea and you will find out very soon what it is,' I reply.

On to Dave's, as Sean, "Dave, I'm sorry to bother you yet again, but can I use your typewriter once more? A sheet of plain writing paper would also be nice."

"Sean, you are becoming a thorn in my side! I might even go as far as saying: A Pain in the Ass."

"Yes, I know I'm being a nuisance, but if I can drop by your house this evening, I may have that story I promised you."

I really and truly hope that this is my last hover over Big Fred's mansion.

With only two things to do, it's soon over. I then fly to Kate's Caf and order beans on toast, a pot of tea and await Phen's enquires.

'Don't ask me your questions Phen. I already know your thoughts. Your main question is: why I have blocked you out of my thoughts since we hit dry land. Am I correct?

'Yes Jake, I thought it unfair. I may have wanted to make a contribution.'

'I was happy with my plan Phen. I didn't want it confused with a lot of chatter.'

'So, that is what you think of me now is it, a chatterer!'

'Now, don't go all moody on me, I swear you are becoming more human by the minute. Do you want to know what was in the letter, which I posted through Fred's letter box?'

'Of course I do. Why do you think I am annoyed?'

'Well it reads: -

Dear Big Fred,

As you know, your incoming new stocks of drugs are feeding the fishes. I will continue to harass your drugs business as long as you remain in it. I want you to know that there is nothing personal in my campaign. I'm only against drug traffickers in general. I suggest that you give up drug dealing completely. If you do you will never have to experience me again. You can concentrate on your betting shop business without harassment.

If in the future, you decide to return to drug dealing, you can be sure that I will find out, and the whole sorry saga will re-enact.

If you agree to my suggestion, please run up a white flag on the flag pole in your back garden. I have left you a white flag at the base of your flag pole for your convenience. You have until tomorrow noon (*Tuesday*) to comply.

If I don't see the flag, be assured, that I will not only continue to wreck your drugs operation, but give my attention to your betting shop business, as well.

Yours sincerely,

The Wrecker. '

'Let us hope, Jake, that that is the end of Liverpool's "Wacky-Backy" dealing.'

'Where did YOU get that from?'

'Oh! Just something I picked up along the way!!!' says Phen nonchalantly.

9

Swiss Banking

I have now finished telling David Jones a story that he can print, but add while departing, "Provided Dave, I give you the go ahead by tomorrow afternoon. If I don't give that sanction, there may be a much bigger story to follow."

'You know, Phen it would be nice to think that we have changed the face of Liverpool's drug dealing permanently, but I fear it's only temporary. Still, I think we've called a halt to it for a while. That at least, is something to be proud of.'

'Jake, if I were able; I would give us a slap on the back.'

'If I remember right Phen you did give me one once but it was more like a kick from a Mule.'

Tuesday finds me at the cove with my Holdall and my four canvas kit bags. I hover over the crevice that I'd left Fred's million plus pounds in. After half an hour, with all four bags packed loosely with Fred's money, which is now project money, I take off for my longest flight ever. I'm off to Switzerland, where I'm told that bank accounts can be opened without too many questions being asked. Well, we'll see?

After an exhilarating flight, with my four bags and Holdall tied to my back, I search for a remote spot, as close to Zurich as I can get.

'There, that should do it, Phen.' I've spotted a heavily wooded area with lots of very tall trees.

'I see your plan,' Phen thinks, because this time I'm including him in my plans, well I don't want him sulking do I. 'You are looking for a tree that has many branches that crisscross each other and with plenty of foliage, to hide the money in; am I right?'

'Yes, Phen and I'm open to suggestions as to how we should proceed from there?'

'To my mind, your main problem is to become a believable character as you walk into a bank; carrying one to four canvas bags full of money.'

'I think one at a time is the way to go Phen and the obvious character and the most likely to be carrying a kit bag would be a sailor, but would a sailor carrying a quarter of a million pounds in cash, be believable?'

'Probably not. What about an Admiral though or someone like that?'

'Could even an Admiral have gathered that much money together? I suppose it's just about possible? If we deposit the money in four different banks, we may get away with it. The real snag comes when we want to make withdrawals. Admirals are few and far between. The banks would find it easy to check-up if our Admiral actually exists.'

'Mmmm.'

141

'Don't start with the Mmmm's Phen, especially as I'm perched, on a not too thick branch, at the top of this tree.'

'Okay Jake but Mmmm's do help me focus when we have difficult problems to solve. We do not have problems like these where I come from. However, it seems to me that we are trying to complicate things too much. I think Jake; we should go in as Gordon, who is an in-between character. Gordon could easily explain the use of a kit bag and could somehow explain how he has come by a million pounds or does he need to explain? Perhaps, as you said before, they may not ask questions.'

'Yes, that could work Phen but we would have to dress Gordon in something more appropriate than his usual gear. I'm thinking a nice white roll neck shirt, grey slacks, a smart jacket or blazer and nicely polished black shoes.'

'The other thing that Gordon has got going for him is that he is an imposing character. Plus, Jake, he also solves the problem of making withdrawals.'

'What's his surname?'

'So far, he has not got one, has he Jake?'

'No, and banks will want a full name, so that they can identify me by signature. How does James sound?'

'Yes Jake, Gordon James, sounds good.'

'That's it then. Now let me get down off this branch, my bum's gone to sleep. You wouldn't think that could happen; bearing in mind I can't be damaged by bullets or rolling pins etc. but, as you know, I can increase or decrease my, let's call it shielding, in the same way as my vision or hearing.' I'd thought to Phen, some time ago, that there are going to be times in my life when I want to be able to feel things. Like a tender touch for example or, as in this case, a sleepy bum and that I don't want to use me powers unnecessarily.

The bank we choose to go into is a bank that sounds the most attractive to us. It's called, "The Independent Bank of Zurich". I walk in as Gordon. Dressed smartly as per plan, with one of the kit bags nonchalantly held on my back and two fingers holding the strings.

I walk up to a counter with a confident air and say, "Good morning, would you tell the manager that I would like to see him, or her."

Before the Teller can protest, I say, "I will be over there when you have arranged it," pointing to a comfortable looking Tub Chair.

"How may I be of assistance Sir?" says a pinstriped suited man with slicked down dark hair, who by his demeanour, is obviously the manager.

"First of all, I would like to speak to you in private Mr?"

"Herr Dribaultes. If you would care to follow me Sir."

Herr Dribaultes leads me into an inner office with beautiful wood-panelled walls and tasteful furniture. It has two three-seater settees positioned opposite each other, with a long coffee table in between. On the other side of the room there is a handsome desk. Herr Dribaultes walks toward it.

I say, "Please, Herr Dribaultes, can we use the settees."

"As Sir, wishes."

We both sit and I open the conversation with, "Could you please tell me this Bank's policy with regard to a customer wishing to deposit one million pounds sterling, in cash?" "Well Sir" ....

"Gordon, Gordon James, please."

"Herr James. Gordon. Would you care for some coffee or tea?"

"Thank you, tea please," he gets up and goes to the intercom on his desk, and speaks the order into it.

Now back on the settee he continues... "This bank would be pleased to accept such a deposit providing it was not illegally obtained."

'Phen, this guy is so cool; you would think that people were walking in of the street with a million pounds every day!'

"The legality of the money is a moot point Herr" ....

"Hans, please, Gordon."

"Hans, it is then."

We pause while the tea it brought in and the young lady, who I take to be Han's secretary, pours the tea, enquires about milk and sugar and adds, "Please help yourselves to biscuits."

"You were saying about the legality of your money Gordon. Would you please explain?"

"I feel, Hans that I can be completely honest with you but please tell me first if what I tell you will remain confidential between the two of us?"

"You have my word, Gordon. In fact, it is the banks policy to respect confidences."

"The money that I hope to deposit with you was not legally obtained, unless you can say that money stolen from drugs dealers is legal."

"I see, In that case!" Hans goes to get up as though the conversation is at an end.

"Please Hans, let me finish before you make a judgement."

'Phew! Phen, I had to get in there quick.'

"For the record, I did not obtain the cash by selling drugs. But I did obtain it by closing down a large illegal drugs operation and relieving them of their ill-gotten gains.

There's no way the now defunct drugs baron will be coming after this money. He knows that it would cause him more trouble than he's in already.

Besides, he has no idea it was me who destroyed his drugs ring, and definitely no idea that the money has arrived here. Now the most important thing for you to know is: this money is only in my care. It's money that's to be used to set up an organisation which helps people who need a helping hand …. All that Hans, is the complete and honest truth."

Hans, sits still and silent, mulling things over for what seems like an eternity. Finally, he says, "I take it Gordon that some of the money is in that kit bag?"

I open up the bag and show Hans the cash. He says nothing.

I say, "This is one of four identical bags, with at least this amount of money in each."

He looks down at the cash again for another seeming eternity, then looks up smiling, and says, "Would you like a pass book or statements sent to an address?"

I smile and say, "I think a pass book would do the trick."

"In that case, if you would bring your bag through to the vault, I will have two of my most trusted Tellers count it; while you bring in the remaining bags. Let me let you out of the back-security door, and would you please give four loud knocks when you return."

We shake hands and I go back to my tree, untie the bags and so that I don't create suspicion; I take my time getting back.

I Give the requisite knocks and re-enter the bank.

"Ha! Gordon, please place your bags in the vault and come with me."

We walk through, out of the Bank, and enter a very elegant tearoom across the road from the bank. Hans passes me a menu, and says, "Please select whatever you wish. It will take time to count the money; we may as well take the time to have a pleasant repast."

During my sampling of the local food, Hans, tells me something of the Bank's history and some interesting things about Zurich.

We return to the Bank about an hour and a half later. A Teller passes Hans a pass book. Hans looks at it and countersigns the Teller's signature. He then says to me, "Please sign here Gordon and also the banks sample signature, card."

I do as requested with a flourish, having had a quick practice before setting out from the bags hiding place.

I finally open the book to the entry page and read £1,200,860 pounds. In my head I hear Phen go 'WOW!!' and considering they don't use money on his planet, that was some exclamation. I, merely thank Hans, shake his hand warmly and say, "Hans it's been a pleasure, I'm sure we will see much of each other over the next few years but the next time we meet you must allow me to treat you."

'Phen, we will have to get a spurt on if we are to get to Fred's by noon.'

I change back to myself, as I prefer, *as you know,* flying that way. It's that feeling of freedom thing. I collect my Holdall from the tree and whiz off.

It's actually twelve thirty as I fly high over Fred's mansion and see a beautiful white flag blowing in the breeze. I say out loud to myself, "Well done Fred I think you've finally got it!"

After changing into Sean, I call to see Dave and dictate to him the article to be published in "The Inquirer". Then, as a treat, take him to lunch at a nearby pub. Afterwards I wish him all the luck in the world and say, "I'm sure this won't be the last time we'll meet."

That done, I walk round to the 'Gazette,' and stroll up to Jane, who looks up at me with a quirky inquiring look. I say nothing; I just lean across her desk and give her a kiss on both cheeks. She goes red. I smile, and mouth, "Thank you SO much."

"Hello Mom."

"Oh, Hello son, when did you get back?"

"Just."

"Did you have a nice time?"

"Yes thanks, Mom."

"Cup of tea?"

"Have you got any cake?"

"I've got some bread and butter pudding and I can make you a bit of custard."

"Mom, you always say exactly the right thing. By the way, could you do a bit of washing for me?"

Following my pud, I retire to my bedroom and within two minutes I'm asleep. I wake up to Dad knocking my door and saying, "Cup of tea son?"

He comes in with it and we chat, I can't tell you how good it feels to be home, even for a short while.

By eight fifteen I've dragged "The Don" out of the garden shed, and cycled to the weight training club.

The first face I see can't be missed, because I never saw such a beaming smile in my life. The next thing I know, two massive arms are hugging the life out of me! "OK Stew, I give in!"

Harry, the coach comes over, shakes me hand and says, "Great to see you Jake, we've missed you. By the way," indicating with his thumb, "This is not just Stewart, but, Mr England – and – AND, he goes to

America next month for the Mr Universe contest."

Next day, I stand in front of Doris's door; go to ring the bell, but before I can, the door's opened wide by Bill. "Gordon, come in…come in."

He takes me to Doris's lounge. There's no one in there. "Where's Doris?" I ask, in a panicky voice, "Is she alright?"

"Relax Gordon, as soon as she saw you coming, she was straight in the kitchen to put the kettle on."

"Phew! Thank God, you had me worried there, Bill."

After tea and a chat, I say to Doris, "Can you let me have that briefcase I left with you a while back."

"I thought you hadn't come to see me."

"Doris, you know I love you like a second Mom."

"I'm only teasing," she says as she gets up, goes upstairs, and comes down with the briefcase.

I open it and take out five thousand pounds and hand it to Doris, saying, "When are the boys playing Football next?"

"Saturday afternoon, but it's an away match, against the Wickendon Boys Club on the Wickendon Park pitch."

She tells me how to get there and I say," "Will you tell the boys that I will be there to see them play, and tell me Doris, do you think there is enough potential in the team that they could do without Winston and Joel?"

149

"Well Freddy has become a very good lad and a good player. I think he would love to take over the team along with Syd but why do you ask?"

"Nothing solid at the moment, just an idea that's running around my brain; I'll let you know if it comes to fruition."

Saturday afternoon arrives. I've made my way to the ground and stand and wait for the match to start.

Bill comes over and stands by me and says, "That five grand you gave Doris could not have come at a better time Gordon. We are raising funds at the moment to build the boys a permanent, fit for purpose, Club House."

"Why didn't Doris say? Tell her if she needs any more money, to let me know."

"You know Doris, she probably thinks you've already done your bit."

"That's nonsense Bill, the day-to-day grind is the hard work. She should be put forward for a gong. At least an M.B.E;" Bill nods in agreement as we enjoy the rest of the match together; which our boys win four/two. As they come off the pitch, having had a Doris hug and a chat, Winston and Joel come over to me and greet me warmly.

Winston says, "Doris, mentioned some obscure idea you're thinking over."

"That's true Winston but I can't tell you anything more now, apart from, I'm hoping to involve you and Joel in an entirely new scheme I'm thinking over.

150

Congratulations on your win, by the way."

Saturday week sees me watching my old mate Dave, getting married and as I stand there, I'm thinking to Phen, 'I dare say this will happen to me one day but in the meantime, I'm looking forward too many more adventures that you and me can share. Starting with an A.F.T.D.A.'

'What is an A.F.T.D.A., Jake?'
'You'll find out Phen!!!'

10

A Gang of Penny's

This early 70's Summer is coming to an end. Autumn's looming. Phen and I are becoming quite restless, apart from a couple of minor things that Winston & Joel where able to sort out on their own. There's been nothing for Phen and I to get our, or should I say my teeth into. I'm beginning to feel the frustration that "Sherlock Holmes" used to experience when he had no cases to solve.

I had managed to persuade Winston and Joel, who still know me as Gordon, to join me in my new venture and leave the running of the football team to Freddy & Syd.

The aim is to set up an A.F.T.D.A. which stands for, "Aid For The Desperate Agency". It's not an ideal title but it's the best I have been able to come up with.

'Ah! So that's what it is,' thinks Phen.

The lads are determined to change the name the moment they can come up with something better. The agency is to be funded from the cash Phen and I've, got stashed in our agency's Swiss Bank Account.

Phen and I haven't been totally idle since the 'Big Fred' saga. We've been busy establishing my self-employment as a furniture restorer. Phen has kindly allowed some of the remaining money, that we relieved the drug dealing character Scarface, of, plus a bit from our Bank in Switzerland, to acquire a pleasant back street premises that used to be part of an old country house's outbuildings. The country house has long gone. The area in now built up; with just a few bits left untouched. The bit that we have taken over was the old Estate's Forge. In fact, we call the buildings "The Forge," which I think is a nice name for a furniture restoration business.

The premises comprise: A wide building that goes back about thirty feet, which I shall be using for my restoration work.

The space in front of this building is a yard where horses would have been shod in the old days.

There's a smaller building to the left-hand side of the yard, standing proud of the main building and measuring twenty feet long, by fifteen foot deep. This building and the yard are enclosed by two eight-foot high- gates. The main building as an upper floor that has one large room, a slightly smaller one, and two smaller still; I have moved into these, because I'm finding it more and more difficult to hide my powers from Mom and Dad.

Mom doesn't mind so much, as she sees me fairly regularly anyway. Like when I take my washing round and drop in for a bath.

This thinking about taking a bath takes me back to when I was a child. Bath night was Friday night and it was a case of dragging the tin bath from the yard into the kitchen; where it was filled with slightly warm water. If I lingered to long my Dad would come in and tip a saucepan full of cold water over me. Brrrrr or what!

The ground floor, as I say, I'm using for my fledgling business. Winston & Joel are to use the smaller building as the headquarters of the A.F.T.D.A.

Doris and the committee that she set up to fund raise for the gang of twelve's football team and youth club, paid some time ago for Winston & Joel to have driving lessons.

They both passed their driving tests first time. See, I told you they are bright! The committee's thinking was that the boys may need transporting to away football matches. Doris's lot agreed to buy them a second hand "Mini Bus." It's white and can seat twelve, fourteen at a pinch. Joel, with Winston's approval, has nick-named it "Scrapyard".

Joel & Winston are with me today, me still being Gordon, at "The Forge". We're here to brainstorm how we can get the ald agency enterprise up and running.

I open with, "Before we start, there is something's that you both should know. First you must both make a solemn promise not to reveal what you are about to see, and hear, to a living sole. That includes family and friends. Do I have your promises?"

Winston says, "Joel and me haven't told anybody about your flying abilities etc. so why wouldn't you trust us to keep secret whatever else you might tell us?"

"It's because I do trust you, that I'm about to tell you a shortened version of the story I told you I would one day tell you. It was the day you asked me if I'm from another planet. I said that I'm not and that is the absolute truth. The reason I must ask you to make solemn promises is because your loyalty, till now, is to a person you know as Gordon. What if I was to tell you that Gordon doesn't exist! That he is another person entirely. Would that person, who has the same values and cares for you in the same way that Gordon does, command your loyalty and trust also?"

Winston & Joel look at each other with quizzical looks on their faces and say, almost in unison, "We don't know." Joel, continues, "The thing is: we only know and trust you Gordon."

"I can see that this is very difficult for you. Would it help, if I, as Gordon were to ask you to believe in and trust this other person exactly as you do me?"

"Yes, I think it would," says Joel, looking at Winston who nods in agreement.

"On that basis then, are you prepared to extend your promises to whoever you see Gordon change into?" There is a look of utter astonishment on both their faces but they make their very hesitant promises.

"Yeeerrs… we ...pr.. pr.. romise…."

"OK lads, prepare yourselves. You can either watch or close your eyes. If you choose to watch you will need to be alert as it will happen very quickly." With that I change into the young man that I am; a young man only

155

two years older than the two in front of me. "So, lads, what do you think?"

"How do we know that you are you?" says Winston, after he and Joel have recovered from the shock, "you certainly don't look anything like Gordon."

"You only have my word for it. This, is the real me, the person I am and was before I was granted my extraordinary powers. This is the person I've always been, even when you knew me as Gordon. Any other person that you may see me change into now, and in the future, is only a disguise. From the look on your faces I would say that's enough to take in for now. I'm going to make us some tea while you both wrestle with what you have seen. After the break we'll get down to our A.F.T.D.A. business."

The lads are too stunned to speak. They just nod. They've been doing a lot of nodding this last half hour.

'Phen, I hope they're not changing into horses or I may have to use "The Forge" for its original purpose.'

'Very funny Jake, Ha! Ha!'

The lads decide to drink their tea in the unit that is to be the agencies office; they need to get their heads around the revelation they have just witnessed.

After thirty minutes they come back into my workshop and stand there looking at me, shaking their heads.

Joel says, "We still can't believe you're Gordon; the guy we've been through so much with."

"That's because I'm not Gordon, Gordon is me, ask me anything you like that you think only you and

156

Gordon would know about."

"What's the breed of the dog, what's its owner's name and the dog's name that Gordon tamed while watching us play football?" asks Winston.

"That's an easy one. "Crusher" is a Pit Bull Terrier whose master is Freddy."

"OK, we think we're convinced. ... So, what do we call you now then?" continues Winston.

"Jake unless I'm in disguise, in which case call me by whatever name attaches to the person I'm disguised as. The hard part for you is remembering not to let slip, that I'm not who I say I am."

"Well we're pleased to meet you Jake," says Joel, "however strangely. Accepting Gordon is you; how do you think we should proceed with the aid agency?"

"From my perspective it would suit me if you two where the front men and I came in where and when my special skills are needed. The room that you had your teas in, is to be your office, and the H.Q of the A.F.T.D.A. (*At the mere mention of the acronym they flinch.)*

You have the use of "Scrapyard" and I would like you to take over from Doris the responsibility for its maintenance, tax and insurance.

The costs will be met by the project fund, as will our upkeep. This workshop and my furniture restoration business will act as a front for me in concealing my identity.

In other words, I'm not going to work on project business as myself. No one must know that I'm involved in the aid agency. Should by chance anyone get curious; merely tell them that you rent your office off me. That you and I have no connection other than that. The upstairs rooms are to be my living quarters. Any comments?"

"Yes, Jake," says Joel. "The set up seems sound, but I must say it sounds a bit impersonal."

"I'm sorry about that Joel but that's only the official line in order to shelter me from nosey parkers. You may think that it would be a good idea to use my skills to publicise the project's work but let me put it to you, more or less, the way a very close friend of mine put it to me."

'Could not get much closer,' thinks Phen.

'Thanks for that Phen. Ha! Ha!'

"He said: don't court publicity, if you involve yourself, as yourself, in projects; it won't be long before the media track you down. Once that happens your life won't be your own. If you only use your powers when you are disguised as someone else, you will be able to use them freely, as the person you become will not actually exist."

Winston, looking confused says, "Jake, I thought you said that we shouldn't tell friends and family about you. Yet you've told this close friend of yours?"

"Good point Winston. But my close friend is a special case. As you two are. Without him I wouldn't have any powers."

"Are you saying that .... It's your friend .... Who's from another planet?"

"Hole in one Winston; my friend's name is Phen. We communicate with each other by thought transfer. If I appear to be talking to myself, without actually saying anything, I'm probably talking to Phen. Now! Can we get down to agency business?"

Having grasped this latest bombshell, Joel proceeds with, "Did you say Jake, that project monies have been used to set up these premises and if I've got this right, project money is not to be used for personal gain? If, that is the case, are you personally, not gaining from having your business and living accommodation paid for by project money?"

"Leaving aside, your salaries are to be paid out of project monies; your summing up is correct Joel. Phen and I thought deeply about it before we went ahead and acquired these buildings. Phen's rationale was that there are three things that matter in setting up our A.F.T.D.A. One is: we need a base to operate from. Two: we need a cover to protect my identity, and three: that I must not consider any part of the premises as mine. The premises in their entirety belong to the agency. If the agency takes off and needs to expand; I have to move out. Does any of this put your minds at rest?"

Joel, looks at Winston; I'm waiting for nods, but only get broad grins, and this comment from Joel "Are you usually this easy to wind up? Besides, apart from the other things, we use "Scrapyard," and he's also to be funded by the agency and occasionally used for our

159

personnel benefit when ferrying the football team about."

"OK, you got me! Can we now get down to business, please? How do you think we should promote our aid agency?"

"Well," says Winston, "You've so far done alright from advertising your restoration work. You're getting a few jobs trickling in; perhaps we should do the same for the agency?"

"That's fine guys. I'm going to leave it to you to come up with how you should word the advert, and what publications it should be placed in. If you come up with a better name for the agency, include that too. Just bear in mind what I said about protecting my identity."

Two weeks later, our advert's been in the 'Post & Mail' newspaper for a week. Joel & Winston have been busy getting the telephone installed, so that they could include the phone number in the copy.

They also included the new name they've thought up for the agency.

It now, apparently, is to be called "N.E.C.H." standing for "Nobody Else Can Help" and the advert reads: - "**We have the N.E.C.H [Nobody Else Can Help] to help those no one else can. Telephone ------- etc. etc. and finishing with. Discretion guaranteed."**

Both of them went in "Scrapyard" to an Auction of office furniture, and bought a desk, filing cabinet and four office chairs. Under my supervision, me being the expert, they've tarted them up.

'Hmm! You talk about my boastfulness,' thinks Phen.

'Like you Pal, it's just a statement of fact,' I think with laughter.

Imagine the excitement! Joel has taken a phone call this morning from a possible first meaty client. "The call was from a Mr Stokes" says Joel excitedly. "He has an Antique Shop in Soho Street.

Apparently, a big white guy and an even bigger black guy have for almost a year been demanding money with menaces. They have threatened even worse treatment if he or any of the other shopkeepers bring in the police. He's at his wits end and says that we could be his last hope before deciding to sell up and get out."

"We had better get over there straight away," says Winston.

I say, "Do we all need to go? How about if we get more calls while we're out?"

"As this is the only call we've had all week; I don't think it's going to hurt that much if we all go. Besides, as this is our first meaty enquiry, it would be unfair if we don't all share in it" says Joel.

"Hang about for a while. I have an idea; I'll be back soon."

'Where are we off to Jake?' thinks Phen.

'Do you remember Jenny?' I think to him.

'Yes, she is the girl you saved from being raped by John & Ken.'

'Correct Phen and as she is still on her school holidays, I thought I would ask her if she would like to earn a few quid, manning our phone.'

Less than half an hour later I'm walking into the N.E.C.H. office with Jenny in tow and say to the lads, "Winston, Joel, this is Jenny. She is going to stand by the phone for us while we're out. I've filled her in about the fact that we are two businesses here. She's aware that she needs to answer calls with a simple Hello; until it becomes clear which service is being asked for. Then saying, that none of the management are here at the moment, but if you would care to leave your details, someone will contact you in the near future."

All three of us now pile into "Scrapyard" and drive across the city to Soho Street. On the way I change into Gordon.

"Will we ever get used to that?" says Winston.

As we enter the shop, that was once a big old Victorian house, there's a tinkling of chimes as the door knocks into them on opening. A grey-haired gentleman with a small grey moustache approaches us and says, "Good morning, you are welcome to look around, if you require assistance please ask." "Would you be Mr Stokes?" Joel asks.

"Yes, who are you?"

"We are from N.E.C.H., you rang us this morning. I'm Joel, the person you spoke to. This is Winston and the big feller is the senior partner of our business. His name is Gordon."

'Mmmm,' thinks Phen, 'I do not recall you agreeing to be senior partner? It may mean you having to be in two places at once, on occasions.'

'I think Phen, that the lads feel more comfortable with Gordon in that role. If it helps them, I'm sure, if the problem arises, we can work it out. I just hope they won't get the two of us mixed up.

Mr Stokes, who is about five foot ten, and has the bearing of an ex-military officer says, "Well, as you are using first names, you had better call me Reg. I must say it is very nice that you have answered my call for help so quickly. I trust that you all know the problem that I and the other shopkeepers are faced with?"

"Yes," I say, "and if you don't mind, I would like to start by looking around your shop; while Joel gets some more details from you."

"Winston, will you go and have a look around the area and visit a few other shops? But don't let on yet, who you are. Just get the feel of the people & places at this stage."

Reg, who I could tell is not too impressed by the size of the lads, as the Bozo's are a lot bigger. His confidence is helped, by the fact, he as to crane his neck to look me in the face; atop my six-foot four frame.

"Joel," says Reg, "would you like to follow me into the office and Gordon, Miss Burke my secretary will show you around the shop, and answer any questions you may have."

Miss Burke, I think to myself, this is going to be nice, an attractive young lady to show me around. Yummy!

Then she appears, and if you can remember my disguise when I boarded the "Coastal Queen" cruise ship, I reckon my interpretation of an elderly spinster, was not far out, except, this lady has a warm and pleasant smile.

She says, "Where would you like to start?"

I say, "Anywhere you like Miss Burke"

"Amy, please and I believe your name is Gordon?"

"Yes, how did you know?"

"I'm afraid, Gordon, that I am an inveterate eavesdropper.

Anyway, the tour: in these downstairs rooms we stock mainly furniture that is too heavy to carry upstairs. We use a few bits of porcelain, as you can see, to decorate some of the items, and of course the Grand Piano there, definitely can't be taken upstairs."

"It's a grand looking piano! If you will excuse the pun," I say.

"It certainly is, and by a very good maker. It was made in Germany by the famed "Bluthner Company".

I think to Phen, 'Perhaps, if they would like the piano upstairs, we could carry it up for them. Ay Phen?'

'Jake, you are digressing again. Phen knows I do a lot of that, concentrate on the job in hand.'

'OK. Mom! God, you're getting like an old granny.'

"If you follow me upstairs," says Amy, "you will see that this room on the right is given over to cabinets of porcelain. Silver and antique glass items are displayed on the antique tables and chiffoniers. In the room on the left we have our dining sets displayed. Of course, most of the dining tables can easily be dismantled."

I notice also, that there are other sundry items scattered about.

"Tell me, Gordon. Do you like cats? Without waiting for a reply, Amy continues, "I have two, "Cindy & Mindy", they are lovely but they can be naughty. Mindy came in this morning with a bird in her mouth. I had to chastise her. It really upset me. I wouldn't mind, but I go to the butchers every day, and buy them fresh meat & chicken breasts. There is no need for them to go killing innocent little birds, is there Gordon?"

As we make our way back to the office I reply "I wouldn't have thought so Amy." I couldn't tell her what I really thought! Like, I wouldn't mind a bit of fresh meat & chicken myself, never mind her cats.

We arrive at the office, and Amy, goes off to make us all some tea with biscuits.

On Winston's return, we make our excuses and leave with the parting comment from me, "We'll be in touch."

We get back to The Forge. I pay Jenny and as myself, fly her back home. On the way I thank her for her help, even though there were no calls in our absence. "Jenny, can I ask you something?"

165

"Of course, you can" she replies. "If you are about to ask me if I can help you out some other time, you only have to ask, and although I appreciate you paying me, you didn't have to. You know that, don't you?"

"Yes Jen, I do know, but that's not what I was going to ask you. What I was going to say to you is: what are you going to do when you leave school?"

"As I see it at the moment, I have two choices, either I can go to college or I can find myself a job as a trainee secretary or something. I'm quite good at English."

"Supposing I said that there might be a middle way, a way that you could learn to be a secretary on the job, and have a day a week at college. Day release I think they call it."

"That would be unreal. Where would I find such a job?"

"Working for us; us being, Winston, Joel and me." I explain to Jenny, about our set up and ask her to think it over and let me know. "You've got our telephone number. I shall have to speak to the lads of course, but I'm confident that if you want the job it's yours."

I think the old saying goes, meanwhile back at the ranch, in this case "The Forge". The lads and I go into conference about what we have gleaned so far from our excursion to Soho Street.

"What did Reg, have to say, Joel?" I ask.

"The first thing he asked me was how much our services cost? I could see, because of the menacing he's going through, that he's worried about money. I told him that we don't charge on a normal business basis. That we wait and see how much our services have meant to the people concerned. If they are pleased, we ask them to offer a donation to our cause, according to their means; a bit like the way John & Ken, do."

"Good answer, Joelee boy! I think we should make that our standard charging policy, don't you Gordon. Err, I mean Jake," says Winston.

"You'll have to watch that Winston! But yes, I agree that we adopt Joel's answer; anything else, Joel?"

"Yes, I asked him when the two goons come around, and how frequently. He said they are usually round during the first week of the month, not always on the same day; they vary it. I also asked him if the goons are answerable to a higher-up, or if they work alone. He said that he didn't know. He has always been too afraid to ask."

"Excellent Joel, great job. Now Winston, how did you get on?

"I had a good look around the area. I wouldn't say that it's a particularly affluent area, but not poor either. I visited six other shops; I don't know if it's my looks, (*Winston being a tough looking black lad with dreadlocks,*) but the shopkeepers looked at me nervously. I would say that they are definitely jittery."

"Well done, that's exactly the kind of information we need."

The lads and I have taken the weekend to come up with a plan of action. Phen has taken a back seat during negotiations. He thinks that I and the lads have developed a sufficiently good working relationship, that his input is not needed at the moment.

Monday's, August bank holiday Monday, which we have off. It's Tuesday when Joel telephones Reg to say we're on our way over. I go ahead, as I want to make sure that one of us is there before the goons turn up. Winston and Joel follow on in "Scrapyard" and Jenny's come over on the bus to help out again.

"Good morning Reg, how are you today?"

"Well, but worried Gordon."

"No need to be now. We at N.E.C.H are going to handle the situation from now on. Winston, is going to the barber's shop, as he has some previous experience in that area. Joel, is going to the greengrocers for the same reason. (*I didn't tell him it's because he used to nick fruit from the greengrocer's outside display.*) I will be staying here with you."

"What about the other shops; they will have no one to protect them?"

"At this stage Reg it isn't about protecting you all, it's about learning as much as we can about the enemy."

'Good thinking, Jake. That should appeal to an ex-service man like Reg.'

'Thanks, but will you please keep quiet while I'm outlining the plan.'

"For example, do you know the names of the aggressors?"

"I'm afraid not, they are always very careful about not referring to each other by name."

"Not to worry, we'll soon find out. How do you and the other shopkeepers usually hand over the money? Do you put it into an envelope or give them cash in hand?"

"They have always insisted it be put in a sealed envelope."

"That's very interesting, as it could mean they're not working alone, but tell me, how do they know how much money you've put in the envelopes?"

"They know! The Butcher tried to fool them once. He put some, trimmed to size, pieces of newspaper in amongst his money. The next day, he turned up at his shop to find that all his shop windows had been smashed."

"I understand, Reg. Now, what I would like you to do is telephone all the shopkeepers who haven't got one of us in their shop and tell them to pay the goons in the usual way. Down the line, I'm hoping we'll be able to get at least some of their money back.

Winston and Joel will be asking their proprietors to do the same. The only difference will be: they will be handing over the envelopes instead of the shopkeepers. That is also what I would like to happen here. Do you have your envelope of money to hand?"

"Yes, Gordon but I thought the idea was that you sort these Bozo's out!"

"We don't work like that Reg. If we did what you say, we would not be able to find out if they are working alone. The plan is to pay them. Then follow them to see where they go after they've collected all the envelopes."

"I see what you mean Gordon. You will have to excuse me, only I'm rather nervous and anxious. Having lived with this problem for so long; I now can't wait to see an end to it. You have obviously put a lot of thought into your plan, so I'm going to trust that you know what you're doing."

"Thank you, Reg. That's very gratifying. Now, when your two thugs decide to turn up, I want you to make yourself scarce and leave everything to me. OK?"

It isn't till Wednesday, that Reg, comes rushing into the office, where I'm sat talking with Amy and says, "They've just pulled on to the frontage."

"OK Reg, go and hide somewhere. Amy you stay in here. Lock yourself in if it makes you feel more secure."

The chimes tinkle. Both Bozo's enter the shop and call out, "Major, it's that time of the month again. Come out from wherever you are!"

I leave it for about a minute, then slowly emerge from another room and say, "Good day gentlemen please feel free to look around. If there is anything I can help you with please don't hesitate to ask."

"What you can do feller, is to get Reg out here," says the white guy, while opening his overcoat to reveal a shortened baseball bat like object.

As I suspected, the white guy is huge and heavy set. His coloured mate is even bigger.

I say, "Ah! You must be the gentlemen that Reg told me may call. I'm sorry but Reg isn't here."

"Don't fool around if you know what's good for yer. We saw his car outside, so call him out."

"His car is here, because he wasn't well enough to drive. He went home in a taxi. You guys are obviously making him ill. However, he has left me with an envelope for you, but he said to make sure that you are who you say you are. Can you tell me your names?"

"Do you think we're idiots, just hand over the envelope, we've never told the Major our names and we're not telling you," Says white guy.

"Well, it's obvious that you're not an idiot, but I wouldn't know about your mate? He hasn't said anything yet, so I have no way of telling," I say.

With that they start to take their batons out of their coats. I quickly say, "Okay! I don't want any trouble, here you are, here's your envelope."

"That's better, and if you're here next time we call, let's have less of your lip." With that they leave the shop.

Back in the shop's office, I phone Winston & Joel to warn them that they're on their way, and tell them what was said; so that they can vary their stories.

'Two very unsavoury looking characters,' thinks Phen.

'Too true Phen. Did you do what we planned?'

'Yes Jake, I look careful note of their features, size and the way they spoke.'

171

'Thanks, Phen.'

The idea now is that I find the goon's vehicle that Reg has described to me. I'll then wait out of sight until they return to it on completion of their rounds.

Winston & Joel will then go around to all the other shopkeepers on the list, that the Barber has supplied them with, introduce themselves and offer as much reassurance as they can. They will then go home. Their work will be done for the day. I have no idea what time me and Phen will be getting home.

I say, "Bye for now" to Reg and warn him to keep a low profile for a few days. I then head off to find the bozo's Ford Cortina Estate.

I've come across it almost straight away. It's only parked four hundred yards up the road from Reg's.

I lift off, and fly around for a while, until I finally spot them returning to their car. In the absence of their real names, I'm calling our menacing duo, Bill and Ben.

'They haven't opened any envelopes, Phen. As you know I've been X-raying them in their car, to see if they would. It could prove whether they're working alone.'

'I see that, Jake, if they are working alone, you are thinking they would be opening the envelopes and stuffing their pockets with the money.'

'Right on, Pal,' I reply.

As they drive off, I follow them from on high and listen to their conversation. Strangely enough, the one that I've called Ben, is named Ben. But the white guy's name is Steve. These are the only useful facts that I've gleaned. The rest of their conversation's been general chit-chat; mainly about football.

Steve who is driving, has turned into the driveway of a large detached Victorian house in the "Mosby" area of the city and parked at the side of the building. They've now walked to the front carrying the shopkeeper's envelopes. Steve opens the black panelled door with a key, he and Ben go in and close the door behind them.

I don't bother with X-rays as the door has a large highly polished brass letterbox, which I open as quietly as I can, revealing a wide hall, at the centre of which is a large circular hall table. Steve and Ben go to it and add their envelopes to a pile that are already there.

'That is lucky, Jake, we can get the shopkeepers money back straight away!'

'Think about it some more, Phen. We've had this situation before.'

'Ah yes. I suppose because I have done such a good job with your training, I am becoming more and more redundant. My mind must have been asleep. What you want to do, if I am reading your mind right, is to wait and see what happens to the envelopes next?'

'Correct. Besides we have no way of knowing who the other envelopes in the pile belong to?'

'Of course. I should have thought that,' thinks Phen. With the time creeping towards two p.m. and having observed that there are two other cars outside, besides Steve's.

I squat on the roof of the house in order to see if any more cars arrive or any leave.

It's two-thirty. A car is turning into the drive. It's a pale blue Austin Healey sports job, and it's pulled up right outside the front door. The occupant opens her car door, climbs out revealing a pair of shapely long legs, and wearing high heel shoes. She's an elegant looking lady with short blond hair and wearing a female version of a pinstriped men's business suit but with a pencil skirt instead of trousers.

Beneath her jacket, she's wearing a white blouse and an expensive looking necklace.

'I would say that she is about thirty-five of your years, wouldn't you, Jake?'

'That's about right Phen, although we rarely talk about a lady's age in this country.'

'You have some strange traditions. It is taking me longer than I thought to understand your country's eccentric ways. That aside, what is our new plan? Only the old one looks like it has gone out the window.'

'Well Phen, when you have finished nicking my role as weird sayings user. I think what we need to know is what role this lady plays in this saga. Let's do our usual trick and try round the back for a possible way in or a place where we can pick up on any conversation.'

'There doesn't appear to be a way in without making a lot of noise, Phen. I don't see anyone in any of these back rooms, including the kitchen. Let's take a look through the upstairs windows.'

'Ah! Yes. It appears that one of the larger bedrooms is being used as some kind of boardroom, Phen.'

There is a long table, onto which the pile of envelopes have been stacked. Seated at the head of the table, with her back to me, is the attractive lady. She seems to be holding sway over a meeting of herself and six men.

With my enhanced hearing I hear her say, "Thank you for your reports, gents. Once again you have done well. Please take an envelope each as you go out. Steve, will you hang back a moment?"

"Sure, what's up boss?"

"We're alone Steve, there is no need to call me boss."

"Sorry Penny, what did you want to talk about?"

"I'm a bit concerned about there being strangers in three of the shops in your area. It seems like too much of a coincidence."

'This lady's on the ball, Phen.'

'Yes, and you have just taken back your weird sayings role.'

"It bothered me at first, Penny. If they had all told me the same story explaining the absence of their proprietor's, I would have been more suspicious," says Steve. "I think we should let it go this time; especially as they have all paid up. If it happens next month, we will lean on them until we get some answers."

"OK then Steve; see you next month and thanks again."

175

I don't know why but Phen and I are expecting the men to leave the house but when we get back round to the front, all the men's cars are still there. It's Penny who comes out the front door, lowers herself into the Austin Healey, deposits the small suitcase she was carrying on the passenger seat and zooms off to wherever? Phen and I follow her from a safe distance.

She has driven out of the city and seems to be heading towards the wealthy suburb of "Stoll Green".

'If that is where she lives, either she or her husband must be in the millionaire bracket,' I think to Phen.

She has turned into "Lady Barton Lane," which, by reputation, is where only the wealthy live.

All the houses are on the right and they're all lavish.

On the left is a golf course. Instead of waiting to see which drive she turns into; I follow the lane to its conclusion. As I suspected, the lane finishes in a dead end. I quickly fly back up the lane, turn into the drive of a house, that through my studies into antiques, I'd say features the Georgian Palladian style. Either side of the portico are two columns with Corinthian Capitals. Over which and supported by the columns is a classical pediment.

Penny, goes inside, and me being a gentleman, and of course, Phen, being the gentle phenomenon. We don't look into any rooms to see if she is changing her clothes; we wait. Finally, we see her emerge and go round to the garages. She opens up one of them and drives out in a "Morris Minor Traveller." If I didn't know better, I'd swear that she's not the same women that

176

Phen and I saw earlier. She's still looking expensively dressed, but dowdy in comparison, with flat heeled shoes, plaid skirt, a woolly top and a scarf over her hair.

Her journey, takes her to a private infant and junior school, where she picks up three children ranging in ages from about six to eleven. She then drives them back again to the house.

I observe for a while, and see that they have all gone into the kitchen where Penny, with the aid of a Nanny/Maid, feeds and waters her brood.

'Jake, I think we are going to have to re-evaluate the whole thing,' thinks Phen.

'You're right, Phen. I noticed a park as we came along. I'm going to take a walk to clear my head and rethink everything.'

It's getting near 5.30, and Phen and I, still haven't totally got our brains around the subtleties of the situation.

I go back to the house and hover around, watching some golfers fluffing shots.

I now see an "Aston Martin" car turn into Penny's drive. As the man gets out of his car, the front door bursts open and the three children come running out shouting Daddy, Daddy. He gathers them and they go indoors.

I put a spurt on, hoping to catch Winston & Joel before they leave for the day, and arrive just as they're getting into "Scrapyard."

"Hi guys, I was hoping to catch you. We could either talk now, or meet later for a drink; if you need to get away."

"A drink later would suit me best," says Winston.

"Me too," says Joel, "especially if you're buying."

"OK. Shall we say 8 o'clock in the Fox and Dogs?" They nod, and I say, "See you later."

I've made myself beans on toast, listened to the Archers on the radio, washed and changed into something resembling smart casual. Now I'm off to meet the lads.

It looks like I'm the first one here. I enter the one room in our local that's been set aside for non-smokers, buy a pint of Shandy and find a table that still has some late evening sunlight shining on it. I'm about to sit down, when in walk the other two.

Having bought them a drink and generally chatted mainly about how well the youth club and football team are doing, we get down to business. Joel, opens with, "Before Jenny, went home, she told us that she would very much like to take the job! When were you planning on telling us about it?"

"I'm sorry lads. I meant to discuss it with you this morning, but with everything else going on, it slipped my mind. Obviously, Jenny, has decided not to do a full-time college course."

"Do you think it wise, to employ another person who will know your secrets? We know she knows about your flying, but, what about the rest?"

"That's why I tried to persuade Jenny to join us. We are going to need a secretary before long. There's no one, other than her, that I would dream of offering the job to. Do you remember, my telling you of my first contact with John & Ken?"

"You mean," says Winston. "That she is the girl that ...you know, that they ...you know ... tried to ...you know?"

"Yes, Winston and thank you for putting it so delicately and so clearly!"

We all laugh. I now tell them of my experiences after I left them at Reg's and how puzzling it all is.

"How do you both think we should proceed from here?" I ask. Then add, "Winston, you go first then you Joel."

"I think we first need to understand this Penny's motives for what she is doing."

"I agree with Winston," says Joel, "but thinking about it, she obviously doesn't need the money. What else? A frustrated housewife. A bored housewife or What?".

"Thanks guys, those are some things to think about. I suggest we sleep on it and meet up at TF in the morning. Again, I'm sorry for not discussing Jenny's appointment with you before going ahead."

"We understand. Sometimes when a solution seems obvious, it's possible to get carried away and make decisions on the spot, without thinking of the need to discuss things with others first," says Winston.

"You know, Winston, you are sometimes wise beyond your years. Now guys I'm off to my bed. See you in the morning," I say sleepily.

Next day, the boys arrive at TF around 9am. After a mug of tea, and with the radio playing in the background, we discuss our overnight thoughts; ending up all agreeing that we get to Penny through her six thugs, especially Steve. "Hang on a sec lads," I say, "What's this I'm hearing on the radio? Joel, will you turn the sound up please."

The news reader is saying: -

"Many people this morning have been reporting, in the south of the city, feeling earth tremors. The experts say that they are not something to be alarmed about, as they only measure about three point five on the Richter scale. ….

Excuse me listeners I have a news flash. I am sorry to report that there has been in the last half hour a building that has collapsed.

I am told the owners of the building had been warned many times, that their building is unsafe. So, this is probably a one-off. …. Some more news is coming in. Yes, I am told that there is a small boy trapped in the debris, and that it is going to take two hours before rescue teams can get to the site. More news as it comes in.

Now back to the music. Here's the Beatles."

"Guys, I'm going to get over there and see what I can do, and so that you don't feel left out of my decision. I'm going as Ben the big Bozo."

"We assume you have a reason for thinking that may help the situation?" says Joel.

"Yes, guys I will be encouraging media interest in the child's rescue, and dropping out the address of Ben, and his mates.

With the media dogging his/their movements, it may rock Penny's organisation a little. Hopefully you're both with me on this one, because if I'm to help this child I must get going?"

"Yes, fly off. We'll hold the fort/forge here," says Joel.

A few seconds later I'm at a place called "Frinton," at the site of the collapsed building. With Phen's, help, I have changed into Ben, on the way. I land beyond the police cordon. The police are looking towards the crowd of onlookers. Hopefully the crowd will think that my presence is part of the rescue procedure. I enhance my hearing, and target my listening into the bowels of the collapsed building; listening for any faint noises that a child might make. Yes, I'm picking up a small whimpering sound. Now, using my X-Ray vision, I'm able to pinpoint the child's location. At high speed I start removing the fallen masonry etc.; careful not to make the building collapse further. The people looking on are gaping at what they are seeing; a blur of rubble, seemingly throwing itself aside. I've now found the child. I slow right down and gently talk to the little boy, and when he's calmer, lift him and walk from the corridor of rubble that I have created, with him in my arms. Or should I say Ben's arms.

The police come rushing forward aggressively, until they see the child, and then stand still, staring. The media cameras are clicking away causing me to rapidly reduce me hearing.

"Are the parents of this child here?" I shout to the crowd.

Without answering, a woman comes rushing forward with tears running down her face. It's at times like this, that I wish I could have done the rescue as myself.

'This is no time for regrets, Jake. You have an act to put on,' thinks Phen.

The woman takes the child from me and clasps him to her bosom, wailing to me, "Thank you. Thank you."

As she walks away, the media come rushing forward, with microphones jamming towards my face and questions firing at me like bullets from a Sten gun. "Where did you come from?" "How did you know where to look?" Etc. etc.

I hold my hands up, and when calm is restored, I say, "I was listening to the radio while breakfasting In my kitchen in "Mosby" and immediately thought I may be able to help, so I raced down "Salsy Road" and got here as quickly as I could.

That is all I've got to say, now I must get off to do some work. There are six of us men, who live in the house, and we all have our jobs to do; it being such a big house. My jobs include, polishing the brass letterbox, on the black panelled door, etc. so goodbye."

A minute or two later and pleased with myself that I'd managed to lay some pretty neat clues for the press to follow, I arrive back at TF.

Joel says, "It's still being talked about on the radio. I rang my Mom and asked her to turn on her tele. She reports that it is on all three channels."

"That should occupy Penny's mob for a while boys and it gives us time to come up with some other little schemes to frustrate them."

Over our midday sandwiches, I say to the lads, "Now that our original plan has been superseded, we need to gather more information before going any further.

What I was thinking for you Winston is to check out Ben's house to see if the media turn up there and observe what effect that has on the household. You Joel, I would like you to go and see if you can find out where the other shops are that the remaining four bozos are menacing. Then we'll catch up sometime tomorrow and compare notes."

As for me, I'm going to spend the afternoon catching up on my restoration work. I have a couple of handsome Victorian chairs to repair and polish. For the evening I'm going to see Mom and Dad. Then come back here and get a good night's sleep. Tomorrow morning I'm off to have a quiet chat with Penny!

11

After breakfast the following day, I fly to Penny's children's school, as it's about the time when they would be taken there. I spot Penny's Morris Minor and as Gordon, lean on it and wait for her to come back to it; after depositing her kids.

"Excuse me! Would you mind getting off my car?" says Penny on her return.

"Oh! This is your car is it? I've always liked these Morris Minor Travellers. Have you had it from new?"

"That's none of your business. Now if you don't mind, I need to get home."

"I'm afraid that I do mind, Penny."

"What! You know my name? … Who are you and what do you want?"

"It won't mean anything to you, but my name is Gordon."

"Well Gordon, I would advise you to get lost! My husband is a very powerful man. You would NOT, want to get on the wrong side of him."

"Not to mention, of course, Ben, Steve and the other four goons you have working for you, in your extortion business."

"If you know so much, you will know that they are not to be trifled with either. Now for the last time get off my car."

"Not until you agree to a little chat. Unless you would rather, I spoke to your husband?"

'With that one Phen, I believe, I've at least made her colour up.'

"Okay," she says, "let's get it over with. What do you want? Is it money? Is this blackmail?"

"I would prefer to call it retribution. Over the past year or so, you have swindled a lot of money out of many struggling shopkeepers. Many of whom are talking about having to give up their livelihoods; they can no longer cope with your demands.

What I want you to do is empty out the secret bank account you undoubtedly have, and give me the cash. Then I can redistribute it to all the shopkeepers you have been swindling. On my reckoning, you must have an account with around £170,000 pounds, plus interest, on deposit."

"Do you, honestly think me such an easy pushover, that I will meekly walk into my bank and hand over all my money to you? I suggest, Gordon, (*said with a sneer,*) that you go ahead and tell my husband. I am absolutely sure he will laugh at you."

'I didn't expect that Phen. What do we do now? Penny is more of a cool customer, than I have given her credit for.'

'It seems to me Jake that we will have to attack the problem from the other end.'

'I'll try one more tack. If that doesn't work, then we'll do as you thought.'

"You may be right, Penny. Have you noticed by the way the amount of media interest that's being shown in your gang of six?"

185

"What media interest?"

"Your boy Ben has been performing feats of strength over at Frinton. The house in "Mosby", is surrounded by reporters & photographers?"

'You do not know that for sure,' thinks Phen.

'I know Phen, but it's a good enough guess.'

"When you get back to your house Penny, give Steve a ring and hear what he has to say, I'll be waiting out by your car; in case you want to talk further."

Penny drives home and out of her sight I follow her. She parks in front of her front door, gets out of her car and without stopping to lock it, swiftly moves to her front door, lets herself in, and dashes to the hall phone; leaving the door wide open.

There's a pause while the connection is made. There is no need for me to increase my hearing, as I can hear what she is saying through the open doorway. I can imagine what is being said the other end, by the fury on her face.

The phone is lowered to its cradle. Penny drops and slumps into a nearby comfy hall seat, with a look of bewilderment on her face, which only lasts about a minute. Meanwhile I'm again with arms folded, leaning on her car and facing her hall.

The once cool lady, fighting hard to regained her composure, comes back out to me and says, "I suppose you think you have won, but let me tell you what I will be telling Steve next time I ring him. I shall be saying, there is no need to panic. We do not have to collect our next envelopes until next month; by which time the media will have moved on to some other story. By the way, Ben claims he never left the house this morning. How do you explain that?"

"Penny, I don't have an explanation. I can only tell you the facts. Let's take a moment to think things through, shall we? …………"

Five minutes later I say, "OK Penny this is how I see it; you're an intelligent woman so I don't need to tell you that some reporters never give up on a story. It would not be difficult for me to rekindle their interest. Shall we say at the start of next month?"

"Are you threatening me?" she says.

"No, I'm just trying to get you to think about it. You've had a good run, and it's my guess, it hasn't been about the money.

Tell me if I've got it wrong: Before your marriage you had a promising career. You were out every day using your intelligence. Your husband, who is undoubtedly a very wealthy man, tells you after the wedding that there is no need for you to work.

You at first kicked against it, but because you respect him you went along with it. When the children came along your desire to work got pushed into the background but twelve months or so ago, the old yearnings came back. You thought, what can I do, that hubby won't suspect me doing. Gradually, possibly through old contacts, you came up with your idea. But Penny, couldn't you have come up with something a little less threatening?"

"You're close, but you can't possibly know how it feels to be stifled all these years. As for my choice of idea: I wanted something adventurous, even dangerous. I already knew Steve from when I worked as an insurance fraud investigator; it was something he and I came up with. There is no intention to harm anybody, not physically anyway. We find the threats sufficient to get the shop owners to cough up. Hang about! Why, am I telling YOU, all this?"

"I don't know. Why are you? Could it be that you are, you being very bright, thinking that you may after all consider changing tack? Don't be offended if I try a bit of flattery because in fact it wouldn't be. The point is…"

"I was wondering if you were ever going to get around to it?" she says acidly.

"The point is, Penny" I say pressing on, "I have noticed how beautiful your garden is. Front & back."

"How would you know about my back garden? You've never seen it."

"That's another story and I WILL get to the point no matter how many times you interrupt me.

The beauty of your garden may not have been down to you doing your own shovelling but I'm sure the creation and planning of it is down to you."

"How can you be sure of that?"

"Well, your husband is a high-flying business man. I don't think that he would have the time to create such a fine landscaped garden. Plus, you don't strike me as the sort of lady who could say to a gardener. Just get on with it, anything will do."

"Alright, you've got me there, but so what?"

"The so what, Penny, is that you have the confidence of six strapping men; who could do with a lot more exercise than they're currently getting. It would do them no harm if you got them involved in a landscape gardening business. Before you say anything, looking around this area alone, I've noticed a lot of gardens that could really use your touch.

"How do you think I should hide such a business from my husband?"

"The simple answer Penny, is that you don't!"

"What! Are you mad? My husband would do his nut."

"Let him. You have shown, albeit in the wrong direction, that you have the talent, confidence and the brains, to run your own business. Penny, you are now an adult. You no longer need to, as you said to me, meekly go along with everything your husband wants."

"I understand what you are saying Gordon but you need to understand this money you are seeking to take back is what was going to be my shot at gaining some independence; should my husband trot out his usual diatribe about how I couldn't possibly manage without his financial support."

"On that point, I'm sure we could come to some arrangement whereby you keep enough of the money to get you started. Once it is up and running and you have sold your house over at "Mosby". You will be able to return more money, through me, to the shopkeepers.

189

As for your husband, I honestly believe he will eventually come around. After all he loves you, correct?"

"Or, he loves the idea of me; as the archetypal housewife and mother."

"Give him a chance, he may surprise you but don't be upset at the first things he says. When he starts thinking about it, he will, I'm almost certain, begin to realise he's much better off with you than without you."

"OK. I'm done thinking. As an ex-American, you would think I would be a bit feistier wouldn't you. How much of the money can I keep?"

"My God, Penny straight to the point or what! Okay, down to business, let me reverse the question and ask you, how much you think you'll need to get a landscaping business up and running?"

"That depends how big you wanna go from the outset. Conceivably you could start with a few forks and shovels, but if you wanna invest in huge diggers etc.?"

"So, Penny let's take the middle ground regarding the set-up costs. If you kept a third of the money back, on my reckoning, and you can choose to show me your bank statements or not; you would have, without the sale of the "Mosby" house, about £60,000. If your husband wants to know where you got the money from to start up a business, tell him you have been putting a bit aside for years; ready for when the children are old enough for you, at last, to be able to do something for yourself. If you are prepared to go along with this idea, I promise you, I won't reveal to the shopkeepers who has been behind their menacing."

"Telling my husband that I have been salting a little money away will not be too difficult; as it's true. How do you think I got the money together to buy the "Mosby" house in the first place? Now I come to think on it, the proceeds from that house do not belong to the shopkeepers."

"I'm sure what you say is true and, on that basis, you will only owe them the money that you are going to withhold.

As for the money you have been paying your six heavies; providing they go along with your landscaping plan I won't go after them for it."

"Do you; honestly think you could persuade them to hand it over? They may decide, after I have told them of my withdrawal, to go it alone."

"I think, what you are asking me is, can I, just one man, take on six burly men on my own? To answer your question let me show you something that you can relate to your men. It may help them come to a decision and save them from prolonging the inevitable."

With that, I lean off Penny's, car, turn around, stoop down and lift it. Then carry it to the end of her Drive and back again. Then ask, "Any questions?"

Penny's too stunned to speak. She just stands there open mouthed and with wide open staring eyes.

"A-a-a how did you do that?"

191

"That doesn't matter. What is important is that you can convince your men that continuing to menace people is no longer viable."

"Are you some kind of alien?"

"No, but I do have a number of powers that your men would be unwise to challenge."

Penny looks at her watch, almost in a far-off way as though in a dream, and says, "Look it's nearly lunch time. Would you care for something to eat and drink?"

"I thought you would never ask; I would be delighted to accept," I say while presenting her with one of my more charming smiles.

Over a nice lunch which includes a glass of wine for her and a beer for me, Penny and I cover many topics. From her husband's job. To the state of the economy. As it all seems to be heading in the right direction, I ask Penny if I could make a phone call?

"Providing it's not to the police, go right ahead," she says with an unsure grin.

"Thanks Penny, I only want to make sure that none of my people have told anyone of your involvement, in the, you know what."

"Hello Joe, Gordon here."

Joel says, "Joe? Do I take it that you are with someone?"

"Yes, I'm at Penny's, we have been having quite a chat. I'm pretty confident that we have come to an amicable arrangement. I just want to check with you, that none of our people, have told any of the shopkeepers about Penny?"

"No, Gordon. As you know, I've been busy finding the other two shopping areas that are being menaced, and Winston, until he came in five minutes ago, was still watching the Bozo's house. I can say for certain that none of us has mentioned Penny to anyone. We wouldn't anyway without your say so. While you're on, here's a bit of news for you: Jenny, would like to start on Monday. She said that you had discussed day release with her. Winston's going to enquire about secretarial courses at Buckton College. He thinks it could be arranged. He will talk to Jenny on Monday."

"OK, good work. I should be back by late afternoon. I must go now. I'll be with you, as soon, as I can."

"I'm sorry about that, Penny; it took longer than I thought. Regarding your problem you are in the clear. No one yet knows of your part in your extortion racket."

"Yet! What does that mean?"

"Only that if our arrangements go through; no one will be any the wiser."

"Fair enough Gordon. While you were on the phone; I dug out my bank statements. There you are, there's proof that I, at least, trust YOU. As you can see, you weren't too far out."

I look at the bottom line of the statement, and it reads £180,550-00.

"Come on, let's get round to the bank and get this over with before I change my mind. Then I can go pick up my kids."

193

Penny fetches a suitcase from her garage and drives us to the bank. Fortunately, it's one of the big high street jobs. Otherwise, they may not have enough cash available. On the way I tell Penny that my full name is Gordon James.

We're shown into the manager's office. As Penny is well known at this bank, the manager says, "How can we help you today Mrs Robertson?"

"I wish to make a sizeable withdrawal and this transaction must remain confidential; as usual."

"Of course. How much would you like to withdraw?"

I jump in at this point, and say, "£120,000 was the sum agreed, I believe Mrs Robertson."

Penny looks at me with a knowing look, which says you have let me off, of the odd £550.

"Yes, Mr James. That is the agreed sum." Then looking back at the Manager, she says, "Mr Jones, if you will have one of your tellers deposit the cash into my suitcase; I will be off to collect the children from school."

"Mr Jones lifts his internal phone and gives the order, gets up and shakes Penny's hand and says please give my best to Mr Robertson. If you would like to go to the end window, my assistant manager will load your money, and get your signature on the withdrawal slip."

Back in Penny's car she hands over the case saying, "No doubt you will be in touch."

I hand Penny a slip of paper, that I took from the bank, and wrote our office phone number down for her, saying, "Ring me when you have got your new business going, and your "Mosby" house sale has gone through. Sincerely Penny, should you need any support along the way, or your men give you any trouble, don't hesitate to contact me."

Ten minutes later, I'm walking into TF with Penny's, suitcase full of money. Both the lads are there. After changing into myself and saying, "Hello." I hand them the case and say, "There you are, lads; a job for you tomorrow. Give each of the shopkeeper's, about £2000 pound back. I'll leave the exact details to you.

This money still leaves them short of what they have paid out but there maybe some more coming in a few months' time and of course they will no longer be bothered by the Bozos."

I fill the lads in on all that has happened. Tell them about the deal I've struck with Penny and add, "Any chance of a mug of tea?"

Winston says, "You know you're amazing, and I don't mean your super powers, but this way you have of manipulating people into bettering themselves"

"That's very kind of you to say so, Winston, but Phen and the powers that he's given me are always the clincher in these negotiations."

'Thanks Jake,' thinks Phen, 'I must say that I thought you had forgotten all about me.'

'Don't be silly. We both know without you, none of what we are doing would be possible; including my intellectual powers.'

"Nice cuppa Joel."

"Winston, will you find a good hiding place for that money until tomorrow and when you see Reg, please tell him that I'll get along to talk things over with him as soon as I can."

12

The Kidnapping

'**Do you know Phen** there is something about the autumn in this country, that makes me feel sad one moment, and glad to be alive the next. The sadness, I feel is bought on by the prospect of winter coming on. Gladness is the sight of all the lovely colours that can be seen as the autumn leaves of bushes and trees change colour.'

I particularly notice this as I'm flying across our wooded park to "Little Marston". Hang on. I'm getting ahead of myself. Let me tell you why I'm headed this way.

The Boys have delivered the £2000 each to all the shopkeepers that have been menaced by Penny's six Bozos. Who, I hope by now, are busying themselves helping Penny to establish her Landscape Gardening Business?

Winston & Joel are having this Sunday off. They're to turn out for the football team they started; now run by Freddy & Syd.

As for me, I'm following up on a phone call we received. It came in as we were about to pack up for the day on Saturday. Joel took the call and wrote down the details. He explained to the lady that all our senior agents are out on assignment at present but one of them will contact her first thing tomorrow and make arrangements to see her. In the meantime, she should stall any demands.

"All our senior agents?" I'd queried.

"Well, if you keep changing your appearance, it may seem to some, that we have more than one senior."

"Good thinking Joelee boy!" said Winston.

Finally, Joel reported to Winston and me what the lady's problem is. I could, of course, have enhanced my hearing and listened to what she said directly but I thought, I'm going to have to hear it again when Joel tells Winston, so I may as well wait.

Joel reported: "The lady has seen our advert and is desperately praying that we can help her. She told me that her 10-year-old daughter has been kidnapped. I asked her about police involvement, and got the expected answer. There is one thing you both should know from the outset. The ladies name is Christine, she is the ex-wife of Dick Dizzley the famous Pop Star."

"That's amazing lads," I'd said. "Who would have thought that a famous Pop Star could possibly become a client of ours already? We've only been operating a few weeks."

"To be fair Jake," Joel, said, "it's his ex-wife who's making the running on this but that doesn't mean that he's not equally concerned for their daughter's safety.

By the way. Dick Dizzley is the Pop Star's stage name. In private he prefers to be called by his given name;

which is, Richard Duval."

"Thanks Joel. The name Duval, that's French isn't it?" I'd said.

"Yes" answered Joel, "I think his Grandfather was French; he himself is a true Brit. He must be because he supports Torquay United F.C.!

Christine is up here visiting her Mom. It is from here, that her daughter Lucy was abducted. The family home is in Devon. Richard is on his way from there as we speak."

"I thought you said they are divorced?" said I.

"They are but it's an amicable separation and because Richard is away a lot, he doesn't need a separate house to himself. He uses, what for a better description you might call a Granny Flat. That way he gets to see his daughter as often as he can," replied Joel.

"You seem to have gathered a hell of a lot of information in a short time Joel."

"It's called charm. You aren't the only one that's got some," Joel had said, with a smile on his face.

"Thanks for that, Joel," then I said. "What I would like you to do is phone Christine and tell her that you have managed to get in touch with a senior agent and that his name is Sean Brooks. Tell her that he will phone her at 8 o'clock in the morning."

"Sean Brooks? Where did that come from?" Winston had asked.

"Sean was a journalist character that I adopted to help with a problem I had in Liverpool. I feel for this

199

situation, Sean will be best suited. I think Gordon would be too over powering."

Early Sunday morning, I rang the number Joel had given me, and said, "Good morning Mrs Duval. My name is Sean Brooks.

First of all, may I say how sorry I am to hear your sad news. Tell me, have there been any demands from the kidnappers?"

"Yes, they rang a short while ago, demanding £100,000 pounds in ransom for the safe return of my daughter."

"What did you tell them? It is them, I take it, and not an individual?"

"I'm sure it is, because the man I spoke to said we want, not I want. I told them what Joel told me to say. Which if you don't know is: I can't do anything until Mr Duval, gets here; he's on his way up from Devon. If you leave me a number, I will call you when he gets here. They said we're not that daft. We can't have you getting someone to trace the number. We'll ring again between 9 and 10am, and remember, no police."

"Good, you did the right thing. What time do you think Mr Duval, will be with you?"

"Shortly, if he doesn't get any hold-ups"

"OK, I believe you are staying with your mother. Did you leave her address with Joel?"

"Yes, but I will give it again. It's "The Roses," Lazyridge Avenue, Little Marston. As you come down the avenue from the main road it's the forth house on the left."

"Thank you, I will be with you around 8.30."

Now you know why I'm flying over the park and noticing the tree colours on my way to Little Marston.

Just after 8.30, I'm ringing the doorbell of "The Roses". There are two cars in the drive. On the way to the door I touch the bonnet of the "Alpha Romeo". It's still hot. Richard must have arrived.

The door's answered by a lady; who once must have been very beautiful. She still has the high cheek bones and is still slim. It's only her age that has dimmed her beauty.

"Hello, can I help you?" the lady says.

"I'm here to see Mr & Mrs Duval. My name is Sean Brooks."

"Oh yes, they are expecting you, please come in."

The Duval's and I shake hands and drinks in the form of tea and coffee are prepared and served. We all sit down including Christine's Mom. Mr Duval opens with, "If it's okay, I'd prefer to use first names. I'm Richard and my wife's," after a quick look from Christine he revises that to, "my ex-wife's name is Christine. My EX Mother in law is Beatrice," he says irritably. "If I may Sean, how do you think we should handle this mess we're in?"

"Before I answer that, I would like us to get to know each other better, so that I can assess how much pressure we can handle. We have about an hour in which to do so."

Richard says, "I'm sure I can speak for Chris and I about how much pressure we can handle and the simple answer is: we don't know." For which, this time, he receives a nod from Christine.

"Would you tell me about the layout of your Devonshire house?"

"It's a lovely house" says Christine, "Art Deco in style, it is built on the cliff top overlooking Braxam Bay. Looking towards the sea, it's on the right. There is another cliff top on the left of the bay, which has no dwellings, only a Lighthouse. In the valley between the two, lies the lovely town of Braxam, with its sea front, harbour and beach."

"And the house itself?" I enquire.

Richard jumps in with, "It's wide rather than deep, painted white, with six bedrooms, two of which I use as my quarters; a four-car garage, front and rear lounges, large breakfast/kitchen, laundrette and a balcony that runs across the whole length of the rear of the property on which, apart from patio furniture, I keep my telescope. I enjoy looking at other people's boats, apart from keeping my eye on my own yacht. At night my hobby is Star Gazing, and of course we have a large swimming pool."

"Thank you both, your descriptions are a very useful contribution towards a possible plan." I look at a Mantle Clock and note that it is a quarter to nine and say, "Allow me to pour us a proper drink and I'll tell you my thoughts. If afterwards you honestly think you won't be able to cope with the idea please tell me and I will have to think again."

I get up, pour the drinks and say to Richard, "When the phone rings I want you to answer it. What they will probably say is that they want the money left at such and such a site; no later than such and such a time.

This is not going to be easy, because you have the fear of what might happen to Lucy, but you must try very hard. I believe this is our best chance to get her back unharmed. (*having passed the idea through Phen.*) Stay calm and say to the kidnappers: that they don't hold all the cards. That you don't have anything like the money they are demanding up here. If they are prepared to come down to your Devon house where you have ample cash?" He nods so I continue, "you will pay them double their demand, providing Lucy is returned totally unharmed.

If you like, you can get bolshie and say, if they harm one hair of her, you will hire the best private detective's money can buy to track them down. Tell them you'll then take a contract out on them. Then slam the phone down and let them stew over what you have said."

"No! No!" Christine, screams, "Let's just pay up now."

Phen thinks, 'I can see now why you chose Richard to answer the phone, Jake. He certainly seems to be keeping his nerve better.'

203

'It's not easy for either of them Phen, we will just have to see how it goes.'

"I'm sorry Christine. I know this is nerve racking but this idea stands the best chance of Lucy coming out of this unharmed."

'I nearly said alive there, Phen.'

'Yes, be careful Jake, her nerves are already at breaking point.'

"I'm afraid Sean is right Chris," says Richard, "we have got to prevent the perps from thinking they have all the control over the situation. They will be the ones who want to put the phone down on us, so that the call can't be traced; if after all we've got the police involved. By putting it down on them, will help to prove we haven't."

The conversation continues until 9.25am, when the phone rings. Richard rushes to answer it, I say, "Slow down. Let it ring four or five times before you lift the receiver. Then take a deep breath and respond."

I enhance my hearing so that I can hear what is being said the other end. It means that Richard will be too loud but because of the recent practice that Phen has been putting me through; I'm now able to accurately target my hearing on what I really want to hear. The technique I use to achieve this is that I'm now able to increase & decrease my hearing so rapidly I'm able to filter out some noises, while increasing the loudness of others. In this case, what I'm listening for are any background noises, which might give a clue as to where the call may be coming from.

The exchanges between the abductors and Richard, go more or less as predicted but the background noises haven't revealed much; only a television or radio playing quietly. The only useful things I picked up were the conversations of another male and a female voice but nothing pointing to their location.

"Now we wait" is my reply to the looks that Richard and Christine are giving me, which without words are saying, what now? "In the meantime, we rehearse the next bit."

"Which is?" asks Richard.

'Yes, I would like to know that too,' thinks Phen, 'this not being part of our original thought out plan.'

"If we can, we need to get the perps to agree to let you see Lucy. Hearing her is not enough. I'm sure they will kick against this; they will fear you will have someone in hiding waiting to snatch her.

The way round this, as I see it, having listened to your descriptions of your home and its surroundings, is to say that you have a powerful telescope at the rear of your property, with a wide bay between you and a Lighthouse on the other side.

If they bring Lucy to the Lighthouse. Then bring her out from behind it at a designated time to suit them. You will be able to see her through your telescope. They can then arrange to exchange her for the money; at a place and time of their choosing."

"Yes, that could work," says Richard. "There's a large area of open ground to be crossed before you get to the Lighthouse. The kidnappers would see anyone

205

coming if they suspected a trap but what good would it do us, other than seeing that Lucy is alright at that moment?"

"To answer that, I would need your solemn promises not to reveal to anyone what I will show you?" They all nod in agreement, "In that case do you have a telescope here?"

"No, but I have a powerful pair of Binoculars" says Beatrice, "my late husband was a keen Twitcher."

I say, "Let's go out to your back garden. .... OK, this is super. If all three of you stand here and take it in turns to focus the Binoculars on that far hillside, you should be able to see me standing on top of it."

Before they can ask questions. I oscillate to invisibility. Fly off, take form again and stand waving my arms about long enough for them all to see me. I fly back and land Just as Beatrice is putting the Binoculars down. I say to Richard, "Well does that answer your question?"

"How! How! Did you get there and back so quickly?"

"Actually, that was slow, but that folks is what I need you all to keep strictly between us. As to how I did it, I'm afraid is too long a story to go into now. I must simply ask you to trust me."

Richard having recovered and we're all back in the lounge says, "I'm beginning to see your idea: when they signal they are ready to let us see Lucy and I look through my Telescope, you will be able to get across the Bay and rescue her."

"Not quite, when I was listening to your conversation with them, I picked up the sound of a female and second male voice. We are dealing with three of them. I would like to put a stop to them all. In such a way that makes it unlikely that they'll try abducting anyone else's child or out of anger; vandalise your home. However, I promise you that my first priority is the safety of your daughter."

"What is, your plan then Sean," asks Christine nervously, her concern naturally, being for her own child.

"When the background man and woman were talking, they were saying something about when they have the money, they will be able to start their new lives in Spain.

What I would like you to do Richard is agree to pay up and make the exchange. I will keep an eye on Lucy and make sure no harm comes to her; during and before the process.

Once they have your money and you have Lucy at home with you. If it is still their plan to smuggle the money into Spain? I will relieve them of it there. Their Passports also if given the chance. Thereby stranding them in Franco's Spain without money or Passports."

"Sean, you have a twisted mind but I like that and don't think I haven't noted that you must have super hearing as well as your other abilities," replies Richard.

"A good friend of mine often accuses me of the twisted mind bit" I say.

Privately I think to Phen. 'Don't you Phen?'

Phen replies, 'Mmmm.'

'You know Phen; I've missed your Mmmm's. I haven't heard them for awhile.'

It's not until nearly noon that the phone rings. Once again, the plan goes pretty much as before; except this time, they get the phone down before Richard. With the parting salvo: "We'll be in touch about the details of the exchange. What is your Devon phone number?" Richard tells them, "Be by it, no later than tomorrow afternoon."

Earlyish Monday morning, I've flown ahead of the others, as I want to get a preview of the layout and to check out the Lighthouse. Is there a Lighthouse keeper for instance and do they keep the entrance locked?

These questions, I'm hoping will be answered by a gentleman that I've just bought a newspaper and a "Mars Bar" from, in a local Newsagents.

"If you don't mind my asking? I would love the opportunity to have a look around the Lighthouse while I'm here. If I go up there, do you think the Lighthouse keeper would let me?"

"You won't find nobody thar this toym ar the day, young fella. The Lighthouse tis only manned at noyt now, some toyms durin the day, if tis foggy.

Nobody lives thar now, so tis kept padlocked most ar the toym. In any case, the Keeper's away this weekend."

"Thank you very much, you have been most helpful."

"You know tis funny, you's the second one ter day, that's been a askin arter Lighthouse."

"That's very interesting. Can you describe the other person?"

"Oy can only tell you that it were a woman. She hard er hed covered wi a scarf, an wor dark glasses."

I say, "Thanks again," and depart but not before Phen thinks to me, 'I am pleased you understood all that, Jake. I was struggling to comprehend him.'

After an early pub lunch and a stroll down by the harbour; looking at the yachts etc., I make my way up to the Duval's house. I have to say it is an impressive building and on an imposing site.

It has a wide drive leading to it, with trees either side, and each one different, what might be called a mini Arboretum. Parked in front of the garages is Richard's Alpha Romeo. I stroll up to the front door but there is no need to knock or ring as it's opened by Richard as I approach.

"Welcome" he says, "Come in, make yourself at home. Chris will be down shortly. She and Beatrice have gone to freshen up after the journey. What would you like to drink? Have you eaten?"

"Nothing thanks, I had a pub lunch a short while ago."

"In that case, come and see my Telescope."

He leads the way through his annex and out the back. The view from the Balcony, out across the Bay is stunning. I say, "You're a lucky man; it must be wonderful waking up to a view like this."

"Yes, it is lovely but as you know, I'm away a lot so I don't see it all that often. Ah! Here's Chris and Beatrice. Ladies, Sean's here."

After a lot of chat and the grand tour of the house & grounds, we return to the lounge that opens on to the Balcony and await the abductors call.

It's 2.30 and the phone has just rung. Richard, who now from experience, takes his time answering, says, "Hello, yes my Telescope is outside the patio doors.… Okay, but remember what I said about any harm coming to her.… I'm going there now." Richard puts the phone down and says, "They have her on the Lighthouse balcony, that circles the top of the structure."

"Right I'm off." I go out through the front door, in case they are watching the back through Binoculars, and within seconds I'm hovering outside of their eye line but at an angle from which I can see them.

There are only two on the Balcony, the woman holding Lucy and one of the men. He's looking across the Bay through his Binoculars. Both are wearing ski masks.

'Phen please take careful note of as much of their appearance as you can.'

'You, do not need to tell me to do this stuff anymore, I know my place.'

'Thanks, Phen,' I say, smiling at his attempt at humour. I increase my sight and look across the Bay at Richard who has looked through his Scope and given the thumbs up to the kidnappers. They move off the Balcony, emerge a few minutes later and attach a new, but similar lock, to the Lighthouse door; having Jemmied off the original.

I'm expecting them to make their way across the open area. But no! They are going around to the other side of the Lighthouse and boarding a Launch; which they must have come on. They steer toward the Point and remove their masks.

Phen thinks, 'Smarter than we thought Jake; but at least we can now see their faces.'

'Yes Phen, that's useful, and they of course don't know, that we now know, what they look like.'

We follow them around the Point, and watch as they moor up near Godmington beach. They disembark and get into a car, which was obviously parked there earlier. The car is being driven by the man, who turns five minutes later into the grounds of a caravan site.

Their caravan is opened by the second man, who says, "How did it go?"

"Perfect. Now we need to plan the next step," answers the women.

The car driver says, "It's, as I see it, about where the safest place is to make the exchange. Wherever we choose, our exit strategy is the most important thing. Anybody got any ideas?"

"We could use the same location we've just used, as Judy said, it went perfectly," says the second man.

The woman, whose name we now know, says as she shuts Lucy in the caravan, "The location is as good as any. It's made easy by are being able to use the Launch my Dad keeps down here. The hard part is getting hold of the money without releasing the girl."

'I'm astonished by what I've just heard Phen and it looks like the two men are also.'

They recover quickly and say, as one. "You are joking surely?"

"No, think about it Rick, Phil, she is able to identify us, there is no way we can let her go free."

Rick, who is the car driver, says, "I hope you're not suggesting we eliminate her?"

"What other option do we have? We can't take her to Spain with us."

"Judy, don't forget what Duval said he would do if we harmed her," says Phil.

"There are a few things in our favour in that regard," replies Judy. "Duval doesn't know we're going to Spain. If he does find out and sends someone after us? He or she will be looking for a group of three people. When we get to Spain, we are going to divide the money and go our separate ways. When we make the exchange, we will be wearing our ski masks again. Apart from the girl, the Duval's still won't know what we look like."

"How do you propose to do away with the girl and still get hold of the money?" Rick asks.

"The area immediately around the Lighthouse is paved. In other words, hard. We only allow Mrs Duval to come forward with the money and to collect the girl. We tell her to open the Lighthouse door, and leave the money just inside, and close the door after her.

In the meantime, we will have the girl up on the Balcony, with a rope tied round her and she will be dangled over the safety rail. Mrs Duval will be told that as soon as we have confirmed that the money is as it should be. In other words, not cut up newspaper, we will lower the girl to the ground, but of course that won't happen. What will happen is we will let the girl fall; from that height and with the hard ground, she is very unlikely to survive. While the woman's tending the child, we make our escape in the Launch, telephone my Dad to let him know where to find his boat, get to the nearest Airport and fly off to Spain.

If we arrange the exchange for tomorrow, we will have this afternoon to make the flight arrangements.

You Phil, have already had our special secret compartment luggage made."

"It seems that you have thought this through, so if this is the only way, it looks like Rick and I will have to go along with it, even though there are two things I'm not happy about: killing the girl and parting from you when we get to Spain.

Back with Richard, Chris and Beatrice, I outline the abductors deadly plan.

213

Chris breaks down and sobs. Richard is stony faced. Beatrice looks grim and says "Of course there's no way we can allow their evil plan to succeed. We will have to send in the Police to raid this caravan site and rescue Lucy now."

"Please Richard, Sean, let's not delay. Do as Mom says," pleads Chris.

"Sean, unless you're prepared to go back there, and rescue Lucy; I'm sorry; I have to agree with the girls."

"If tackling the three, especially as they are now all together, was an option, I would have done it while I was there but I'm afraid I'm not allowed to do physical harm to anyone; even scum like them. So, I completely understand your position. You must do as you see fit. You know of course that I would not be able to give evidence in any ensuing court case, but with the Police evidence and Lucy's testimony, it should be enough to convict them. You should know however, that I think this is a mistake. I only hope that I'm wrong."

The phone call made and the descriptions of the perps, given by me, but conveyed to the Police by Richard. He's told them nothing about me but has told them the location of the site and the specific caravan. He then says to us, "Come on we'll drive to the site and be there for when Lucy is rescued."

"Although I could fly there quicker. I may as well come with you. It's no good my being there before the Police.

I'll fly back after Lucy's release so that she can be comforted by you all without me there. The more normal we can make it for her, the better, she will have had enough shocks for one week."

Within half an hour, we are all at the caravan site and making our way through the Police cordon.

A plain clothed Policeman comes forward, shows his warrant card, introduces himself as D.C. Bradley and says, "I'm sorry Mr & Mrs Duval we were too late, they've cleared out."

The faces of the Duval's sink so low, you would be forgiven for thinking their jaws would reach the ground. They turn on me saying, "Why couldn't you have broken your non-violence rule, and rescued her, while you had the chance?"

The Policeman begins to ask what that means, when Richard intervenes with, "It's nothing officer, just lashing out. Come on let's get back home," he says to us, and then re-addressing the officer, says, "I'm sorry for getting you out on a wild goose chase D.C. Bradley."

We arrive home; Richard's apologising to me but before he's finished, the phone rings. I answer it. With Phen's help, I try to mimic Richards's voice as best I can and say, "Hello."

"Listen Duval, you have been a very naughty man. You were warned not to involve the Police. So, what do you go and do! Now, it's going to cost you another hundred thou. We'll be in touch, and no more Police, or else!" The phone goes dead.

I relate the message and get the unison response "What can we do now?" said with heavy despair in their voices.

"I'm afraid, it's back to plan A. We have to wait for their next call and let them carry out the plan that I overheard them talking about."

"NO!" screams Chris with wide staring eyes, "We can't risk it."

"Listen Chris" I say as gently as I can. "We will be very lucky if they continue with their original plan. Their suspicions must be aroused by what happened.

I mean how did the Police know where to raid? If they do go ahead as planned, it will still be our best chance of getting Lucy home alive. Especially as we no longer know where they are holding her."

'I note, you didn't hold back that time Jake,' thinks Phen.

'No Phen, circumstances have changed.'

"HOW CAN YOU SAY THAT?" shouts Chris.

"Because, as I said before, I won't let them harm your daughter."

"Chris," says Richard, "Let's calm down and listen to what Sean has to say. After all, our plan was a dismal failure. On reflection, we should have held our nerve and gone along with Sean in the first place."

Chris takes a few deep breaths and says, "Go ahead Sean, I'm listening."

"You, Chris are the one who is going to have to hold your nerve more than anyone. A lot is going to depend on your ability to act, and at the same time, get Lucy to

216

act along with you. When, you have left the money behind the Lighthouse door. You must go and stand below the balcony, as though you are expecting them to lower Lucy down.

When they let go of the rope; you must scream out. I'm sure the one letting it go will rush down to join the one with the bags and that the third one will be with the Launch. Revved up and ready to make their getaway.

As they make their escape, they are not going to have time for more than a quick glance in your direction. What that glance must reveal is you bending over your dead child sobbing your heart out, except she won't be dead. You can stop going pale Chris because I will catch her on the way down and lay her at your feet, where you must encourage her to play dead. Do you get the picture Chris?"

"Yes, I think so, but are you sure you can catch her in time?"

"Chris, you've already seen how quickly I can move, and I wasn't joking when I said that my earlier demonstration was slow. To convince you further, please come and stand facing me, and really look at me.

Can you see me?"

"Yes."

"Can you see me now?"

"No, I can hear you but I can't see you."

"Even though I'm still here in front of you, you can't see me. The reason is that I'm moving too fast for the human eye to make me out. I'll start slowing down; you tell me when you begin to see me."

"Now, I can see a blur, and now you are taking shape. Now, I see you properly, and now you have convinced me! I will do my best not to let you down on the acting front. Let's hope, as you say, they are prepared to adhere to the plan you heard them plotting."

"Talking about plans, I'll be changing the final scenario. I'm no longer, in the light of their intent to kill Lucy prepared to let them rot in Spain. I will be encouraging you to seek their extradition to stand trial here. The Spaniards from what I hear are very fond of children. Even though it is a dictatorship, I don't think you will have too much trouble."

I stay overnight, at the insistence of the family, in case anymore phone calls come in.

It's not until 10-30 Tuesday morning that a call comes through; I answer again but only say "Yes".

The perps say "How did you know where to send the Cops; yesterday?"

"That was my fault, I'm a friend of the family. I'd been waiting in sight of the Lighthouse all afternoon for you to show up. I had you in my sights as I followed in my car and saw you round the Point.

When you turned into the caravan park, I drove to the nearest phone box and rang the Police. It's not my fault they took so long to get there. Richard and Chris knew nothing about it until I told them later." I hear

218

murmuring going on in the background and just about make out the words; he didn't hear the plan.

"Get off the phone asshole and put Richard on."

I hand the phone to Richard with a thumb up signal.

Richard says, "Hello. I'm sorry about the Police, it was a big mistake. I'm ready to follow any instructions you lay down, I just want my Daughter back. Yes …, yes … OK …yes. OK we'll do that. …Yes, and definitely no Cops. We're not going to make the same mistake twice…yes only Chris will approach the Lighthouse and she will follow your instructions to the letter.

…Yes, I've got the whole £300,000 together."

Click! The connection is severed. "The plan is going ahead, we've got to be there in one hour exactly and as you heard it's now £300,000, they want," concludes Richard.

Chris, carrying two Holdalls, her shoulders pulled down by the weight as though she has been hauling heavy shopping for years, makes her way slowly across the open area towards the Lighthouse.

She is now near enough to see her daughter on the balcony but can't allow herself to focus on her or she could break down and not be able to carry out her tasks.

Now at the Lighthouse, Chris opens the door and exhaustingly drops the bags behind it. She then goes, as instructed to the front of the structure and starts screaming, "Come on lower her down, you promised, come on lower my baby down."

219

Both Chris and I can see that it is the woman who is holding the rope that surrounds Lucy. With my hearing tuned to what's happening in the Lighthouse I hear Phil shout, "all's fine with the money".

Judy let's go of the rope and races down to join Phil.

I fly past the Lighthouse collecting a screaming Lucy on the way. Then circle back, saying to Lucy on the way, "When I place you at your mothers' feet pretend to be dead; it is vital that you do."

I gently deliver her in front of her mother. Chris quickly lays her down and leans over her screaming, "Oh my baby! No! Oh no! Please no! And Lucy God Bless her, lays perfectly still. What a little actress and she must be double jointed. She's twisted one of her arms and both her legs around so they appear broken.

Chris sees the abductors coming out of the lighthouse and screams at them, "You bastards you've killed my baby, you evil swine," while continuing to sob uncontrollably.

The two race towards their Launch with Phil carrying the bags. They jump aboard. The Launch sets off immediately and I follow them from high above. All the way to the nearest Airport.

While they Check in. I drop into a fish and chip shop and buy a 'Fleur de Lys' chicken and mushroom pie. Then hang around until I see them board an Iberian airways flight.

I follow the plane and watch it land at Malaga airport. I stand by as they pick up their luggage and watch as they climb into a taxi. Which drops them off at a small hotel. I observe, from their balcony, that they've booked into two adjacent rooms. As luck would have it, they've thrown the suitcases, with the secret compartments on the nearest bed.

I hear Phil as he goes to the bedside phone. He asks for room service and orders two bottles of their best Champagne to be delivered to Judy's room number.

'Great Phen, they should be occupied in Judy's room for a while. It will give us time to go in search of their Passports.'

'Will not the receptionist have put them in the hotels safe?' thinks Phen.

'Yes, but they check them first. Let's hope they're busy and haven't got around to it yet.'

I land with invisibility speed behind the reception desk, search rapidly for the three's documents and strike lucky again. Overhearing, according to multi lingual Phen, the reception staff complaining about the draught in here today. We then fly off to pick up the suitcases.

It's no trouble for me to use my finger nail lasers to burn out the simple lock on the balcony door.

I silently enter the room and grab the three suitcases off the bed. I'd love to hang around to see the three's reactions when they return to divvy up the cash but time being of the essence, I fly off and head back to Devon.

An hour later I'm sitting in Richard & Chris's lounge drinking a long cool glass of Lemonade & Beer Shandy.

Lucy's brought in by Beatrice to say hello to the man who saved her.

I say, "Hello Lucy. How's my little star; that was some act you and your Mom put on this afternoon."

At Beatrice's prompting she says, "Thank you very much for rescuing me." With that she puts her arms around me and gives me a big hug.

I respond, "You're very welcome Lucy. I'm only glad that you are home safe and sound."

Lead by Beatrice, Lucy goes off to play or in the light of her ordeal to get ready for an early bedtime.

Richard and I discuss extradition rules, with the conclusion that Richard will be contacting the British Embassy at the earliest opportunity and hopefully, Judy, Phil and Rick will be caught before their trails go cold. With their Passports in our possession it shouldn't be too difficult.

"Now Sean, we have to discuss your fee."

"Richard there is no fee as such. My organisation acts as a kind of charity. We don't charge a fee. We only ask people to make a donation to our cause; based on what they can afford and what our help has meant to them."

While Richard and I have been talking, Chris has been busy emptying out the concealed compartments of the suitcases and putting the money back in their huge safe.

"As a donation to charity Sean I would say that 10% of the recovered money would be reasonable and affordable, but as to what it has meant to Chris,

222

Beatrice and I to get Lucy safely returned to us. No amount of money is too much."

"Ten per cent will do fine Richard in fact it's generous."

"No, it's not generous at all, and you know it.

Chris, before you put all that money away please leave £30,000 out for Sean's charity and Sean, I would like to say on behalf of us all if you ever need a friend or anything else; let us be the first people you turn to.

I will also let you know if the band is playing in your neck of the woods. There will be as many tickets in your name, as you can use."

I stay overnight again and after breakfast I say my goodbyes to all the family including Lucy from whom I get another even bigger hug. Then, from their back garden I take off and fly back to "The Forge".

13

Road to Damascus

As I walk into "The Forge" I'm greeted by Jenny, "Hello Jake, did you have a good weekend?"

"Not bad Jen, where are the guys?"

"They will be a little late this morning. After they delivered the funds to all the shopkeepers, they had a call from a woman whose husband beats her up, they have been all weekend trying to sort it out and given your directive not to do any physical harm to anyone; it's not been easy for them."

"I shall be interested to hear how they managed it, Jen."

'I also will,' thinks Phen, 'It is much more difficult for them as they do not have the benefit of your powers to back them up.'

'I agree Phen but that is no reason not to let them try. Like me, the more they have to find ways around not using physical violence, the more they will increase their abilities to avoid doing so, but I take your point; they may well need us and our powers, to finally drive home the clincher.'

"Jen, tell me, what arrangements has Winston made for you?"

"He's enrolled me on a secretarial course at the college, which covers shorthand & typing, answering

& making telephone calls and guidance with regard to a secretary's support role for her boss and or the company she works for."

"That's good Jen but there is one more thing I would like you to study at the college and if you need more time off to do it, that's okay. What I want you to study is bookkeeping, in fact in the short term; it's the most important subject. You can start by depositing this £30,000 in our N.E.C.H. fund account and keeping a ledger of all fund transactions."

She starts to ask how I came by it but appears to think; don't ask! Instead she says, "I'll look into the bookkeeping. It may be possible to study it at night school. With regard to banking the money, if it's alright with you, I'll get one of the fellers to go with me, for security you understand?"

"That's fine Jen, but right now, what's even more important is: how's your tea making skills?"

"They are pretty good Jake. I assume you're asking because you would like a mug of tea and I'm absolutely sure these two; who have just pulled up in "Scrapyard" would like one also."

After warm greetings and sitting in my workshop, drinking our tea I relate to the others my experiences over the weekend.

"It seems you had quite an adventure says Winston but you aren't the only one. We've had one of our own."

"Yes, Jen was telling me, you had some poor women asking for your help because she is being knocked about by her husband. How did you handle it?"

"The first thing we did was observe when her husband went out, that was Saturday night, we assumed he was going to the pub; as the women, whose name is Sadie, told us it's after he's been out drinking that most of the beatings occur. Our priority as we saw it, given that we are not allowed to give the husband a good thrashing, was to get Sadie away. So, until we can sort something out, we booked her into a guest house. At the moment, she's still there. The money won't be a problem; will it?"

"Not at all. When one of you go with Jen to the bank, you'll find out why."

Joel picks up the story, "After that, we went looking for her husband in the local pubs, we finally tracked him down in "The George" and waited for him to set off for home.

We got there before him. Used Sadie's key to let ourselves in and with the lights off, we waited for Greg to follow us in.

"How, did you know his name's Greg?" I ask.

"Sadie told us when she was showing us a photo of him," replies Joel. "Anyway after five minutes he came staggering in and slurring, Sadie, … Sadie, … come on you lazy slut, cook me up some Bacon & Eggs or you'll feel the back of my hand."

"I said," says Winston, "Sadie isn't here and if you ever want to see her again you'll have to quit hitting her."

"He said," slurring even more. "Who's the...that? Who's the...the... that in my h..h..house? Ge..ge...get out or I'll c..call th...the Co..o..ops."

"Good accent Winston, but please stick to normal speech," I interject.

"I replied," say's Winston, "please, feel free; we would very much like to tell them about the beatings you have been giving your wife."

Greg, then staggered to the wall light switch and after a couple of goes, managed to switch it on.

"He then said, where is she? What have you done with my Misses?"

"She is somewhere safe," continues Winston, "Somewhere you can't get at her," and adds, "we're going now, but we'll be back in the morning to talk to you, when hopefully, you've sobered up."

"We returned about ten o'clock Sunday morning and let ourselves in again. No sign of Greg was found on the ground floor, so the search continued upstairs, where we found him slumped on the bed, still dressed as last night and with a pool of sick on the floor beside the bed."

"I said to Winston," says Joel, "Go and make some coffee and if you can find some disinfectant, put some in a bowl of warm water.

I shook Greg four times before he started to become conscious. When he finally did, he said, "Are you still here?"

"Gone and come back. At least you remember us being here at all. Now get yourself to the bathroom and clean yourself up; coffees on the way.

I went to the window and opened it wide to let out the stench of booze and sick. Winston came up with the coffee and bowl. I took the bowl and tipped some of the disinfectant water over the sick patch and using a towel mopped up as much as I could.

Greg came out of the bathroom in no better mood than he had been last night. He demanded to know what we had done with his wife. Winston poured the coffee and said to him get that down, then we'll talk."

"OK. Talk," said Greg as he drained his mug of coffee.

"One way or another, you are going to stop harming your wife and start behaving like a man instead of a pathetic sot," says Winston.

"What makes you think you can make me?" replied Greg."

"How did you respond to that?" I ask.

"Joel told him," continues Winston. "We can't make you, you have got to want to reform, join A.A. or something; anything that helps you stop drinking. Sadie told us, it's mainly when you're drunk that you are abusive and violent."

"What would she know about it; it's because of her that I drink in the first place."

"I said, Typical drunk, always blaming someone else for his short comings. We're sure Sadie isn't perfect, no one is, but that doesn't give you the right to knock her about. You must have loved her at one time?"

Greg's response to that was, "What do you mean one time? I still love the bitch. It's that she doesn't love me, that's the trouble, every time I try to have sex with her, she refuses, that makes me mad, so I hit her."

"That's when Joel went over to the dressing table and removed one of the triple mirrors," says Winston still continuing the saga, "he held it up in front of Greg and said, take a good look. Bearing in mind you look ten times better than you did last night, tell me honestly, given the choice, would you want to make love with someone looking like you? If it was the other way around and Sadie was the one coming in drunk, slapping you around and being sick all over you; would you be happy to make love to her, if she demanded you to?"

"JAKE." Jenny shouts from the office.

"Yes Jen."

"Phone call for you."

"Excuse me lads. Who's it from, Jen?" I say, while striding into the office.

"Richard Duval," she says.

"Hello Richard, this is a surprise! I didn't expect to hear from you so soon."

"Yes, I'm sure we would love to… and that too. ….. Four if you don't mind. …. looking forward to it already. How're Chris, Lucy and Beatrice? …. Good, that's great. Yes, see you soon. Bye."

"Jen, ask Joel & Winston to come in please."

"Guy's, Dick Dizzley's invited us to one of his concerts at the Palace Theatre in October and he wants us to go back stage afterwards.

He's there for a week, and he will leave four tickets for us at the door; for whichever evening performance we choose to go. Apart from the pleasure of it, he wants to talk to me about a problem that a friend of his is having."

"That's super," says Winston, "there's some perks to this job after all!"

"Anyway Guys, back to your Greg adventure."

"With our last comment," says Joel, "we left him to chew things over, but not before we searched his house top to bottom for any alcohol stashes. We didn't find any, which didn't surprise us, as he seems to favour the Pubs for all his drinking."

"Is there anyway, you think, I can help?" I ask.

"While the Pubs are open this evening, could you keep an eye on him for us. If he sneaks out to the Boozer, perhaps you could find some way to frighten him into seeking help for his addiction."

"Like what?" I ask.

"I don't know!" Joel says, while at the same time thinking. "Perhaps like," he says, snapping his fingers and pointing, "Like that character I saw last year, in that Christmas film, "Christmas Carol." … You know, Oh, what's his name? Don't help me … Marley, that's it, "Marley's Ghost." I had to think of "Bob Marley" to get it!"

"Now, you're talking about my hero, Joelee boy!!!" pipes up Winston.

"OK, I'll watch him for you but I can't guarantee how I'll handle it if he should decide to go to the Pub."

This Monday evening, with the Pubs about to open, I think to Phen, 'I've been thinking Phen, Joel's idea of "Marley's Ghost" is not a bad one.'

'Jake, during the two years before we encountered each other I scanned all the great works and ancient novels including "Dickens" and I have to point out; I am not able to bestow on you the power to go forward or backward in time. My people have been studying time travel for many of your centuries but as of now, they still have not perfected it.'

'I know you can't Phen but I do have the ability to change my appearance. Let's see how things pan out. Maybe, borrowing a scene from one of the other great books you've scanned, will come in handy?'

'Like what?'

'I don't know yet Phen. If Greg doesn't sneak out, it will be a waste of effort thinking it all out now. As I say let's wait and see.'

I block Phen and think to myself; on the other hand, it does no harm to be prepared.

Let's see, where did I leave my Torch? In fact, I may need two if my half thought out plan is to work. Here's mine and I think there's another one in the office. I grab them both, lock up and go.'

I re-engage Phen and he immediately asks, 'what do you need two Torches for Jake?'

'A vague stirring in my devious mind only at the moment Phen but best to be prepared, as I and the "Boy Scouts" say.'

Two minutes later, I'm hovering around Greg's house. As it's getting dark, his lounge light is on. I look through the window and see him sitting with his eyes glued to his television, but he doesn't look as though he's actually watching it. His eyes have that blank faraway stare of a man in mental trauma. Now he's up on his feet, pacing the floor, and wringing his hands; then sits back in front of the tele for another half hour. Now he's up again, repeating the pacing.

'I do not think it will be long before he gives in to the urge,' thinks Phen.

'I have to agree, Phen.'

No sooner the thought, but the deed. Greg's half way out the front door. No! He's gone back in again. Several minutes later, after a bit more pacing, he's out again and this time he's making his way, we assume, to his Local pub.

He has his head down and his hands buried deep in his trouser pockets.

'Well Jake!! What plan are you cooking up?

'Let's wait a little longer and make sure he's going to the Pub, after all, he may only be going for a walk?'

'To use one of your sayings, Jake, "Pig's might fly"'.

'OK. Phen, here's the plan and I have to admit it's a close fit to the one I was vaguely cooking up when I blocked you out. You may have noticed on your travels that where there are lots of Pub's, a Church is not far away. I plan to steer Greg in that direction.'

'Good luck with that,' says Phen sceptically.

Greg is about to enter his local Pub when he hears an angelic voice behind him. I've changed my appearance into a being, with an elderly, but angelic face and white flowing robes. By hovering above the ground and holding the two Torches at arm's length, with their beams shining down on my head, I oscillate and rotate my arms just enough to make me look ethereal; like an angel that's complete with a halo.

I'm saying to Greg, "Greg my son, do you really need to go in there? The answers to your problems do not lie in that direction!"

Greg's head whip's round, he tries to focus his eyes on me, and blink's a few times. He finally stammer's out, "W...w...hat are, you?"

"I am your guardian Angel. I am here to guide you along a better path. Please come with me." I say spectrally.

Greg follows me as though in a dream state. I guide him into "St Barnabas's", a church at the other end of the street from the Pub. Evensong finished quite some time ago. The only soul left in the church is the Vicar who's doing a final check of his church, prior to retiring to his Vicarage for the night.

I say to Greg, "If the Reverend sees you and approaches you, neither you nor he, will be able to see me, but do not worry, I will be here, watching over you."

The Vicar has seen him and is coming along to talk to him.

I, before I'm seen, turn off my torches and secrete myself behind a nearby pillar.

The Vicar, who is, what I would call, cracking on a bit, says to Greg, "Are you troubled my son? Would you like to tell me about it?"

Much to his surprise, Greg finds himself pouring out all his troubles, with the Reverend patiently listening and nodding sagely from time to time.

The encounter concludes with the Vicar saying, "Greg, I'm the Reverend Mathew Philip's and I have to say that you may need medical help for your problems, but if you feel, that coming to church can help in anyway, you will be made very welcome."

"Thank you, Rev., It's been good talking to you. I can't promise anything but will try my best to get along to an A.A. meeting and who knows, if I keep my nose clean, Sadie might come back to me. What, honestly do you think of my vision of an Angel?"

"It doesn't matter what I think. It only matters that you believe you saw a vision and through that, you now have an opportunity to reform your life.

Go with God my boy. I will be praying for you and I sincerely hope to see you again. If Sadie comes back, I will be delighted to see her also."

Tuesday morning, and the four of us are sitting

around drinking tea, I've regaled them with the story of my exploits last night, and I'm saying, "Winston, it might be an idea if you went to see Sadie this morning and put her in the picture of what's happening with Greg.

I'll leave it to your discretion of what to tell her and what to leave out."

"Joel's not coming with me then?" says Winston."

"No, I'd like Joel to come with me this morning, if that's alright Joel?"

"Fine, where are we going?"

"It's a personal thing, combined with a follow up after Reg's experiences with Penny's menacing thugs. Will you ring Reg and ask him if it's convenient for you to call on him this morning and if it's okay to bring along a friend who would like to meet him."

We've arrived at Reg's shop, and Joel says, "Hello Reg, good of you to agree to see us. I'd like to introduce you to Jake Edward's. Jake is our Landlord at the office. He has his workshop in the adjacent building, where he Restores Antique Furniture," says Joel.

"Pleased to meet you Reg," I say. "Joel and Winston have told me a lot about you. I thought it would be good if I came and say hello."

"I'm pleased to meet you Jake. Especially at this juncture. An elderly lady has been coming here two days per week, for more year's than I care to remember. She goes over item's that need some restoration. But she, poor thing, has had to go into

235

hospital and sadly it doesn't look as though she is ever likely to come out again. Tell me Jake have you been a Restorer for long?"

"Since I was sixteen Reg. I served an apprenticeship with Coburn's and then, more or less, started on my own from there."

"Coburn's, ah yes, very good; they were a fine firm of Cabinet maker's; such a pity to see how much they've declined."

"If, you should have need of my services Reg, I would be happy to give it a go. I would prefer to do any work at my workshop. I'm sure Joel or Winston wouldn't mind me asking them to do some transporting for me occasionally. I don't drive, myself."

"I haven't got a workshop as such here, so that would be fine. Have you got a telephone number I can ring; when I have some pieces that need restoring?"

"There is only one-line Reg. We share the phone and secretary; she will call me into her office each time you ask to speak to me. I'm looking forward to working with you Reg. I hope we do business for a long time to come." After a little more chit-chat, I say, "Thanks again for seeing me, speak to you soon, bye for now."

Back at the N.E.C.H. Office, Winston reports: "Sadie says she will eventually go back to Greg if he genuinely reforms but it will take quite some time for her to be convinced. I think we'll have to monitor the situation for some time to come."

Phen and I, have a private, Mmmm each, at that, but I only say, "Whatever you think best guys and as we're reporting stuff, Reg seems to be doing Ok now."

14

This Serial is a Killer

Apart from keeping an eye on Greg, Winston and Joel have been busy helping Doris. She and her committee have been granted planning permission to build a club house for the football team and youth club. With the help of a few fathers, who are experienced in the required trades, they are attempting a self-build.

I've been busy on some restoration work Reg has put my way, and Jen's been concentrating on her college work.

Who would believe it, mid-October is here already, and the four of us are on our way to see Dick Dizzley in concert.

We arrive at the Palace Theatre, this fine Saturday evening and collect the tickets that Richard has left for us in the name of Sean Brooks.

As we make our way into the auditorium, Jenny and Joel are jumping up and down with expectation and excitement!

"This is going to be great!!" says Winston looking at the tickets and realising that they are some of the best seats in the house.

We find our seats, and as there is still half hour to go before kick-off, I say to the others, "I'm going to see if I can get a quick word with Richard."

Have you ever tried to get an audience with a star, as he/she is about to go on stage? It's not easy, you find your way blocked by a whole host of security people, not to mention, secretaries, wives, brothers etc. But I digress, as I'm prone to, because as you know I could easily use some of my powers to get into Richard's dressing room. On these social occasions though, I like to be as normal as possible; besides Phen wouldn't like it.

"Excuse me," I say to the first line of defence, "I realise that you can't just let me through to speak with Dick Dizzley but would you pass the word along that Sean Brooks is here, and would like a quick word with him."

"Mate," says this tough looking guy, "even if I told him the queen wanted to see him. NO chance. Besides I've heard all the ruses to get to see Dick before. You're wasting your time."

"That's a pity," I say, "I'll try later."

'I can see there is no way this guy is going to pass on a message Phen yet alone let me through before the show. I'll try again later.'

But as I turn to go back to my seat, I hear, "Sean! ... How lovely to see you!"

"Chris, my God, you look stunning," I stammer.

"Never mind that," she says, "come here and give me a hug." With the hug done and enjoyed, Chris continues, "Were you trying to get in to see Rich?"

"Yes Chris, I would have liked a quick word with him but if it's not possible, just tell him I'm here and that I'll see him after his concert."

"Nonsense," she replies. Turning to the security man she says, "Bill it's okay, Sean is a good friend of ours." With that Chris takes my hand and says, "come on, let's go and see Rich, he'll be delighted to see you."

Chris taps on Richard's dressing room door but doesn't wait for an answer. She opens the door and walks straight in saying, "Only me Rich, look who I've bought with me!"

Richard looks up from applying his Pop Star makeup and exclaims, "Sean! So glad you could make it. Where are your mates?" he asks looking passed me.

"They're here, I'll bring them along after your show, I just wanted to let you know we're in the audience and get a pass; so that we can get through your security later."

"Chris'll sort that out and by the way, you'll be pleased to know we're back together. Now sit down and tell me how you're doing."

"I'm delighted with the news about you and Chris but I won't stop now Rich; it's nearly time for you to go on."

"Oh, sit down; they can wait for a few minutes."
"Isn't that rude or unprofessional," I ask.

"Yes, if you are more than 15 minutes late going on. Up until then, it just increases the excitement and the audience's expectation."

I say, "I'll bow to your long show biz experience."

Having given Rich, about a five-minute précis of our organisation's recent activities, he briefly tells me about the problem he would like my help with. "Sean, my cousin Charlotte Grant who by the way is the daughter of the well-known Show Biz agent and impresario Conway Grant, owns and runs two high class escort agencies. I'm not saying it is but you know what that can mean? Anyway, I digress."

"Yes Rich, I'm pretty good at that too... Sorry for the interruption, please, go ahead."

"The problem, Sean is that Charlotte has a number of young ladies and one or two handsome young men who she hires out as escorts.

Some of her girls over the last one or two months have been brutally murdered. It's this that she and I would like your special help with.

But, enough for now. After the concert, I would like you and your staff to join me at a local restaurant. I've booked it out for an after-concert dinner. I'll see you all later. Come back here, so that we can sneak out. Chris will organise the cars and get you past Bill and his crew. Enjoy the show." Rich, gets up, puts his left hand on my shoulder and shakes my hand with the other as he's showing me to the door.

The four of us thoroughly enjoy Richard's concert. Afterwards we make our way back stage and get waved through by Bill. One of the other guards shows the way to the back door and loads us into a "Limo". After a five-minute drive, we arrive at the door of a very nice-looking Restaurant. The chauffeur opens the car door for us and then opens the Restaurant door also.

We walk into a very elegant room, whispering to each other, "Anyone would think we're royalty".

A waiter, who has obviously been warned of our imminent arrival, shows us to a table set out for nine, and says, "What would you all like to drink? I have been asked to look after you until the rest of your party arrive. My name is Paul. I will be your waiter for the evening. Anything you want, just raise a hand."

Half hour later when we are on our second drink, Chris and Richard arrive, talking excitedly with three other people, one very attractive woman of about thirty-five years of age and two men.

One probably in his late fifties, with loads of wavy grey hair, and the other, a world worn looking man of about forty plus? It's hard to tell.

The mirth stops as they get to the table and Richhard says, "Sean, let me introduce you all to Conway and Charlotte Grant. This tired looking gentleman is Detective Inspector Andy Morrison."

We stand up, shake hands, and I can't help noticing a slight reluctance on the part of the Grant's when Winston and Jenny offer their hands but I might be being over sensitive. Anyway, I say, "These are my colleagues, Jenny, Winston and Joel."

Now seated, Richard raises a hand for Paul's attention and we all place our orders. Rich then turning to me, says, "Sean, I'll let Charlotte tell you a few more of the details of the problems she and others in similar businesses are having."

"To be straight forward Sean, I don't see how you and your meagre crew can help and I'm sure Andy will attest to that? But Rich assures me, although he wouldn't go into any details, that your organisation has abilities beyond the norm. I hope he's right?"

My response to Charlotte is, "When we've got all the facts to hand, we'll see."

"Charlie can be rather sceptical at times," interjects her father, using the version of her name that she's better known to her friends and family as, "but I'm sure she will co-operate in anyway she can. After all, the conventional route hasn't turned out to be much use, so far." Conway adds looking slightly piercingly at Andy.

"Of course, Daddy. What would you like to know? Sean."

'Daddy has spoken ay, Phen?'

I don't wait for Phen's response but reply to Charlotte, "I don't think this is the place to go too deeply into it, Charlie, if I may call you that? For now, how many of your girls are victim to this murderer and how many other girls to your knowledge have been murdered?" I ask.

"Two of my girls. Andy will fill you in on the others and please, do call me Charlie. Andy's one of the detectives who have been involved in the investigations from the outset and the only one who's continuing the investigation, albeit in his own time. Andy, would you mind explaining that further for Sean?"

"Not at all Charlie. Sean, I have been trying to solve these murders for over twelve months and frankly I'm no nearer now than I was nine months ago. We're up against the cleverest homicidal criminal mind I've ever come across.

He, to my knowledge has killed ten or more sex industry people. I say people because two of the victims have been young male adults. The latest victims are Charlie's two girls. One at the beginning of September and the other near the end. On Richards say so, I'm willing to share with you any and all information that I have collated so far.

The reason I'm continuing with this in my own time is because the resources of our police force are finite and as the investigations weren't getting anywhere; the powers that be decided, in their wisdom, to shelve the cases but I'm determined to catch the bastard who's committing these murders."

"That's great Andy. Before we go tonight let me have your phone number and we'll arrange to get together. The same goes for you Charlie. In fact, it might be an idea if the three of us met at the same time?"

"I'll consult my diary tomorrow and liaise with you both as to a suitable date," responds Charlotte.

The rest of the evening is spent in pleasant chit chat about the show etc. The four of us, stuffed to the gunnels with delicious food, are then driven home in the Limo.

We, of course, don't let the driver take us all the way, but get him to drop us within walking distance of our ultimate destinations.

On Sunday we all have a restful day off, followed by a Monday morning meeting of the four of us in the N.E.C.H office, to discuss current and past cases.

"Joel and I" says Winston, "are still keeping an eye on the wife beating case but there's not much left to do now that Sadie's gone back to her, now pillar of the church, husband."

"In that case. What I would like you guy's to do is gain access to as many newspaper and radio reports as you can of sex industry murders going back at least twelve months. We may be duplicating work that Andy has already done but later we can compare the two to see if anything's been missed.

As for me, I'm going to take a quick trip to see how Penny is getting on with her Landscaping business and see if she is anywhere nearer to letting us have the remaining £60,000 of shopkeeper's money. In the meantime, Jenny may get a call from Charlie with a date for our meeting.

As I land on Penny's drive she has just climbed into the cabin of an open truck, with two of her gang of six.

Steve is at the wheel and brakes as he sees me standing in front of the wagon, disguised of course as Gordon.

He turns to Penny and exclaims, "That's the big guy that was serving in the Antique Shop on my patch." Steve winds down his window and shouts, "What the hell are you doing there, get out of the way you idiot!"

"It's okay Steve; it's also the guy I told you about, the guy that carried my car up and down the drive. You and Ron carry on to the sight; I'll catch up to you later."

Penny jumps back down from the truck and greets me with a lovely smile. "Well hello stranger," she says. "Come inside the house and have some tea."

"Thanks Pen, I'd love a cuppa."

Penny makes the tea. I take a look at a mug of dark treacly looking stuff that she has handed me, and say, "I'm sorry Pen, but I need to give you a lesson on how I like my tea! Guys on a building site might like it like this but... me no. Sorry."

"Heck Gordon, there's the kettle, milk, tea, sugar. Make it yourself," she says with no sign of animosity, and adds, "I suppose you've come to see how things are going regarding the £60,000 I still owe the shopkeepers?"

"Well yes, slightly, but mainly I've been wondering how your landscaping business is doing?"

"It's going great for a fledgling business, most of the profit at the moment is being ploughed back, and I'm not saying that because you're after the shopkeeper's money, it just happens to be true."

"Whoa! Pen, I trust you. I know you'll honour our agreement as soon as you can. I only want to show support and that I'm interested in how you're getting along."

"I'm sorry Gordon, only, although the business is fine and hubby and the kids are okay with it, I'm finding it tiring, which makes me a little grumpy.

But ay! There is some good news; I've just sold the "Mosby" house. I should think that in about eight weeks I should have the proceeds to hand. I can then use the remainder of that money to fund my business and release my grip on the sixty grand." Pen concludes her news with, "If you'd like more tea help yourself, only I shall have to go, the guys will be waiting for me.

By the way, two of my gang have gone on to do other things, nothing crooked I might add but as you saw I still have Steve, who's my foreman, and three others including Ben. Pull the door to when you leave."

"No thanks, to the tea Pen. How will you get to your site?"

"I'll take the Traveller; one of the other guys can drive it back later."

"If you promise to keep secret, even from your nearest and dearest, another of my powers, I'll get you there a lot quicker."

"Intriguing," replies Penny, "I promise, even if it's only to find out what it is."

"OK, lock up here and we'll be off, but first tell me

where your site is, and if you're afraid of flying?"

"Ho! Ho! Don't tell me you can fly?" exclaims Penny, as she locks her front door and tells me the whereabouts of her site.

"If you don't mind me putting an arm around you, we'll get you to work." Without waiting for a reply, I do just that and whisk her away. We land a few seconds later in a secluded part of the garden that she's making beautiful. She looks at me glassy eyed, reaches up, pecks me on the cheek and says, "Thanks, see you soon." After another brief stare and quizzical look, she turns and heads towards her now, gang of four.

I can't help thinking: even wearing Overalls, she's still very attractive.

It's a thought I've forgotten to block Phen from. He thinks to me, 'Is it normal for human men to find other men's wives attractive?'

I smile broadly and think back, 'Any kind of beauty is there to be appreciated Phen.'

Back at The Forge, Jen says, "Charlle rang, can you meet her and Andy, at Andy's house this afternoon?" as she speaks, she hands me a note containing his address and phone number.

"Thanks Jen, ring her back and say that I'll be there at two thirty. Now, what are you doing for lunch?"

"I've got sandwiches," she replies.

"How would you like Fish & Chips instead?"

"Oh, yes please, yummy!"

"OK. You get the kettle on; I'll be back with them shortly."

Over our lunch I ask Jen how she's getting on at College and how she's finding the Job?

She fills me in on those and other subjects, concluding with, "As I say I love the Job but I'm finding it hard to cope with the boring gaps between the active and inactive periods. I wish sometimes, I could be more involved on the investigative side."

"At the moment Jen, our set up is still very young, as we become more established your job will get busier and busier. Then I'll remind you of what you've said when you start complaining about being run off your feet," I say smiling. "But I will try and involve you as much as possible, providing you're not put in too much danger. Now I must go and meet Andy & Charlie. I don't know how long I'll be away. I'll, see you when I see you."

"Come in Sean," says Andy as he opens the door to his nice suburban semi.

He leads me through to a back room that's laid out as a study. On the walls instead of pictures he has hung charts, maps and cardboard incident boards.

"Have a seat," he says, "Charlie, apparently is on her way. Would you like some coffee?"

"No thanks, I've just had lunch. Some tea later, would be nice. While we're waiting, talk me through your wall hangings." I say doing a 360 around the room.

'Phen, if you're awake, what do you think?'

'You get cheekier by the minute. I do not think much at the moment but I have scanned all Andy's investigation hangings. I can pass the information into your mind, as and when needed.'

'Thanks Phen, good job.'

There's a knock on the door. Andy goes to let Charlotte in.

She appears dressed in a figure-hugging outfit and high heel shoes. After greetings, I say, "Andy is about to tell me what this is all about," I say, waving a hand around the walls of the room.

Andy takes up the hint and explains: starting from the left of his main incident wall: "This of course is a general map of England. The next one, with the flagged marker pins, are the locations of the relevant murders.

Each flag has a number that relates to this next chart, which as you can see, has a numbered photo of each dead victim in order of the approximate date of their death. I say approximate, because not all the bodies were discovered soon after death.

The last chart on this wall sets out how the victims were killed, and as you can see, not one of them has been killed using the same modus operandi.

The charts on the other walls contain my notes on the facts surrounding each victim and my thoughts about each case. There you have it; my obsession for the last, at least, twelve months."

"Very thorough Andy, congratulations," Charlie, and I say almost in unison.

Andy says, with a world worn face, "I suppose you'll

want copies of all this, Sean?"

"Not necessary Andy. I'm blessed with a photographic memory."

'Since when did you have a photographic memory?' thinks Phen.

'Would you rather I tell them that I have this alien living inside me, who is actually the one with the super memory,' I reply.

'Take your point Jake. Carry on.'

'Thanks, I'll try!' I say, with a slight hit of sarcasm.

"You're lucky," says Andy, with a big sigh of relief.

"True, but what's important, it saves me time and, in this case, you also." I say smiling, having clocked his reaction to the news.

"Let's take a tea break, then we'll get down to the details of each case," Andy says.

"If you don't mind, after the break, can we talk about my girls first, so that I can get away?" Charlie says.

An hour after our break, Charlie takes her leave, having repeated for my benefit, all she knows about where and how her two girls disappeared. The first, named Hattie had been found strangled to death in an area known as Halesowen.

The second, Betty had apparently died of poison and was later found half buried in another Birmingham district, called Great Barr.

"Those causes of death were two of the simpler and straight forward. Some of them have been far more elaborate, especially the murders of the two young men," says Andy. "One of them, Raoul, was found with a wooden stake forced down his throat, and another one rammed up his rear end. He was discovered near Tamworth. Trevor was the other one. He was found three months later. He'd had his genitals removed and rammed down his throat; then hung in a tree in Walsall Woods."

"Don't tell me anymore Andy; I've never heard anything so gruesome."

'My faith in the behaviour of some humans is not being helped by these stories Jake,' thinks Phen.

'Mine neither Phen.'

"Sorry Sean. The only reason for telling you how these young people died is not to shock you but to let you see how diverse are the techniques this fiend is using to muddy the waters of any ensuing investigations."

"I can see that Andy. Tell me, how quickly, on average, were the bodies discovered?"

"On average, about three days, some longer and some within a few hours."

"Do you conclude from that, that this killer hasn't taken too much trouble to prevent the bodies from being found? In other words, he wants you, the Police, to see how clever he is."

"Yes Sean, we feel that he's cocking a snook at us; which is another reason I want him caught. I say him; because I'm sure our killer is a man. Otherwise, unless a she had an accomplice, how could a she, have the strength to hang a deadweight body in a tree?"

'Yes Phen … thank you Phen …' Phen has just passed me his thoughts on this point, and shown me the relevant sections of Andy's notes to back it up.

I respond to Andy by saying, "I'm inclined to agree with you Andy. Everything in your notes, flags up that we are dealing with a loner and a strong loner at that.'

Andy looks at me somewhat puzzled and says, "Amazing, so that's what having a photographic memory's about!"

"Yes, but I have to do a lot of filtering out; otherwise my brain would become totally blocked.

Tell me Andy; from the witnesses your people interviewed, you seem to conclude, our criminal is some kind of master of disguise. Is that so?"

"Yes, nearly all our witnesses reported having seen a stranger lurking about; two or three days before our Pathologist's gave us the death date of each victim. However, their descriptions are different in every case. In fact, in one case, the person seen lurking was a woman but the witness thought something didn't seem right about her. Maybe it was the way she walked or held herself, but if she had to make a judgement, she would have said that the person she saw was a man, dressed as a woman."

"So, to sum up then Andy, we're looking for a strong male, master of disguise, loner."

"That's how I read it Sean but that's as far as I've got. Any and all leads have led nowhere. The question now is: where do we go from here?"

253

"I noticed from your charts," I reply, "that the murders have been committed widely throughout the Midlands. No doubt you've tried to pin down how he's getting around. Have any of the witnesses to a strange loiterer noticed, for example, whether he had a bike, or a car? Or saw him getting on a bus, or train?"

"No to that, Sean, but it's possible because of the gap between attacks, he could have walked from one to the other and still have had time left over to do his research into who's to be his next victim.

I'm telling you Sean this man is very cautious and clever. He covers his tracks extremely well, but that may eventually be his downfall, because as you said, he wants us to KNOW how clever he is. Those sorts of criminals do eventually get too cocky & slip up. So far though, that hasn't happened. I've simply got no idea, if or where, he will strike again???"

"Don't worry Andy we'll get him. He used a gun on one occasion, didn't he? Where might he have got that from? Also, poison, where from?"

"We've done all that Sean. It's turned up nothing. I'm in touch with all the Midland police stations. I've asked them to let me know if any of their beat guys notice, or have noticed, any strangers wandering about near any escort agency businesses or massage parlours, in their areas."

"Seems to me Andy, you've done all you can. I didn't see on your charts (*Phen's, feeding me the info as we go,*) a listing of any Midlands known escort agencies?"

"No Sean, that's because not all the murdered girls were agency girls. Two of them were freelance high-class prostitutes and one from a massage parlour."

"Did their demises happen consecutively?"

"No, but I already told you, only Charlie's two, were consecutive."

"Andy, I think that's about enough for now; how about some dinner?"

"There's a nice pub, just around the corner from here that has an adequate menu. Would that suit?"

"Lead on Mc Duff!"

Andy and I sit back after a good stuffing of Cottage Pie, Peas and chips. Swilled down with a pint of Ansell's beer (*Yes, I've moved on from the Shandy's)* and get back to discussing our shared interest in catching Serial Man, for want of a better term, to describe the fiend we're after.

"What I would like to do Andy, if it's alright with you, is to re-interview the witnesses that have given evidence surrounding Charlie's girls. Can that be arranged, do you think?"

"I don't see why not," Andy says while standing up. "I'll give you a ring when I've set it up." He shakes my hand, and we part company.

I'm up early on Tuesday morning and get in a good hour's restoration work before Jenny and the lads come in.

Jenny arrives first, looking a bit bedraggled because she's had to trudge through the rain. It's okay for Winston and Joel they've got "Scrapyard" to come in. By the time they arrive Jenny's had the kettle on and made us all a cuppa, or more accurately, a mugga.

I ask the guys how they are getting on with their search for news clippings. Joel answers, "Not bad we've unearthed references to three of the murders but it's early days yet. We'll be out there again today."

"How about you Jen? Was there much activity yesterday?"

"Not a lot, a few phone calls and some post. One letter reminding us that we haven't paid our electric bill, so if you could sign a cheque before you go out, I can clear that up. The rest of the day was spent trying to come up to date with the account books. It's not easy keeping track of you three and your expenses!"

"Yes, I can imagine, especially these two," I say pointing at Winston and Joel.

"Actually," says Jenny, "You're the worst. I can never pin you down long enough to find out what you've spent or haven't."

Laughing I say, "Sorry Jen, I will try to improve." More seriously I say, "I forget sometimes that you've got a job to do, and you don't need me making it more difficult."

"Sometimes? Try all the time!" Jenny quips. Just then the phone rings; Jen answers it and says, whilst handing me the phone, "It's Andy, for you."

"Yes Andy… right I'll see you there… in half an hour… okay, no problem, see you later."

Apparently, the street I've just met Andy in, is one street down from where our witness lives.

Andy asks, "How do you want to play this Sean?"

"As low key as possible. I think we need to stress that this is not official. That It's off the record. I don't know about you Andy but I feel that witnesses sometimes open up more when free from the intimidation of an official investigation?"

"You may be right. Let's go and find out. Her name is Brenda Smith."

"OK. If she should ask, tell her I'm Sean, of "Sean Brooks Investigations". How did you get here by the way? I don't see a car nearby?"

"On the bus," reply's Andy, "I had to sell my car to afford carrying on with the investigations. Come to think of it, how did you get here?"

"That, I may tell you when we've had time to build up the trust in each other's discretion. Until then, as you say, let's go and see Brenda."

Brenda's, a middle aged, pleasant looking lady, who lives in this nicely kept, Great Barr Semi. After introductions and my making things clear, as agreed with Andy earlier, she tells us about the stranger that she had noticed, more than once, hanging around near a premises known to be an escort agency. What she's telling us, unfortunately, doesn't differ from her earlier evidence. However, I try and pin her down on a couple of points, "Brenda what you have told us is great but can I get you to cast your mind back and try and picture this man, say stood next to Andy, who is five foot nine. How would they compare?" Andy stands up to help her memory.

"It's difficult to say, the man was old and bent over, I suppose if he stood up straight, in military fashion, he would have been taller, possibly at least six foot."

"Was there anything that struck you as strange about him?" I ask.

"Now, as you say, casting my mind back, and I can't think why I hadn't thought about it before. He looked straight at me on one occasion. I must admit, I took him at face value but thinking about it now, I would say, that he wasn't old at all. Although he looked old from afar, there was something about his eyes and the way he walked, despite being bent over, that now makes me think that he was only pretending to be old. Does this make any sense?"

"It makes a lot of sense Brenda, thanks," says Andy'

"Brenda, you say you noticed the way he walked, focus on his feet if you will. An old, but great actress once said that when she is trying to get into a new role she starts with the feet. For example, were his feet splayed out, or anything like that?" I ask.

"No, I didn't think to look. But hang on it's just occurred to me. His shoes, they didn't look right. They were not the sort of shoes you would expect an old man to wear. Although they appeared a bit worn and scuffed, they looked too modern for someone of his age."

"Now focus on his eyes, what did you find strange about them?"

"They didn't look like the eyes of an old man. Although there were wrinkles at the corners, they didn't seem real. Sort of painted on, and something else, while I'm thinking of it, his eyes looked dead, if you know what I mean; as though there was no-one alive behind them."

'There you are Jake,' Phen chimes in, 'You now see what I was saying months ago when I said you should change your appearance completely, not just wear a disguise.'

'Yes Phen, you're right as usual.'

"Last question Brenda. Looking past this man's disguise, if you had to put an age to him, what would you say it was?"

"Difficult to say," she replies, "but pressed I'd say about forty, maybe less but not much more."

"That's great Brenda. Thank you very much for your time, you've been a delight, and more help than you realise," I say, as Andy and I take our leave.

"I noticed a café, as I got off the bus. If you fancy a bacon-butty and a cuppa, we can recap what Brenda has told us," says Andy.

"Sounds good; lead the way."

Sitting with a steaming cup of tea, coffee for Andy, and the smell of fried bacon in our nostrils, I say, "Brenda has, I think, broadened our picture of Serial

259

Man. Without boasting, I'd say my line of questioning has yielded a model for questions that can be used on the rest of your list of witnesses?"

"I'll concede that, Sean and say we are now looking for a man of about six foot, not much more than forty, has a strange look to his eyes, and has suspect footwear."

"I think that about covers it mate, so let's finish up here and go and see your next witness."

"It's going to take us about an hour/hour and a half, to get there. We have to catch a bus into the city and another one out again."

'What do you think Phen? Can we trust in Andy's discretion yet?'

'I take it you are thinking of flying Andy to meet his next witness?' thinks Phen.

'Yes, unless you think the risk is too soon?'

'Mmmm, I think on reflection it might be alright. Andy has too much bound up in this project to risk giving away any chance he has of solving these cases. Knowing one of your secrets shouldn't cause too much of a problem.'

'I think you're right Phen. Apart from which, I feel Andy and I could become very good friends throughout this joint venture. Hopefully, after it's all over he'll respect my anonymity.'

'Only one way to find out Jake!' says Phen daringly.

"Andy, did you arrange an exact time to meet our next witness?"

"No Sean, I only said we'd be along sometime this morning."

"In that case, I take it that you would have no objection to getting there an hour or so, sooner than the bus could get us there?"

"Don't tell me you've got a helicopter handy?" quips Andy.

"Better than that Andy, but I need a solemn promise from you to keep my secret."

"I will, once I know what it is."

"OK. Don't get the wrong idea, but come and put your left arm round me and allow me to put an arm round you." Andy looks at me quizzically but complies and says, "Is this where I find out why Richard thought you were the only man who could help me solve these crimes?"

I don't answer, but after another quick look to make sure no one is watching, I take off and land about two minutes later in a deserted area in Halesowen.

"Wowee! That was exhilarating. No wonder Rich insisted I encourage your help. Are you some kind of alien?"

"No, I'm as human as you Andy, but enough of that for now, point us in the direction of our witness."

"Actually, we're not too far from it. If we walk through there," he says pointing, "we come to the Halesowen Rd. Let's get walking, if that's not too slow for you and I'll tell you when we get to our destination."

"Cheeky," I say, smiling, and add, "as a matter of fact I enjoy walking, but, only occasionally."

261

About ten minutes later Andy stops at the entrance to the "Old Swan" pub, opens the door and walks in. "What are we doing here? It's a little early for a wet lunch," I say.

"We're here to meet the landlord, his name is Bill Trent, he's our witness," says Andy.

"Bill, this is Sean Brooks of "Sean Brooks Investigations." As I told you on the phone, the police have shelved the case surrounding Hattie's murder. Sean is helping me, on a strictly unofficial basis, to get to the bottom of it. I'd appreciate it if you'd tell him all you know about the stranger that came into your pub, even if it means repeating yourself."

"No problem Inspector."

"Bill please call me Andy, this is off the record."

"Fine. Sean, Andy will have told you that what stirred my suspicions was that he looked like a tramp but when he paid for his drink, and I'm sure he didn't realise that I'd noticed, he had much more money in his wallet than you would expect a tramp to have. Plus, his nose looked unreal. When you do my job, you meet a lot of people, and learn to read them fairly accurately."

"Thanks Bill, now can you take a guess at what height this tramp-like feller was?" I ask.

"Well he was a little hunched over but I'd say he was about six foot, maybe more if he stood straight up."

"How old would you say he is?"

"That's difficult to say, his hair and face were dirty, also his hands, but thinking about it now, they weren't the hands of an old man. More like someone of around forty."

"His eyes, did you notice anything strange about them?" I say, continuing the questioning.

"Let me think. I'm trying to recall … you know you're right, there was, they looked very distant, if you know what I mean. Sort of like someone with a mental disorder, not focused on anything, just looking without seeing. Does that make any sense? And another thing now I'm thinking about it. As he was leaving, I noticed his shoes, they seemed wrong for a tramp. I would have expected worn boots, but he had shoes on, dirty, but not particularly worn. Does any of this help at all?"

"Very much so Bill," chimes in Andy. "Now pull us a pint before we die of thirst, and one for you, on us."

"I'll go one better than that, as it's coming up to lunch time, why don't you take a look at my menu, and order up one of my specials? On the house." Even though we'd not long had a bacon butty we think it churlish to refuse, so we scoff a steak & ale pie each and wash it down with a pint each of Bills real ale.

When we finally emerge from the pub, we make our way back to our deserted spot; talking as we go. "What do you think then Andy? I thought Bill to be an interesting character."

Andy says, "More importantly, what have we learnt that's new? What struck me was Bill's description of the manic look in our perpetrator's eyes. It got me thinking whether he has ever spent any time in a psychiatric hospital?"

263

"Yes Andy, I see that, and think it's something we should follow up on. Would you like to come back with me to our H.Q. and see if we can get a few things organised?"

"Yea, I'd like to see where you work from."

"It's not very salubrious, but "Tis Mine Own", as they say. I feel Joel and Winston should be back by now. If so, we can have a proper meeting."

I fly us both to "The Forge" and land in the yard. Scrapyard's parked outside, so I was right, the lads are here. "Hello everybody, I've bought Andy with me for an informal meeting. Have you all had your lunch?"

Jenny answers for them all, "Yes Sean."

"Good. How've you got on with the press cuttings, guys?"

"Fine, we think we've got all the available stuff.

We were putting the final two bits on this board as you came in," says Winston, pointing to a large flat piece of wood, obviously nicked from my workshop.

"Let Andy and I have a look then. See if we can spot anything different from the clippings Andy has already collected."

After about ten minutes of staring at the board, Andy and I with Phen feeding me images at a rate of knots, look at each other, and shake our heads. "Pity, but no lads," I say. "I'm afraid they've turned up nothing new, but it was worth a try; don't you think so Andy?"

"Certainly," Andy replies, "it may have turned something up, in which case we would have been kicking ourselves for missing it. So, well done, and what now?"

"That depends on what you two have discovered?" says Joel, looking at me and Andy.

I defer to Andy and ask him to fill the others in on the current profile of our "Serial Man"; which, in clear terms, he does. He follows this up by saying, "What Sean & I have discovered makes it worthwhile re-interviewing the remaining witnesses."

"If it's okay with you Andy, I'd like Winston & Joel to follow up on that. While you and I look into your idea regarding psychiatric hospitals." Before any arguments can ensue, I turn my attention to Jenny, "Jen, this is your chance to use that fancy electric typewriter we bought you, and by the way, have we had the new and revised bunch of Sean Brooks business cards from the printers yet?"

"Yes Sean, they came in this morning."

I think, good girl, she's still remembering to call me Sean, not Jake, and I get a quick 'Mmmm' of approval from Phen.

"Good, will you give some to the guys, and unless Andy can remember the remaining witness's names and addresses, I'll dictate them for you to type up, also Jen two copies of a list of questions that Andy and I found effective on the witnesses we interviewed this morning."

"When Jen's done guys, she'll give you some money for your expenses and you can then get off and start interviewing, but please stress that they are entirely informal. Just be your usual charming, gentle, selves."

"When do you suggest we start this, only its four o'clock now and Jen needs time to do her bit?"

"Guys, you're intelligent people. I'll leave you to decide when to start. Just gather as much information you can and as soon as you can. Okay mates?"

Andy says, "Your neighbour's business, in the other building sounds interesting, Sean. Any chance I can sneak a look?"

"I wouldn't," says Jenny, coming to the rescue. "He hates to be disturbed, even by customers.

You should hear him if I have to call him to the phone. Every expletive you can imagine is trotted out; until he takes the call that is. Then of course, he's all sweetness and light. Luckily for him, before I hand him the phone, I cover the mouth piece or I'm sure he'd have no custom at all."

Andy just shrugs and says, "Fair enough."

An hour later, I'm standing chatting with Andy in his incident chart room. Phen is busy refreshing his memories of all Andy's charts. I'm asking, "Where did the first murder take place, Andy?"

'I could have told you that,' thinks Phen.

'I know you could Phen, but I want Andy to feel as much a part of this as possible.'

'How about me feeling as much involved as possible?'

'I understand Phen. I'm sure as this thing progresses your super intelligence will prove invaluable. For now, though, I'm sorry, you'll have to take a back seat.'

'Flatterer, but it is nice to know you have not run out of weird sayings.'

"Worcester," Andy replies."

"Tell me Andy, does Worcester have a Psychiatric Hospital?"

"I don't know, but I'm sure I can find out."

"If you can use your police contacts to come up with that info; I'll drop by and pick you up, so to speak," I smile and say, "tomorrow."

15

After Wednesday's breakfast, and a quick chat with Jen to find out if hers and the boys' tasks are underway, I take off to Andy's. It's a fine, warm for autumn day, so our little trip to Worcester should be very pleasant.

My arrival at Andy's is greeted with a warm smile, which has taken years off him. He now seems more relaxed and has a sparkle about him I haven't seen before. "Come in," he says, "good news, not only have I found out that Worcester has a Psychiatric Hospital but I have also managed to get an appointment with their head of psychiatry, Dr Neville Williams. The appointment is for ten thirty this morning; isn't that great? We will, be able to get there in time, won't we?"

"Yes Andy, even if I fly us slowly. We can take in the views and the beautiful colours of the Autumn Leaves as we go. In case, for any reason I do have to speed up, bring a scarf with you to wrap around your mouth and nose. It will help prevent too much cold air rushing into your lunges. For short slow journeys, it's not important.

About the appointment, I'd guard against getting too excited; it may not lead anywhere."

"I know, I know, but it's great to have some leads to follow up after all this time of getting nowhere and also knowing that I'm no longer fighting this battle alone."

"Pleased to hear it mate but let's get going. If we're early, we can have a look around for a while. I've never been to Worcester before," I say with a look of pleasure on my face and add, "Did Dr Williams tell you the whereabouts of the hospital?"

"Yes Sean, he said it's near a place called Collet Green. I checked on a map and it's about two miles south west of Worcester's City Centre. At a spot called Powick."

Andy and I have enjoyed a pleasant hour looking around Worcester's beautiful Cathedral. Strolled by the River Seven and are now on our way to our meeting with Dr Williams.

We arrive at the entrance door of this imposing building, the central part of which rises two stories above its two flanking wings, ring the bell, and are let in by a giant of a women, who must be well over six foot if she's an inch and broad shouldered with it.

She tells us her name is Freda. Andy and I share a quick look between us and it's obvious we are both stifling a laugh. This goes unnoticed by Freda who says, "Dr Williams is expecting you, and has asked me to show you into the Canteen. As it's time for his tea break; he thought you may like to join him."

"Thank you, Freda, that would be more than acceptable," Andy replies, still fighting for control over his desire to laugh at this huge women's appearance.

Freda shows us along various corridors, which I have to say don't look particularly clean, and have a lingering stench of stale urine. We eventually emerge into a large area set up with folding tables and benches.

At the end of the room near the serving counters, a gent stands up and waves us forward. He smiles, and we exchange introductions. Meanwhile Freda goes off and fetches tea for us all, with the requisite milk and sugar; taking her own tea to another adjacent table.

"Well Detective Inspector, how do you think I can help you," says Dr Williams, with, I think a slight trace of a sneer, and ignoring me completely.

"First of all, Dr," starts Andy.

"Let me stop you there, Inspector. Please call me Neville."

"I was going to say Neville. This interview is entirely of the record. Anything you tell me will not be recorded as evidence in any subsequent trial relating to the multiple sex industry murders, that Sean and I are investigating. We are hoping you can shed some light on the sort of person who would commit such dastardly crimes, and if you have had, in recent years anyone here that would fit your profile? Or the description I outlined on the phone yesterday?"

"On the first point," replies Neville, "It could be any number of things that could trigger off someone to go murdering people. Usually though, it's some traumatic event in their childhood that festers and grows. It then becomes distorted in their brain; which manifested itself into this insane desire to kill.

To answer your second question. Have we had, or got, anyone like that here? I'm afraid I am not at liberty to say and don't think you can bribe it or anything else out of me, because you won't succeed. Others have tried, and failed."

We respect your professional integrity Neville and would not ask you to betray your inmate's confidences. Thank you for your time. Hopefully we won't need to bother you again."

Andy and I rise to go. Neville picks up his keys with his left hand and shakes hands with Andy with his right, still ignoring me. He says, "Freda will show you out, good day."

'You know Jake,' Phen, says, 'having scanned many of earths crime novels since I have been here, I have noticed that it is the small things that eventually trip criminals up. For example, did you notice the strange looking Fob on the good Doctors key ring? Also, that Freda has the self-same Fob on the bunch of keys she has hanging from her belt?'

'No Phen I didn't, but I confess, I don't see the significance.'

'I was only using it as an example of the point, that it is often small clues, like that, that prove the down fall of criminals.'

'Perhaps, Phen, you've read too many of those crime novels.'

'We will see,' thinks Phen huffily.'

Andy and I are surprised when Freda not only sees us to the door but also follows us outside.

"Gentlemen, if I may, I think I can help you," says Freda, "the crimes you're investigating are terrible, so

271

I feel justified in telling you what I know. Three years ago, we transferred from here a patient who fits Dr Neville's profile and also your description of the man you're looking for."

"How do you know the sort of person we're looking for?" I ask.

"Well, I was sitting near during break and I also happened to be in Nev's office when he had you on speaker phone, yesterday."

"OK, what is it you know?" Andy enquires.

"We transferred a patient, as I said, who fits your description, to Highcroft Hospital, in Birmingham and I believe he was released from there about eighteen months ago."

"Why was he transferred from here?" I ask.

"He was too much for us to handle. We were, in all honesty, getting absolutely nowhere with him. It wasn't so much his madness, but his latent intelligence. He thwarted any and all attempts to help him. Even though he had killed his own mother."

Andy asks, "Do you have a name for this gent."

"His name is Ronald Dykes," replies Freda, "and gentlemen, that's all I can tell you. I bid you good day."

Freda doesn't wait for our thanks, she turns and without delay, re-enters the hospital. It's as though she thinks someone maybe watching her.

Highcroft Hospital, as Andy and I land behind a tree with a wide trunk, of which there are many in the grounds of this sprawling hospital, is a jumble of several large buildings. The one we are approaching appears to be the main one. We haven't made an appointment this time; we're hoping to rely on Andy's warrant card to get us into see the head of psychiatry. We enter through two large double doors and saunter up to the reception desk. Andy flashes his warrant card, gives his name and title and asks, "Who is the head of your psychiatric department?"

"Which one?" the receptionist asks, "There are several heads of psychiatry here; covering its various branches."

"The one dealing with the criminally insane, such as someone who might have killed his own mother," Andy replies.

"I see, your best bet in that case, would be Doctor Peter Svendrich. I'll try and contact him for you, but if he's with a patient, you'll probably have to wait."

Half hour later, we are at last introducing ourselves to a man of about forty-five, clean shaven, even his head. I'm sure he sees his head as an extension of his face, so when he washes his face, he doesn't stop there but carries on up. The good Doctor. invites us along to his office, which is on the second floor. He opens the door with a key and allows us to pass him into the office. Unbuttoning his long white coat as he goes, he makes his way to his desk chair and motions us to pull up the two chairs that are either side of his office door.

Phen and I, notice that, although Doctor Svendrich's attire's reasonably tidy; his clothing has seen better days.

"Right gentlemen, my secretary, Mrs Smith will bring us in some tea. In the meantime, perhaps you will tell me how I can help you?

Andy gives the Doctor the usual spiel about this not being official, describes the man we're looking for and why we're looking for him. "We also know," says Andy, "that you released a man from here about eighteen months ago, who fits that description. His name is Ronald Dykes."

"How did you come by that information; if I may ask? It's not the sort of thing that's banded about!"

"We can't reveal our sources, but we can assure you, the information didn't come from anyone in your position. Let's just say a little birdie told us."

'I take it your use of the words, little birdie, is one of your jokes,' thinks Phen.

The Dr does a Phen and goes Mmmm. "So that I can refresh my memory, I'll ask Mrs Smith to bring in the relevant file, but I warn you gentlemen, the information therein cannot be open to you."

I think to Phen, 'Mmmm's seem common among you intellectuals, Pal.'

'Mmmm, I see, thank you!' thinks Phen, and adds, 'While we are communicating are you going to try and use some of that envelope of cash you keep in your back pocket for purposes of bribery, on this good Doctor?"

'I don't know yet Phen. We'll see how it pans out.'

There's a tap on the door, and instead of letting Mrs Smith bring in the file, the Doctor goes to the door and

274

relieves her of it. I take the opportunity to rapidly grab a pen off the Doc's desk and write something on the envelope of cash.

Doctor Svendrich sits back down and takes five minutes to peruse the file and says, "I can see why you may think this may be your man but as I said, I'm not able to help you, even if I wanted to. We monitored him for the first six months after his release but after that we lost all track of him. Gentlemen if that's all …?"

I reply, "Supposing the Inspector obtained a court order, ordering you to turn over the file, would that work?"

The Doctor smiles a crooked smile and says, "I think you already know the answer to that."

'This is it then Phen, here goes.' I take the envelope, containing the cash from my pocket and pass it across the desk to, hopefully, the not so good Doctor and wait for a reaction.

He glances down at the message thereon and I can sense his brain going at a million miles an hour, obviously weighing up all the pro's and con's.

After a long pause he finally says, "If you gentlemen will excuse me for a moment, I need to go and relieve myself, please be gone before I come back. This is goodbye." With that he leaves the room; while at the same time pocketing the money.

I think to Phen, 'Do your stuff Pal'

From Andy's viewpoint he sees me go to the file and in a blur scan the whole thing in less than twenty seconds.

"OK Andy, let's get out of here." I say.

On the way down the corridor we pass the good Doctor on his way back to his office. I smile at him and I say, in a muted tone, "enjoy". I feel sure that in the very short time that has elapsed, he will console himself with thinking, they can't have read too much in that short a time.

Outside Andy says, "What did you write on the envelope you gave the Doc?"

"Let's go and find a caf, I'm starving. I'll reveal all after I've got some food in me."

We walk to Erdington High St. before we find one, but it's clean, and has plenty of custom; which, as I've often thought, is always a good sign. We settle down with an adequate meal and a mug of tea and I tell Andy what I wrote.

"I see. So, you bribed him! I'm not sure, as a copper I can sanction such behaviour!" Andy says a little tongue in cheek.

"Well yes, but it was worth it. When I tell you what I gleaned from the Dyke file, I think you'll agree."

While we were walking to the caf, Phen had been feeding me, a little at a time, the gaffe from the file's contents. In between mouthfuls of tea, I tell Andy, "The most important thing in the file, is the last known address for Ronald. He lived in a flat in Worcester. The rest of the file relates to why he was there, his treatment, and why he was released.

Apparently, he was raised by his Mother, a single parent, who while he was growing up brought men into the house and received payment for services rendered. To cut a long story short, when he reached the age of understanding, he finally, after years of neglect, killed his mother and cleverly laid the blame at the feet of one of her clients; one he particularly disliked.

He felt no remorse at the time, but guilt eventually started gnawing at him, particularly the strange sense that he had enjoyed the intrigue and plotting involved in his mother's murder.

The fact that he had got away with it by laying the blame elsewhere, which he continually laughed inwardly about, was also gnawing at him to a point where he began to feel that he was going mad. He was referred by his general practice doctor. to Powick, where we know he spent some time, before his transfer to Highcroft."

Andy, who has been patiently waiting to say something, says, "Did the file say why he was transferred?"

"Yes, but it all sounded a bit muddled, something about being a bad influence on other patients, uncooperative and objecting particularly at being treated with L.S.D. (lysergic acid diethylamide,) he reckoned it was giving him hallucinations. Anyway, as Freda said, they couldn't cope with him any longer; hence his transfer."

"Did it say how he kept body and soul together, before his committal and after his release?"

"Apparently, he was and is an actor, although the hospital doesn't recall ever seeing him in any stage

277

shows, plays or films."

"My concluding question," asks Andy. "Does it say why he was released?"

"Yes, they say he'd been very quiet for three months prior, had caused no trouble, and appeared to be perfectly sane. So, they released him, and as we now know, checked on him for six months; then lost all track of him."

"He certainly sounds like our man, being an actor, he'd know about makeup and such, and being keen on the planning side of murder, also points toward him being, at least, our chief suspect."

"Let's face it Andy, he's our only suspect," I say resignedly.

As it's mid-afternoon, I've flown Andy to pick up a few toiletries etc. and the same for me, plus picking up some more cash. We're now on our way back to Worcester to see if we can pick up R Dyke's trail.

There being not much left of today, and as it may take quite a while to track our suspect down, we thought a B&B might be on the cards.

We find a suitable Guest House not far from Mr Dykes last known address, and park our overnight bags.

On our walk round to Oldbury St. Andy, asks, "Who's going to lead this enquiry? Should I, in an official capacity, or should I stay in the back ground?"

"For this one I think we should play it by ear, and only warm up to official, if the situation demands it. In other words, don't say, to begin with, who we are or what we want. Act initially as though we're looking for an old mate."

"Sounds like a plan," Andy acquiesces.

We arrive outside Ronald's digs, which is a small block of flats, to find that there's a security lock on the front entrance door. "BLAST!" says Andy. He doesn't understand, as I haven't revealed all yet, that with the special powers bestowed on me by Phen, these things are of very little consequence, but this is not the time to tell him. I say, "I tell you what Andy. You stay here. If anyone comes out, you may be able to talk your way in. I'll go around the back to see if I can find another entrance."

There doesn't seem to be a way round to the back, so I check that no one's looking and fly up and over. I land in a scrubby garden, and inspect the whole of the rear aspect of the building. The only visible access is a small attic window, so I fly up and peer in. I see the window's been left open because it opens on to a landing, not into anyone's room. I Change into Windy, Phen's name for an emaciated character I adopt for such occasions, and squeeze through the tiny space available. After changing back to Sean, I make my way down three flights of stairs and open the front door for Andy to come in.

"How did you get in?" Andy enquires.

"Ask no questions here no lies," I reply.

"What now? Do we knock on a few doors until we find someone who'll talk to us?"

279

"That's about it, Andy, and we may as well start with flat one."

Andy, rings the bell, and we wait, ring again and wait again. No answer. "Oh well, on to the next," I say.

We follow the same procedure at number two.

This time the door's opened a couple of inches, and, "Yes! What do you, want?" says the part of a face that we can see.

"Hello," I say, "We're trying to trace a friend of ours, who lived in this building, about twelve to eighteen months ago."

"No good asking me mate, I've only been here three months. The only one, who's been here for that length of time, is old Ted at number five." No more conversation is encouraged, evidenced by the door being slammed shut.

After knocking on Ted's door, there's no bell, the door remains shut, but we hear a voice the other side saying, "Who is it?"

"Hello Ted," I say, "we're private detectives, could you spare us a few minutes. I'm putting my card through your letterbox."

A long pause is followed by the door being opened, by what seems the standard two inches, and Ted says, "What's it about?"

Andy says, "It would be much easier to talk if we could come in?"

"Not until you've told me what it's about," answers Ted.

"It's about the murders of at least ten people by a serial killer." I say.

"And yea think I'm the killer?"

"No-way Ted but the guy we're looking for may have lived here, maybe eighteen months ago."

"OK, come in, but I don't see how oye can help yea."

We move down Ted's dingy hall and he leads us into an equally dingy lounge, with a kitchenette at one end.

He sits in an easy chair and motions us to the settee that he's hurriedly cleared off for us.

Andy, describes the person we're looking for, and asks Ted if he can remember such a person.

"Yea, he woos a funny un. An actor feller yer know. Yea he moved out about a yer ago. He had number two. Oye think he'd spent some toym in the loony bin."

I say, "Have you any idea where he might have moved to Ted?"

Ted replies, "No, not where he'd move to." Our hearts dropped a few rungs at this news. "But," Ted continues, "Oye did have occasion ter go inter his room arter he'd gone.

Hang on, oye got it here somewhere." Ted rummages in a draw and brings out a Brochure depicting Handbury Hall, Worcester.

He opens it up and a slip of paper falls out. I move quickly and pick it up before Ted can.

"Well, let's see what we have here? Ah! It's a note typed on "Handbury Hall" headed note paper, which says, please be ready, made up and in costume by 8.30am as agreed.

Yours sincerely,

Brian Cox, Events Manager.

"Well Ted, now you can see how you've helped us. Thank you very much; we'll take the brochure and leave you in peace now. Here's a little something for your trouble." I drop a Tenner on the arm of his settee as I rise to go.

"Which direction does Handbury Hall lay from here?" I ask Andy, as we make our way back to our digs.

"I don't know, but I'm sure the brochure will have a direction map on it somewhere."

"Tell you what then, Andy, let's find a nice place to eat and how do you fancy going to the pictures after? I'm sure Worcester's got a cinema tucked away somewhere. Tomorrow will be soon enough to get back on R's trail."

After a leisurely full English breakfast and a read of Thursdays local newspaper, provided by Winifred, (*our Landlady*); we set out, about eleven o'clock, in a north easterly direction.

"Wow! Look at this," Andy says, as we view Handbury Hall from above, "What a spread!"

I land us behind the stable block and we walk round to the front of this beautiful, red brick, William & Mary style edifice. Andy flashes his warrant card, announces himself by rank and name at the pay desk, and asks if we might have a word with Brian Cox the events manager.

"I'm afraid Mr Cox is not in at the moment. He had some errands to run before work," the rather elegant lady at the desk is saying while looking at her watch, "but I shouldn't think he will be too much longer. If you gentlemen would like to wait, you can use that small Anti-room across the hall there," she says pointing. "I will come and get you when Mr Cox arrives."

It's been a least half an hour that Andy and I've sat twiddling our thumbs. Finally, the desk lady, for want of a better title for her, has put her, not unattractive head round the door.

She says, "Mr Cox will see you now gentlemen, go up the main staircase and take the first door on your left."

A tap on the door, followed by a cheery come in, and we enter a very pleasant, elegant room, furnished with eighteenth century furnishings.

Mr Cox comes from behind his desk and greets us with handshakes and a warm smile, radiating from a rotund, clean shaven face. "How may I help you gentlemen?" He says moving back behind his desk, and waving us to two chairs, made ready.

Andy, once again goes into the spiel about our Mr Dykes and Mr Cox says, "Yerres, I remember him now; we dressed him up like Thomas Vernon, our esteemed M.P. and 18th Century owner.

We had a special event month, were the staff and a few actors, dressed in costumes depicting characters from the Halls history. I can remember thinking at the time, strange character, but he played the part of Thomas very well, so I took him as I found him."

"Did he give you any idea of where he went, after he

had finished with you?"

"The only thing he said, because I asked him, was that he felt sure that he'd secured a bit part in one of Shakespeare's comedies for the summer. I assumed he was talking about Stratford, but I can't be sure. I'm afraid that's all I can tell you gentlemen. You're lucky to have got me, tomorrow we closedown for the season."

My contribution, thinking of my stomach as usual, is to ask if the Hall has a tearoom?

Over a cup of tea and a buttered scone, Andy says, "I suppose our next stop is Stratford?"

"I could get used to this," Andy says, as I'm flying him toward Stratford. "It sure beats travelling by bus, train or taxi."

I say jokingly, "Don't get too used to it, or when you have to use other means; you could find it a bit of a come down!"

No sooner said, we land on a deserted part of a canal towpath, and follow the path along to the mouth of the river Avon. There we turn right and follow the river to the "Royal Shakespeare Theatre", that we can see in the near distance.

Andy goes up to the box office. I hang back, as I don't particularly want to hear the opening gambits again. He reports, "I've asked to see the casting director, who has been here at least eighteen months. I'm told, there are four casting directors, and that they have all been here at least that long."

"Oh dear, nothings ever simple is it Andy?" I say.

"Anyway," Andy continues, "There are two of them here at the moment. I've asked for a brief word with them, also their assistants, which they all have. Apparently, they are more likely to have cast the bit parts."

A quarter of an hour later, we are all sat round a table in the theatre bar, drinking teas or coffees. Andy, gives them the thrust of our inquiry, and asks, "Do any of you recall a Ronald Dykes?"

A young assistant raises a hand, and says, "Yes, I do, I cast him in "Love's Labour's Lost" as a forester, and later on, in small roles, in other plays."

"Have you any idea," I say, "when and where he went to after leaving you?"

"He did mumble something about Scarborough and the "Library Theatre". Let me think... da-de-da ...., yes, it was just after we had done "The Tempest"; that would be three months ago."

"Well thank you very much all," says Andy, "we're sorry to have inconvenienced you; we'll let you get back to work now. .... Just one more thing. Do any of you know where he was bunking down, while he was here?

"Yes ... I now recall, thinking about it, he was in one of the local theatrical digs. Let me think ... yes, he was with Mrs Kilbride at the "Riverside Guest House."

Having received directions from the young assistant, we make our way to Mrs Kilbride's.

'Do you think this lady will be able to tell you anymore than you know already,' thinks Phen?

'Maybe not Phen but the young lady assistant didn't seem entirely sure of her information. If R's landlady only confirms what we already know; it will be worth the detour. Apart from that Phen I'm beginning to feel a little uneasy about things.'

'In what way' thinks Phen?

'Well, if he did move to Scarborough, three months ago, why would he come all the way back, to kill Charlotte's, two girls?'

'So, you are thinking, either, he did go to Scarborough and can account for all his movements in the last three months; in which case he is not our killer. Or, he dropped out that little nugget of information, to put any investigation off the scent.'

'Yes Phen, that's my worry. As you thought, will he be able to account for his movements? If not, it's just possible he could have come back a couple of times, to bump off Charlotte's, two?'

'Either way Jake you and Andy have no choice but to continue following Ronald's trail.'

'Yes, thank you Phen. That's a bit obvious, even for you.'

'More sarcasm, but I will ignore the jibe'.

Mrs Kilbride does confirm R's move east. Not only that, she gives us the address of a fellow landlady and friend of hers in Scarborough; which she'd also given Ronald.

Flying Andy over England's rolling countryside, I say, "My number one priority when we get there is to get something to eat, and I'm bursting for the loo."

"Me too. I take it, as you're unusually quiet, that you're having the same feelings of trepidation that I am," says Andy, in a scarf obscured voice.

"Yes Andy, you're very perceptive. This could mean we're on the wrong track."

"Yea, my feelings exactly, but we still have to follow it through to the end, right?"

"Huh, huh," I say, as I land us behind a likely looking Scarborough caf.

We've used the Loo, had a good feed, and obtained from our waitress directions to the "Vint Muller" B&B; leaving her a good size tip, as a thank you.

As we're walking down "Victoria Road" I say to Andy, "This is it mate, the make or break call."

We turn into Mill Street and there before us is this lovely, what used to be, a Wind Mill, plus, additions.

The exterior sign says, "Ye Old Vint Muller B&B" and a dangling sign underneath saying, Vacancies. Two great minds think alike, so they say, because Andy and I without saying it, agree that the best course of action is to book ourselves in. Should Ronald not be in right now, we'll be able to casually meet him here later and talk with him in this less formal setting. In the meantime, we'll be able to chat with the Landlady and her staff, to see what we can glean in advance.

'I swear Jake,' thinks Phen, 'that you and Andy are almost tuned into thought transfer.'

Andy and I sign the B&B's register, introduce ourselves, and mention that Mrs Kilbride had

287

recommended us.

"Ah yes, Audrey Kilbride. How is she? We go back a long way, I'm Maggie by the way."

"Hello Maggie. Audrey's fine thanks," I say.

"You know, you're the second customer Audrey's, sent me in the last three months. I have a very nice man staying here at the moment. Ronald his name is. You'll probably meet him later. He's doing a season in an Alan Ayckbourn play with Stephen Joseph at the Theatre above the Library. Anyway, I'll show you your rooms. Then you can feel at home."

I've insisted on separate single rooms, because who knows who I might turn into in my sleep. Besides which I prefer sleeping as myself.

"I know I'm a B&B," says Maggie "but over the months, Ronald has taken to enjoying an evening meal here before returning to the theatre for the late evening performances. You two gentlemen are welcome to join us if you wish?"

With a nod from Andy I say, "We'd be delighted Maggie thank you. You will be sure to add the cost to our bill, won't you?"

"Without doubt," she says smilingly.

Andy and I take our leave, saying that, "We'll see you later. We're going to have a look around and maybe take a walk along the seafront."

"That couldn't have worked out better Sean. We'll hopefully be able to quiz him over dinner; without raising too much suspicion," Andy, says as we're walking along.

"Yes mate, but I'm not holding out too much hope. I think we have to come to terms with the possibility that we are at a dead end."

"Mmmm."

"Don't you start with the Mmmm's. I have enough trouble on that score with someone else I know."

With that we continue our walk and eventually return to the B&B in time for dinner. After a wash and change, we enter the dining room to find a large looking man with broad shoulders. It's difficult to tell how tall he is, he's already seated. He smiles at us and says, "Hello, you must be the gent's Maggie was telling me about."

'Mmmm, that's a bad start Jake,' thinks Phen. 'Could a man with such a broad open smile possibly be a serial killer?'

'Not likely Phen, but my knowledge of these things is limited. I must remember to ask Andy.'

"Yes," says Andy as we sit to the dining table, "I'm Andy and this is Sean."

"I'm Ronald."

"Yes, we know who you are. We've been tracking you for some time."

'It would seem Phen that Andy's decided on the direct approach. It looks like, our earlier decision, to casually lead up to the purpose of our visit has gone out the window.'

"Oh! Why would you do that?" R. says, somewhat startled.

"I'm actually Detective Inspector Andy Morrison and my colleague and I are looking into a number of Murders that have been committed in the Midlands over the last eighteen months. If I give you a couple of dates, one at the beginning of September and one near the end; do you think you'd be able to recall where you were and what you were doing?"

"Why! Am I some kind of suspect or something?"

"Let's just say that we'd like your help with our enquires. If you could fill us in, as to your movements on September 3rd, and September 29th it would clear up a whole lot of problems for us."

"Let me think," answers R. ... "On your first date I'm not entirely sure but on your second, which I believe was a Saturday, I breakfasted here, went to the theatre for about eleven o'clock and started to rehearse for the matinee performance of the Ayckbourn play I was appearing in at that time.

I seem to remember it was "The Square Cat". Yes, it was, now I recall. I then came back here and had an early dinner with Maggie and then went back to the theatre for the evening performance. After the show, myself and other cast members had a few drinks in the Theatre Bar, till about 11.30 pm, then I came back here for the rest of the night. Maggie and several people at the Theatre; I'm sure will be able to confirm all this. Does that help you?"

"Are you sure you can't remember where you were on the third?" Andy, asks in a crest fallen voice.

"I know one thing for certain. I was not in the Midlands killing anybody." Ronald answers starchily.

"OK Ronald, let's start again," I say as Maggie comes in with the first course. "It's now obvious that you are not the man we're looking for but you can still help us; if you will? We know that you spent some time in Powick Psychiatric Hospital."

"STOP! I choose not to talk about that phase of my life," he says, with a theatrical wave of a hand.

But I press on. "All we want to know Ronald is: did you ever, while you were there, pass any of your skills of makeup, disguise and characterisation on to anyone?"

"Yes, to a number of people. I tried to organise a drama group while I was there," another flourish of a hand, "totally unappreciated by the management. I had endless rows with them."

"Can you think of anyone in particular? I say.

"Come to think of it, there was one staff member who took particular interest in the makeup and characterisation side of it. Huge women. I seem to remember her name was Freda. She was very convincing as a man."

"Why do you say that?"

"There was one occasion, unbeknown to the management, when we put on a little play, entirely for our; our being the other inmates, own amusement. Just a three hander. Freda played the part of a man."

"Who was the third person in your play?" Say I, continuing the questioning.

291

"You know! I don't know! One of those women who are entirely unmemorable," he says with another circular wave of a hand. "Now, if there are no more questions; is there any chance we can enjoy our meal in peace."

Maggie brings the second course and the conversation turns to lighter topics, mainly about the stage, music and films.

I use Maggie's phone, ring Jenny's private number and ask her to make sure, that in the morning, the boys are at "The Forge" for when we get back.

Friday morning, after a quiet word with Maggie, who confirms everything that Ronald told us last night, leaving no doubt that he couldn't possibly have been in the midlands on Saturday the 29th of September. Andy and I have an early breakfast, leave the "Vint Muller" and head back home with heavy hearts and minds.

I fly us slowly so that we can talk; consoling each other on the way. The question that is literately hanging in the air is: WHAT NOW?

16

Apart from a comfort break, we make good time and land in "The Forge's" yard about ten am. With the, WHAT NOW, question still burning in our brains.

There are warm greetings all around and each of us are standing drinking a hot mug of tea. Andy and I speaking alternately, regal the others with the result of our disappointing trip.

Finally, Andy asks, "Boys, how did you get on with your re-interviewing of the remaining witnesses?"

"Almost as disappointingly as yourselves," says, Joel.

"Almost?" I query; clutching at straws.

"It may not be worth mentioning," says Winston, picking up the story, "but a shopkeeper added to her original statement by saying the strange looking man, who she thought could easily have been a disguised woman, fumbled for change and in so doing bought out a bunch of keys. She thought that the Fob was unusual; it was brass, and looked like two tapering squares, one on top of the other.

Joel and I dismissed it as of no particular interest until later; when the newspaper seller/witness happened to report seeing the same thing.

Joel, asked him what originally had made him suspicious.

He said the guy stood reading the headline about the serial killing of a massage parlour girl. It was the look on his face that caught his attention. He'd had a kind of a laughing smirk on it. He thought, how can anyone find that funny? So, he said to him, are you going to buy that paper or just stand there reading it? That was when; hunting for change, he'd dropped his keys, and the newspaper man noticed the strange Fob."

"Thank you, boys," says Andy, "you've no idea how much of a contribution, your report has made. It's cheered me up no end."

'Arrrr,' thinks Phen.

'Arrrr, what's that supposed to mean?

'I seem to remember saying, that it is the little things that finally trap criminals. These Fobs have cropped up before. Dr Neville and Freda both have one if you remember?'

'I do remember, Phen and I suppose you're expecting an apology?'

'Well if it makes you feel better? Mainly, I would like you not to be so sceptical when I have brilliant thoughts.'

'Fine Phen, you win this one. Is that okay your brilliantship?'

'From studying your sayings, that I have had to tolerate; I believe the saying goes: "Sarcasm is the Lowest Form of Wit," but I sense you are anxious to discuss matters with the others, so I will be quiet.'

'Thanks pal. It was just a joke; I didn't mean to offend.'

'I know, and I was only pulling your leg about having brilliant thoughts; even though I do.'

294

This train of thoughts is interrupted by Joel, who is saying, "Before we said goodbye to the newspaper man, I got him to make a sketch of the Fob."

Joel pauses while he spreads a crumpled piece of paper on Jenny's desk. "What do you think it is?"

Jenny says, while we simpletons are stood scratching our heads, "do you mind if I have a look at that?"

"Not at all Jen. Please do," I say.

"I thought so. Last year my Dad took the family on a barge trip up the canals as far as Stratford. To get through the locks the bargee had to use a key, which was many times larger than that sketch, also it had a handle. Like this," Jenny says, pencilling in what the complete thing should look like.

"Nice one Jen," says Andy, "We now know that our killer may have a connection with the canals. It could explain also how our killer is getting around without a car etc. plus, we have two new suspects. My money, for what it's worth, is on Freda."

"Is she clever enough? We know that our killer is very astute. Dr Neville on the other hand knows the workings of the mind, so could easily be bright enough? Those are my thoughts," I say.

'Mmmm, sorry to butt in Jake, only what Andy said got me thinking. I have overlaid my memory of the murder sites on top of Andy's map that shows the midlands and its canals, and guess what?'

Stealing Phen's thunder, I think, 'There's a canal near every murder site.'

'Precisely,' thinks Phen.

Andy, "Mmmm's,"

"Please don't do that, Andy," I say.

"Sorry, I was thinking, we're going to have to go back and interview them both again and find out principally; if one or both have any connection with the canals. I know we said we're looking for a man, but Freda, who is strong enough to lift patients in and out of beds, could well qualify as the major suspect. When you consider; it was she who sent us on that wild goose chase."

"Good points, Andy but why would a woman disguise herself as a man. Then overlay that disguise with that of a woman? We won't know any answers unless we go and find out. What we need is a plan?"

"What's to plan? Let me get on to my Police contacts and have them picked up for questioning?"

"I'm sorry Andy but I don't think it's that simple," I say, having consulted privately with Phen, "the problem is, they're only suspects at the moment. If one of them is our perpetrator, we don't want either of them alerted. Not wishing to tell you your business Andy but we're going to need evidence before we have anyone arrested.

My plan, after careful thought, would be for us to go and speak to them again; not letting on, they are in anyway suspect and see if one or both have any connection with the canals."

"Yeaaaa … I take your point, but it's still a bit vague."

"Is there anything, we can do to help?" interjects Joel.

"I've thought about that too Joel and it's unfortunate that you're the one who's going to have to stay behind.

Jenny you said you'd like the chance to be more active. What I'd like you and Winston to do is pretend to be a couple who are looking to buy a barge to live on after you're married. The idea is that you, without raising suspicion, glean as much information as you can about the movements, or not, of as many barges and their owners as you can.

If either one of our suspects owns a boat, we don't want him or her fleeing. Especially as it's coming up to a month since the last reported murder. Ideally, I'd like to catch whoever is committing these crimes, red handed."

"So, what am I supposed to do?" asks Joel.

"You have to be our liaison. As you'll be manning the phone, both groups will be able to communicate through you. If any problems come up, you're best placed to deal with them."

'Ever the Diplomat,' thinks Phen, 'and I get the "red handed" bit.'

"I don't know about you all, but my suggestion is to take the rest of the day off and have a rest; as the next few days could be arduous.

After your rest, pack some overnight things and I'll see you in the morning, bright and early."

Its 8.30am Saturday. Joel's in the office and Jenny's kindly making tea for the four of us. We only need Andy now, and those of us who are going to Worcester can be on our way.

He arrives, looking bleary eyed, at 8.45 and saying, "I didn't sleep very well. You don't happen to have any coffee on, do you?"

"No, but I'll make you one," says Jenny, and by the look she's giving him, I'm sure she's thinking that the bleary eyes have more to do with his liking for a few evening pints of the brewers best; rather than lack of sleep.

"Right, Jenny, as I've only got two arms, I'll fly you and Winston to Worcester first. I'll drop you at the nearest B&B to the canals as possible. Then come back for Andy. Hopefully by then, he'll have finished his coffee."

"I may be on my second cup. You'll have to wait if I am," says Andy, showing the first signs of a weak smile.

"What's the plan?" asks Andy as we're once again walking up Powick Hospitals drive.

"We'll try and see Dr Williams first. All we're interested in, at the moment, is where he got his Key Fob from? We'll have to dress it up a bit so it doesn't look too obvious that, that's all we're interested in."

Ten minutes later, we're shown into the good doctor's office.

"Hello again," he says, "and to what do I owe this second visit?"

I lead off, mainly because I don't want Andy compromised by the lies I'm about to tell. "We thought we would do you the courtesy of letting you know in person, that we have, and this is strictly confidential at the moment; someone in custody who, shall we say, is helping with our enquiries."

"I must say, that is very considerate of you. I'm sure a lot of people will, when it's made public, be very relieved."

'He seems genuine does he not?' thinks Phen. 'And of course, you have noticed his keys are on the desk?' 'Yes to both, thanks Phen.'

The Doctor continues, "I would offer you tea, but I'm afraid I have a heavy schedule today, so if you will excuse me?"

"Not a problem Doc.," I say, rising to go and staring at his keys as I do. "It's just struck me Doc. where I've seen that unusual key ring Fob shape before. A cousin of mine has a barge. It's a miniature Canal Lock Key, isn't it?"

"Yes, Freda gave it to me. Nice isn't it. I've no idea where she got it from."

"You don't have a barge yourself then?" asks Andy, casually.

"Goodness gracious no. I would never find the time to use it."

"Anyway, Doc it's been a pleasure," I say, shaking his hand, "we'll see ourselves out. Any chance I could have a quick word with Freda on the way? "I'd rather like to get one of those Fobs for my cousin."

'Very smooth Jake,' thinks Phen.

'Shush! Phen, I want to hear Neville's reply.'

"Not at all, the receptionist will tell you where she is."

Ten minutes later we're sitting in the hospital canteen having a cuppa with Freda. Andy and I decided in advance that he would open for us on this one. He's already told Freda that Dr Williams has okayed it, and about my cousin's interest in canal barges.

"This is all very interesting," says Freda, "but I don't see why you're telling me. I don't own a barge."

"Oh! I'm sorry, my mistake," says Andy, "only when I saw you had the same Key Fob as Neville, I naturally thought you had an interest in that direction."

"Oh, this," she says, tilting up the bunch of keys suspended from her nurses' belt, "you can get these anywhere. I bought two, and gave one to Nev."

"Can you remember where you bought them from; only Sean, would like to get one for his Cousin?"

"No, it was a long time ago; I can't remember now. Was there anything else before I get back to work?"

"Yes," says Andy, "we thought you'd like to know that, thanks to you, we have Mr Dyke currently helping us with our enquiries."

With that news Freda, unless I'm reading too much into it, seems to inwardly relax, as though a huge burden has been lifted from her shoulders. She quickly gathers herself and says cheerfully. "Well thank you for that; that is good news. Now I must go, but please stay and finish your teas."

Outside, Andy and I confer. "What do you think? Is she genuine? I thought she was a bit edgy; until you gave her the good news."

"Yes Sean, I think she's lying through her teeth about not knowing where she got the replica Lock Keys."

'Lying through her teeth?' Phen, enquires.

'Don't worry about it Phen, put it down to just another unexplainable English saying.'

"Come on Andy. Let's go find somewhere quiet to take off from and go and see how the others are getting on."

We run them to ground, typically in a canal side caf, and say quietly; after ordering something for ourselves of course. "How are you two lovebirds doing?" which elicits grimaces from both. "Andy, me thinks they do protest too much," I pretend to whisper.

"Alright joke over," says Winston, "we've identified twenty-five Longboats in this immediate area. Ten of which haven't moved in the last two years. Six have never tied up here before and they only arrived in the last one to two weeks. The remaining nine are known to come and go at regular intervals."

"Good work you two," I say, "this nine then, are the ones we need to keep an eye on."

"Unfortunately, they are fairly widespread, says Jenny."

"Never the less, we need to know the comings and goings of these nine boats. Particularly if any of them are visited by a particularly large woman named Freda.

Andy and I'll be booking into your B&B. You won't have to worry about the barges being spread out; we are going to help you with the stakeouts. As far as other B&B's guests are concerned, we for now, will pretend not to know each other.

I don't think anything's going to happen until Freda leaves work but any information is worth having.

Talking about that, I'm going to stakeout the Hospital in the hope of seeing Freda head home. Hopefully I'll be able to trail her to one of the nine barges."

My stakeout is not helped by the heavy rain. 'Thank God, Phen I had the forethought to bring an umbrella. What a strange, funny picture, it would make if anyone could see me hovering in the air with an umbrella over my head.'

'No more than I would expect from an eccentric Englishman,' muses Phen.

'Ha! Ha! Very funny. I don't suppose if anyone could see YOU, that they wouldn't think it a strange sight?'

'Pass! Changing the subject. Perhaps you would like to know that I approve of your current tactics in our investigations.'

'Wow! Thanks, Phen.'

'More sarcasm.' he thinks wearily.

'Hang about Phen, people are starting to come out. There's Freda, you can hardly miss her. Mmmm, she doesn't appear to have a car, she's walking to the bus stop.'

'Ha! Caught you out.'

'What do you mean? Caught me out?'

'You Mmmmed!'

'You're obviously rubbing of on me,' I think back at him.

'Here comes the bus. It's at least pointing in the right direction.'

We follow it, hopefully to the canal basin, but NO! 'Drat, she's got off two stops before. What now, Phen?'

'There is no option but to continue following her,' thinks Phen.

'Hell, she's going away from the canal,' I think as we follow her along two streets. She goes into a grocery shop, we wait for her to come out, which she does ten minutes later.

Five more minutes, she's going up the steps and through the entrance door of a block of flats. She's opened the door with a key. There's no doubt that this is where she lives.

'Double drat, Phen, this has knocked a hole in our theory. I was convinced she lived on a barge and is possibly our killer.'

'She still might be Jake. We do not know for sure that the killer lives on a barge. Only that he/she has a Lock Key Fob.'

'As usual, you're right Phen. I don't see any point hanging around here; let's get back to the others.'

"Hello you two, where's Andy?"

"He's off doing his own thing," replies Jenny, "he said that it's no good staying with us. It would blow our cover."

"That makes sense. Made any progress?

"Yes," says Winston, "we've eliminated three from the nine. One has a young couple aboard and two have elderly married couples on them. Of the other six barges; two have left."

"Any description of who crewed them and which direction they went in?"

"No, says Jenny, we didn't actually see them leave but by process of elimination we know the names of the boats. One was, "Worcester Pot" and the other "Betty". Are! Here's Andy."

"I heard a bit of that as I was approaching," says Andy, "Winston and Jenny, have given you the good news. The bad news is, the two boats that left went in opposite directions and they had gone too far for me to see who was steering."

"OK. It shouldn't be too hard for me to catch them up. Regarding the remaining four, which I assume you have the names of, is there anywhere that keeps a register of owners?"

"I've been asking the same question," says Andy. I believe there is an organisation, set up in the last five years, called the IWA. (Inland Waterways Association)."

"That's great news Andy. Can you use your Police status to get them to open up their files?"

"I'll try phoning, but I suspect I will have to go along to their office. They will probably want proof of my identity."

"We'll see you back at the digs Andy. There's nothing more to be achieved here today. We'll start fresh tomorrow," I say.

Andy, goes off, armed with the names of the six longboats, to make the call. Hopefully, he'll come back with the IWA's address.

"Yes, they're open on a Sunday," says Andy, as the following morning, we're having Breakfast and sitting nowhere near Winston & Jenny. "They are only open till noon. I told them that we'd be along this morning. I've given the names of the boats we're interested in but as I suspected they wouldn't reveal the owner's names over the phone."

I get up to go to the toilet. On passing Winston I whisper, "Meet me in the Loo".

As I'm washing my hands he comes in and says, "This is a bit cloak & dagger aint it?"

"Maybe, but it's best to be cautious for a while longer. What I'd like you and Jen to do this morning is to think up a good reason for visiting Powick Hospital. What I'm particularly interested in, without raising suspicion, is finding out Freda's surname. I'll leave you to that while me and Andy try to find out who owns our remaining Longboats."

Breakfast over. Andy and I fly off to gather the info we want from the IWA's office.

"I'm Detective Inspector Morrison," says Andy, offering his Warrant Card to a gentleman hiding behind a rack of pamphlets, "We spoke on the phone yesterday. This gent is Detective Brooks."

"Are yes, I have the information you wanted right here. I hope it helps in some small way," he says smiling. "You will see that you have the names of five of them. The sixth one is yet to register."

"Interesting?" I say to Andy as we leave, "I'll drop you back to the wharf so you can check those names out. Then I'll go and pick up Winston & Jen."

Because they had to get there by bus and foot, I'm expecting a bit of a wait but thankfully it's not too long.

As they leave the end of the Hospital's Drive, I pssst from the bushes opposite and beckon them into my hiding place. I put an arm round each and fly them back to the canal wharf, landing them almost on top of Andy, who has ceased to look shocked by such antics.

"Well Andy? What have you got for us?" I ask, not bothering now about the four of us being seen together.

"I can see why you found the list interesting; the unregistered one is the boat that headed out on the Worcester/Birmingham Canal."

After a nod to Andy, I say, "Now Jen, What's Freda's surname?"

"Before that, let me tell you how she managed it, she was brilliant," says Winston. "She went up to the Receptionist, and the shortened version of what she said is: I'm looking for my uncle. He is supposed to be in a Psychiatric Hospital somewhere in this area. The only clue I have, is that he once mentioned a very large nurse, whose first name I think was Fenna, Seda, Freda or something like that, but you know for the life of me, I can't remember her surname. Do you have anyone like that here? Only she may be able to recall my uncle Ronald? The Receptionist said we did have a Ronald sometime back. I'll see if I can page Ms …. Go on Jen, you say it, before I fall about laughing …."

Jenny says, trying hard to hold back her own laughter, "Ms Small!"

Winston almost doubling over, garbles, "We excused ourselves and got out of there before we busted our faces."

"That's, without doubt the funniest thing I've heard for a long time." I recover from my own doubling up and manage to say, "Okay, let's go and get a snack, and recap what we have."

We're all seated in the Canal Side Caf, and Andy says, "Although we still can't rule Freda out. She is definitely not the person heading toward Birmingham on the "Worcester Pot". Which I assume is the boat we're interested in. The boat owner heading in the opposite direction, apparently, is well known on the canals and is a man in his seventies."

Stating the obvious, I say, "We need to know the name of the "Worcester Pot's." owner."

"That's not easy," says Winston. "All our investigations have shown that the owner is a loner. Not one, of the people we've spoken to has ever seen him/her."

"OK, here's the thing: I'm going to fly over the Worcester/Birmingham canal until I've picked up our barges trail. If you can get a bit more leave Andy? I'd like you three to keep an eye on our Freda. To my mind, as things stand, we've got more reason to suspect her, than whoever's on that boat."

"Really? So, you're coming around to my way of thinking," says Andy.

"Yes Pal, thinking about it: the person on the barge definitely has a Lock Key, but we don't know if he/she has a Lock Key Fob. We know that our murderer has one, and we know that Freda has one. We know that Freda received training in disguise from what's his name, the guy she sent us on the wild goose chase after?

"Ronald Dyke," supplies Andy before Phen, who is busy following my evidence trail, can pop the answer into my mind.

'Wild goose chase?' thinks Phen, 'you have used that one before but you did not explain it, and if you had thought to ask me, I would have reminded you of Ronald's name.'

'It means Phen, chasing after something to no avail, and I'm sorry I didn't use your memory regards our previous suspect's name, but I am trying, here, to lay out an argument; so, if you don't mind.'

'Pardon me for thinking I might be able to help,' moans Phen.

"Yea, him," I say, answering Andy, "So until we know different, I'd like to keep her in our sights."

"I suppose your right. I must admit, I was beginning to get excited about our bargee."

"It's understandable Andy; you've been after this killer far longer than we have. Let's hope your excitement bears fruit."

'You will have to explain that one also Jake,' thinks Phen.

'For God's sake Phen; will you give me a break? How can I concentrate while you're questioning me all the time?'

'Give you a break?'

'Grrr! —Phen, I'll block you if you don't stop it.'

17

No luck on my first pass over the Birmingham/Worcester canal. Nothing for it but to persevere. I reckon my best bet is "Stoke Prior". There were so many Longboats going through that spot; I could easily have missed my target.

My plan is to ask as many boat owners as possible if they have seen the "Worcester Pot". Andy's lent me a lock picking kit. If I find the boat my plan is to sneak aboard and use it on the cabin door.

The first dozen, reveal nothing. I have more luck with lucky thirteen. It belonging to a nice elderly couple who have been tied up all week. "Yes," the lady says, "it went through this morning. I remember it because I thought it strange that the bargee was fully covered."

"Why would that seem strange? I ask.

"Well, for late October, it's a very warm day, isn't it? I couldn't tell if it was a man or a woman, the face was completely covered with some sort of hood."

"Do you know which route the barge took?"

The gent says, "It's headed up towards Kings Norton."

I say, "Thank you both very much; you've been a great help."

Using my enhanced sight, I carefully check every name, of every boat as I slowly fly high above. Finally I spot my target as the barge is about to enter the "Tardebrigge Tunnel". Hopefully patience will have its reward. I land on the towpath, at the tunnels exit, change my appearance to something near that of the elderly lady I used on the cruise ship and start slowly walking.

Because I'm walking at less than four miles per hour the boat gradually overtakes me.

From the towpath and at my diminutive height and looking up, I can only see the steersman's head and shoulders. Which are turned away from me as the boat passes.

'Do you think that was deliberate or not, Phen?'

'Probably, Jake,' he replies.

'Our target's still an X, then, Phen?'

'Until we get a look at the driver's face, that is a yes,'

I wait till the boats out of sight, change back to Sean, and take off. As X, is about to tie up at "Tardebrigge Old Wharf", I fly a 360-degree path and for the first time, despite the hood, we get a partial look at X's, face.

'That more or less confirms it Jake, our target, is a man.'

'Yes Phen, he's got, I wouldn't call it a beard, more a stubbly face and there's something about his eyes that's familiar, but dam, I can't put my finger on it.

After waiting several hours Mr X, finally leaves his barge. Even though it's now dark, I note that he makes sure no one sees him disembark and he's left a light on. I assume to give the impression that he's still aboard. I follow him to a local pub.

This is my chance. I flit back to the barge, take out Andy's lock pick and work it into the cabin lock. It takes me longer than I would like, as it's not a skill I've had much cause to develop.

I eventually manage it, causing no visible damage, which is the idea. I remain undetected.

A cursory look reveals nothing unusual, that is until I open the rear sleeping compartment. There on a cloths rack, are at least a dozen costumes, and on a small dressing table; pots of theatrical make up. I have to admit, I'm shaking. After all this time here's the poof Andy's been searching for.

'Phen, help me mate. I need to calm down and think.'

'Take a few deep breaths and then carefully look for further proof,' advises Phen.

I follow his lead and explore the rest of the boat. Looking in a draw I find several more Lock Key Fobs.

My eyes now wander to several books on a shelf. What's caught my eye is a novel I've read, by Agatha Christie called "Murder is Easy", in which multiple murders are perpetrated.

On further inspection all the books are crime novels. The knowledge of which, sends shivers up me. I have no idea how long I've been standing here staring at them?"

'Jake, JAKE!' Phen's thought goes bouncing through my brain, 'get out of here now. The last thing you want is for Mr X, to catch you in here.'

'One last thing Phen, I need to find something that reveals Mr X's, real name.'

Using my X-ray vision, I scan the whole of the boat's

interior, including the rear costume cabin, and spot a box tucked under the dressing table. I open it and there inside find some letters addressed to! … I can't believe it. No wonder I thought there was something familiar about the eyes.

'Jake, get out of here I can hear someone approaching.'

'Right Phen, I hurry out, relock the cabin and duck down just in time to see our man coming along the towpath. I'm sure he hasn't seen me as he's got his head down. I do my rapid oscillation thing to make myself invisible and take off.

'I don't think our man is going anywhere tonight Phen. I'm going back to report to the others.'

A few seconds later I land in the garden of the B&B, make my way through the dark and enter the B&B's front entrance.

I find Jenny in the guest lounge and say, "Hello Jen where's Andy and Winston?"

"Hello, welcome back. Winston's staking out Freda but Andy's around somewhere. He may be in his room."

"Can you go and ask him to come down Jen? I'll wait here."

Five minutes later, they both take seats near me. I say, "How's the Freda, stakeout going?"

"No activity there so far. Jenny did the first stint. Winston's there now, and I'm going to relieve him at midnight," replies Andy.

"Good it's important that we keep tabs on her.

Tomorrow Andy, I think it time to contact your Boss and ask him in the light of new evidence, to reopen the cases.

We don't want him going in yet though, so don't tell him everything, just enough to spark his interest and get him to alert all police stations between here and Birmingham. Ask them to standby for your call to move in."

"I take it Sean, that you've uncovered something that connects Freda to our murders?" says Andy.

"There is one thing that does connect Freda but Andy, she's not the murderer. The murderer is the guy steering the "Worcester Pot" toward Birmingham. His name is Eric Small!!!"

With raised eyebrows and gaping mouths Andy and Jen look at each other, then questioningly, back to me.

I say, "The evidence is now overwhelmingly in favour of Eric being our perpetrator." I relate the evidence to them. Then Andy prepares to go and fill Winston in on these latest developments and at the same time, although it no longer seems necessary, do his stint of observing Freda.

Jen and I retire to our rooms.

Monday morning, Jenny had an early breakfast and went to relieve Andy.

When Winston and I walk into the breakfast room, Andy is already there reading a newspaper and nibbling toast.

"Rough night?" I ask, looking at Andy's unshaven face.

"Not particularly. I'm used to stakeouts. Besides there was no activity."

Half way through breakfast, a voice behind me says, "Mr Brooks? I'm sorry to butt in, there's a phone call for you."

"Thank you," I say to our Landlady, "I'll be right with you."

"Hello, Sean Brook's here." I say, answering the phone.

"Jake, it's me, Jen. I'm speaking from a Phone Box and I haven't got much change, so I'll say it quickly. Our bird is on the move. She's just left her apartment carrying what looks like an overnight bag. She's heading for the Bus Station."

"Thanks for that, Jen, you come back to the B&B now. I'll fly over there and see if I can spot her. See you soon."

I finish my breakfast and take a quick flit to the Bus Station and hover. I can't spot Freda. She must have boarded a bus that's already left and I've no idea which one, or particularly care, as it no longer matters.

'She could be going anywhere.' Thinks Phen, 'perhaps visiting a friend? who knows?'

Back at the B&B, I give the news and say, "Guys I think we're reaching the climax of our investigations. Now we've come this far; we don't want to blow it. Andy have you decided on your approach to your chief?"

"Yes, and now we know where the barge is and where it's heading, it makes it easier for the Super, to allocate man power."

"That's great; we're going to leave you to that. When you're finished can you hang around the B&B? I'll pick you up as soon as I can. I'm going to fly these two until we spot the "Worcester Pot" and then drop them further up the barges route. Say as far as Kings Norton. I don't believe anything will happen before he gets, at least, that far."

Half hour later, we've spotted our target and I've deposited Winston and Jenny near the Kings Norton moorings. "You two, relax here for awhile. I think it'll take two to four hours for the "Worcester Pot" to reach us. While you're waiting Jen, it might be an Idea for you to find a phone box and give Joel a ring. Here's some change. Give him our news and collect any messages from him. Winston will you wait here. In the meantime, I'm going to pick up Andy and see if we can get a word with Charlotte."

I've put Andy in the picture and he's now using the B&B's payphone again. This time to ring Charlotte.

I visit the gents, and on my return, I ask, "How did your call to your boss go?"

"Fine Sean, it's all set up. He won't make a move until he gets a call from me or you."

'If I may cut in Jake,' thinks Phen, 'why do you need to see Charlotte?'

'I need to know Phen, if there are any escort agencies in Kings Norton or anywhere else on the route from there to the Birmingham Canal Basin.'

'Mmmm. I can tell you there are none on Andy's charts.'

'Thanks, Phen, your contributions do help me clarify my thoughts.'

'I am pleased, that I am some use.'

'No comment. Is it alright if I get on now?'

'Mmmm, I suppose so.'

Andy's call to Charlotte revealed that she has a 40% interest in an Agency not far from Kings Norton's canal moorings and he has arranged for us to meet there in one hour from now. I fly us back to the moorings, pick up Jen and head us off to keep the appointment.

"Charlie, so nice to see you," says Andy, "you remember Sean and Jenny."

"Yes of course. How are you all? It seems ages since we met up, although it can't be more than a couple of weeks."

"Fine thanks," we all chorus.

Jenny doesn't know why I've brought her along, but she's about to find out.

Andy fills Charlie and Ronda, who is the majority stake holder for this agency, in on our progress and they both look at us with worried frowns.

"Does this mean," says Ronda, "that you think one of my girls, is the killer's next target?"

"It's a strong possibility," I say, "because we don't think there are any other escort agencies near this canal from here to Birmingham."

Turning to Jen, I say, "I haven't had a chance to discuss it with you yet Jen but I'm hoping that with Charlie and Ronda's help you'll agree to disguising yourself as one of Ronda's girls and act as a decoy?"

"Do you mean? You want me to be the bait? Jenny asks."

"Well you did say you wanted to be more involved at the sharp end, and it's not likely to get much sharper than this. You know of course, that I'd never allow any harm to come to you."

"OK! – I think?" says Jen, hesitantly.

"Ronda, if you'd take Jen away, get started on her disguise and how to act the part, I'd like a quick word with Charlie."

"Charlie, what I'd like you to organise is to give Jen centre stage. In other words get Ronda's girls/men to keep a low profile for three or four days."

"Why that long?"

"Because, we believe that's how long it usually takes our killer to decide on his victim and plan his attack."

"In that case," responds Charlie, "consider it done."

"Right, let's go and see how Ronda's getting on with Jen."

Winston, who we'd left watching out for the "Worcester Pot" does a double take as Jen and I come into his view. "Jenny? – Is that you? He says with astonishment."

Jen explains what's happening. Winston looks at me with a worried look on his face, and says, "Is that really necessary?"

Jen smiles at him and says, "Why! Winston, I didn't realise you cared so much?"

Winston, if he could show it, would be blushing down to his socks.

Jen puts a hand to his face and says, "You've gone all hot."

"I think that's enough of that. What's the plan?" He says trying to cover his embarrassment.

"Andy & I want to take Jen for a look around, so's she can familiarise herself with the area and help her to plan the way we'd like this thing to pan out.

Afterwards Jen is going to stay with Ronda. Charlie's partner. Here's her telephone number. When you see the barge come in, ring it. We'll see you later."

Jenny and I walk in several directions using the escort agency office as our starting point. We end up choosing a route that leads to the shops and decide to make it her daily routine trip, ostensibly to buy cigarettes from the newsagents.

'I see your idea Jake,' thinks Phen, "you want Eric Small to observe Jenny doing at least one thing on a regular basis, so that he hopefully chooses that moment to make his attack.'

'Correct, Phen.'

Andy shows his Warrant card to the Newsagent and asks if there's a back way out? The shopkeeper confirms that there is, so Andy fills him in on as much as he needs to know. "Most importantly," says Andy, "You need to stay calm, and act as naturally as possible."

I say, "We'll try to make sure no harm comes to you or your shop but if there is any damage, you'll be well compensated. Don't forget to keep your back door closed only by a bolt, no dead locks on. Finally, thank you very much for your co-operation."

We drop Jen at Ronda's, and accept the invite to eat a sandwich and use her facilities. As I come out of the toilet, Ronda points at her phone and says "A guy called Winston, for you."

"Yes, mate?"

"Right... good. Stay out of sight. When I've finished here, I'll come and relieve you. You can come here and have a break." I give Winston the address.

I turn to the others and say, "Eric's just arrived."

'Jake,' thinks Phen.'

'Yes Phen?'

'You're making all these elaborate arrangements. What if this is not the spot that Eric is planning to make his next attack?'

'Good point Phen. The answer is: we'll have to keep doing the whole thing over and over, until he does make his final choice.'

Andy looks at Jen and asks, "Why does Sean often look as if he's not with us?"

"Oh, that," says Jen. "He's probably talking to his imaginary friend. He does it a lot, especially when he's working out complications. Just ignore it, we do."

I'm hovering high above the canal moorings. With enhanced sight, I can see every detail of Eric's, barge. There was no activity while Winston was here and there's been none, so far, since my arrival.

'Look Jake! He has stepped onto the towpath. How would you describe the cloths he is wearing?' thinks Phen.

'The long coat, with the lapel turned up, I believe Phen, is called a Trench Coat, and the hat that he's pulled well down, covering part of his face, is called a Trilby.'

'Phen & I follow him (*not that Phen has much choice, as he lives within me,*) to a nearby Pub. I dash back to Ronda's and pick up Andy and Winston.

"Alright chaps, we'll wait for Eric to come out again, I'll continue following him, while you two go into the Pub and see what you can find out."

Eric has led me to Ronda's agency. He's loitering out of sight of the office windows.

I make a landing at Ronda's apartment and pick up Jen. I explain to her that I'm going to deliver her to the office's rear door.

"OK Jen, what I'd like you to do is go in, come out the front and then go to the Newsagents as we planned. Buy some cigs and return. I'll be watching, so don't worry. Besides Eric will only be observing at the moment. I'm sure he won't make his attack until he's done reconnoitring."

It's beginning to get dark as Jenny heads home to Ronda's. I watch her go in. Then I go around to the back of the pub and pick up Winston and Andy. We observe while Eric loiters, then after a while he seems to call it a day and makes his way back to his boat. We watch him board. All of his lights go on and his radio starts playing. "Time, we found ourselves some digs lads," I say.

The three of us are sat in the dining room of our chosen Guest House. The meals been served and eaten. We finally get around to discussing the day.

"How did you two get on with the Publican of "The Navigation"?" I ask.

"Fine," says Andy, "I've sworn him to secrecy on fear of his licence and the short version of what he told us is: our suspect said that he's in the area for a while on business, and that he may need to be accompanied to a business lunch; did he know of any local escort agencies? I then asked him what happened after that. He then said, he'd told Eric the address of Ronda's offices. He'd drunk a couple of pints of his best ale, ate a cold beef sandwich and asked after the toilet. The publican told him it's out the door at the end of the lounge and first right past the payphone. That's the last he saw of him."

We chatted a while longer over a few drinks in our digs lounge, then went to bed.

Tuesday, at breakfast, the discussion is about how to divide our labour effectively.

We decide that patience is the watch word for the next two to three days.

"Winston," I say, "would you take the first turn at discreetly following Eric. Andy, now that we are fairly sure that this is the killers target area, will you keep your boss informed of our progress."

'What are you going to do Jake?' thinks Phen.

'I'm about to tell the others Phen. You'll find out then.'

"As for me lads, I'm going to visit Jen to let her know how I think we can turn up the heat of the killer's interest in her, and be surer he makes her his next victim."

How are you this morning Jen? How are your nerves holding up? Beginning to wish you were safely behind your desk at "The Forge"?

"I'm fine, and NO, not yet anyway," Jen replies.

"Good, because things are about to hot up. About midday I want you to go to a Hotel called "The Midway". I'm told by Ronda it is often used as a pickup point by prostitutes. Dress in some of Ronda's most provocative gear and sit at the lounge bar. A suave business type will come and sit beside you and start chatting you up. Don't worry it won't be Eric. It'll be me, in one of my disguises. We'll chat for a while, then go up to a room I've booked for the day. We'll lock the door behind us and hopefully, Winston will observe if Eric has taken the bait."

An hour later, there's a tap on my hotel bedroom door. I open it a crack; it's Winston! "Come in," I say. "What are you doing here? Why aren't you keeping an eye on Eric?

"He's gone off somewhere, not to worry though, I met up with Andy. I've asked him to watch him. I thought it more important to report that our friend has been watching you and Jen. He followed her as far as the bar and he saw you bring her up here. He also saw which room you two went in. When I met Andy, I told him as well."

"Alright, that's good."

There's another tap on the door, this time it's Andy. He doesn't wait to be invited, he blunders in, and in panting breaths says, "Eric's on his way back into the hotel."

"Good, now you two keep out of sight in here, I'm going to do my disappearing act the other side of the door."

"Disappearing act?" questions Andy.

"Don't ask," Winston says, "we'll explain later.

"Jenny, what I want you to do is put an ear to the door and when you hear a faint tap from me, count to ten, open the door, come out, smooth your dress and pat your hair; as though you have been at it, so to speak. Then walk out of the hotel and head for the shops. Go into your usual Newsagents, buy your cigs and finally go back to the escort agency offices. I'll meet you there, and we'll decide what to do next.

   After Jen's gone lads I'll get you both back on Eric's, tail."

   I watch Eric take up a position where he can watch who goes in and out of the room Jen's in.

   Still invisible I flit by and make the almost inaudible tap, as planned, and Jen, does her thing.

   Later, Jen lets me in the agencies back door and I say, "Would you ask Ronda if she can spare me a few minutes, Jen?"

   We meet in Ronda's office and she says, "How can I help?"

   I say, "You know how we're pushing Jen forward; well we don't want it to look too unnatural. I was thinking it may be an idea to let him see one or two more of your girls. If they are too nervous to go out singularly, they could go as a pair, even if it's only to shop for groceries.

   Perhaps you could ask for volunteers but please make it clear, that although they won't be able to see me, I shall be watching over them. Oh, and one more thing, can you ask them to dress down. I don't want our killer picking one of them over Jenny."

   When Jen and I are alone, I say, "Now Jen this evening I'd like us to repeat our hotel act. I shall of course adapt a different disguise but we'll use the same room. The idea is to get Eric thinking, that you are a right slut and have that room set aside for your professional use and to finally decide that you're it."

The whole thing follows the same pattern and at the end of the day, when Andy and Winston get back from "The Navigation", they tell me, that after Eric had watched Jen go into the agency offices, they'd trailed him to the Grocers.

Apparently, he'd dropped his purchases of at the barge. Then continued his vigil. The lads saw him take a fleeting interest in two girls exiting the agency, who were giggling as they headed toward the shops.

"I must say," says Andy, "I admire his patience. He hung around till dusk. After he'd observed Jenny's exit from Ronda's Agency and her repeat performance at the hotel. He'd followed her back to the agency, then went back to the boat. We hung around for a while, until we caught the whiff of his meal being cooked and then came back here."

"That's great. Thanks for that. Let's go and eat."

"Wednesday, follows along similar lines. The only things of interest are: that he'd been in the Newsagents, purchased a paper and enquired if there was a back way out, and that he'd paid yet another visit to "The Navigation".

Andy told me, that he'd followed Eric there.

"Any excuse for a pint," I said.

After seeing Eric return to his barge for the night; Andy paid a return visit to the pub and the Publican told him that our suspect had drunk a pint, used the toilet, and went, as before.

As we enter the hotels dining room Thursday morning, I say, "Don't have Breakfast yet Lads, I'm going to fetch Jen to join us."

"Before you go," says Andy, "There's something else I meant to tell you about Yesterday. I don't know if it means anything but I got the feeling that Eric at times, was going out of his way to let Jenny catch a glimpse of him; as though he wanted to make her nervous, or something."

"You may be right," I say, "but we have no way of knowing if that's the case or why. Anyway, Lads I'll see you later."

I've taken a detour via the canals to be sure Eric hasn't stirred yet. As he hasn't, I flit to Ronda's and ring her bell. Jen opens the door, fully dressed and ready to go. "You must be Psychic Jen?" I say.

"If only! Winston rang to say you were on your way. He knew you wouldn't think of it," she says, smiling.

Now, as we're all sat down to Breakfast, I say, "Well team, I think this may well be the day. We all need to be on our toes. Andy can you alert the local Bobby's to stand by.

Jen, I'll drop you at the agency's back door. When I know Eric's watching, I'll tap on the door three times. I want you then to make your usual trip to the newsagents."

"I have to say Sean, even though I'm entirely confident in your ability to protect me. I must confess to being very nervous."

"Understandable Jen, it's normal to feel that way, especially when things are coming to a head."

"Winston, I want you to position yourself in the Newsagents. When you see Jen come in, ignore her by pretending to peruse the Magazines."

"Jen, when you see Eric enter the shop, glance at him, pretend to notice a threatening look on his face and to feel frightened. Then head for the back door."

"There won't be any need to pretend," says Jen, with a tremor in her voice.

"Andy, when you see Eric enter the shop, which I'm confident he will, otherwise why enquire about the rear exit? After he's gone in, you and your men can come out of hiding and be ready to follow Eric through the back. If he attempts to abduct or murder Jen, I shall be ahead of you to make absolutely certain he doesn't succeed."

Andy, nods and I turn to Jen, "Okay Jen, let's get you back to the agency."

Just after ten thirty I do the tapping thing. I see Jenny exiting the agency and making her way to the shops. More importantly; I observe Eric following her. His Trilby shading his face even further.

I fly swiftly ahead and alert the others to stand by. Out of sight of the counter, I say hello to Winston and stand with him looking at the Mag's.

Only five minutes have passed when Jen comes into the shop but it feels like a life time. I was about to go out and check on her, as it seemed so long!

She goes up to the counter and chats with the proprietor while buying cigs.

'God, our girls good,' I think to Phen as I see her glance toward Eric as he enters the shop. Fear shows on her face as their eyes lock for a split second. She grabs her cigs and asks the proprietor if there is a back way out and he, bless him, looks surprised and just points in the direction of the rear door.

Jenny edges her way toward it and sees Eric moving in her direction. She turns quickly and makes a dash for the door. She wrenches at the bolt in a pretend panic, and finally exits.

Winston and I are now expecting Eric to follow her, but to our complete surprise, he doesn't.

He returns to the counter, buys a newspaper, and then leaves via the front door, straight into the arms of Andy and his four constables. Winston rushes for the rear door and disappears out. I, put my head out the front and see one of the Bobby's handcuffing Eric while Andy, is reading him his rights.

"Sean, …. Help, …. Freda's got Jenny!" Winston shouts, as he staggers back into the shop.

I sit him down and see that he's bleeding from a gash on his head but I have no time to fuss over him. I quickly say. "Tell me what happened?"

"I was trying to stop Freda, from putting a pad of Ether over Jen's, nose and mouth, when she clobbered me with the butt end of a huge knife."

I've never moved so fast. I'm out the back door and flying a grid pattern; the fear welling up inside me, that I may be too late to save Jenny's life.

After what seems ages but it really is only seconds, I spot Freda lowering Jen to the ground and leaning her against a large tree in the wooded area of "Kings Norton Park".

As quietly as I can I position myself at the top of the same tree, tune up my hearing and watch. I'm thinking, thank God I'm NOT too late.

Freda's slapping Jen's face, saying, "Come on you slut, wake up, I want you to know why and how I'm going to kill you."

Jenny stirs, still woozy, looks at Freda and stammers, with her face full of dread and fear, "What have I done to you?"

"It's what you and your kind have done to ruin my brothers and my life over the years.

Enticing our weak father into your filthy, sordid world, until he finally left us." The look on her face as she's speaking is one of twisted hatred.

"Our Mother was heartbroken and survived only a few months.

My brother and I vowed that as soon as we were old enough, we'd get our revenge on your kind. It's taken longer than we'd have liked, but it was important to get the planning of each murder right. I say we, but it's me that does the killing. My Brother helps by carefully picking out each victim, and guiding them into my path, but he's squeamish, he's too much like Dad to do the killing, he hasn't got the guts.

Speaking of guts, you might like to know how I'm going to kill you. I'm very clever. I never kill my victims in the same way twice. Have you heard of the Japanese method of committing suicide, called "Hara-Kiri"?

"No," squeaks Jenny, piteously.

Freda reaches into her coat and says, "I'm going to plunge this razor-sharp knife into your lower bowel and drag it up to your sternum."

"NO! NO!" screams Jen.

"Shut the hell up slut," hisses Freda, as she gives Jenny another slap across her face.

It's agony for me to see what's happening, but it's vital to hear as much evidence as possible, especially as I've been watching Andy and his men slowly and quietly, creeping up, from tree, to tree.

"Prepare to die slut!" says Freda, as she grabs Jenny. Yanks her to her feet, and slams her against the tree, knocking the wind out of her. Freda's right arm goes back, and is starting to drive the knife forward into Jenny. But guess what? She doesn't make it. With minimum force, I've grabbed her wrist and twisted the knife out of her hand. She looks over her right shoulder at me with a startled look of hatred, and moves far quicker than I would have given her credit for.

She twists violently to the left and fetches me a hefty blow on my head with her left elbow. Far from harming me; she screams with the agony of a shattered "Humerus bone".

Andy and his men surge forward and make the arrest. Winston hugs and consoles Jen. Freda is screaming blue murder at me, and calling me a freak.

She can't understand why I didn't collapse in a heap, as anyone else would have done, from one of her elbowings. In spite of struggling like a wild thing, even she can't escape from the combined strength of four burly policemen and finally gives up. She is cuffed and carted off in a waiting "Black Maria".

"Did you hear enough evidence Andy?"

"Yes Sean, those two are going away for a very long time."

'Well Phen, that was something I don't want to go through too often!'

'I need a holiday,' Phen, complains.

Trust Phen to put a smile back on my face and stop me from thinking what could have happened!

18

3 Months Later

This is some spread; Charlotte Grant and her father Conway have put on. We've all been busy making statements and giving evidence at Freda and Eric's trial. But that's all behind us now. Freda has been sent down for life with no possibility of parole. Eric's also got life but he may be considered for parole at some unspecified point in the future.

This "Do", has been organised to celebrate that outcome. We're all here, including Joel, for although he wasn't directly involved, he nevertheless played a supporting role by holding the fort.

Other people that are here are: Ronda and all the other establishment heads that lost friends and colleagues to Freda's vile attacks. Andy, who has received a Police Commendation and a promotion, is of course, here.

His boss is also here, along with all Lawyers and Barristers connected with the prosecution. Also, representatives of each family who'd lost one of their own to Freda and Eric's evil.

I've got Jenny seated on my left, Andy on my right; Winston and Joel opposite us. Charlie and her Dad are the Masters of Ceremony.

During the meal, I have to tolerate a bit of quizzing from Charlie, who obviously hadn't been paying full attention at the trial. She wants to know how Freda knew where to be when Jenny came out the Newsagents back door?

I answer, "You may remember Andy's evidence, when he told the court what the Publican had told him. That Eric had used the Gents on every occasion that he visited the Pub. Well, just before "The Navigation's" loos, you pass a payphone. That's how."

"I see," says Charlie. "I don't want to spoil your meal, but could I ask you one more thing?"

"Shoot."

"Why, when you had been carefully tailing Freda did you stop doing so?

"Because," I reply, "By then, the evidence against Eric was so overwhelming, that we gave up fingering Freda for the murders."

Thinking, after a further, I see, from Charlie, that that was the end of her questions and that I'd now be able to pitch into this sumptuous meal, I've now got Andy starting. "Sean," he's whispering, "you never did explain about your disappearing act?"

"I'm glad you're keeping your voice down," I say sarcastically. "Lean in a little closer. You know already, I can fly and move at great speed."

"Yea, yea, but how do you disappear?"

"It's just an extension of my speed. Instead of going a long distance, I move super quickly backwards and forwards between two points; so quickly that the human eye can't keep up. The only thing anyone may notice is a bit of a draught, but please Andy keep it to yourself; along with my being able to fly."

"Mums the word," he says, squiffily while tapping the side of his nose.

Thankfully Conway has come to the rescue; he's on his feet, making a speech.

"And finally, Ladies and Gentlemen," he says while moving to stand behind me, "It's all thanks to this man here," he leans forward and whispers, "stand up Sean." I do his bidding, but only so's not to cause him embarrassment. It doesn't matter about mine, it seems. It's okay for these show biz types; I'm not used to this sort of thing. I only hope I'm not asked to speak.

Conway takes my right wrist and raises my arm and hand above my head. I'm wishing now, he hadn't come to the rescue.

Everyone in the room is now standing, clapping and shouting, "Speech! Speech!

Oh God, I'm not going to be able to get out of this. When the room settles down, I say my thanks. You know the sort of thing: so pleased to see you all here etc. etc. and adding, "There is no way this could have been achieved without - who is now - CHIEF Inspector Andy Morrison and my team."

I join in clapping them, "to help you all to understand, I have to tell you that the one person called upon to show extreme bravery and guts, is this little Lady here." I turn and clap Jenny.

"All that she went through you know from the trial.

May I say in conclusion," while pointing with all four fingers at Winston, Andy and Joel, "That we are all very proud of her."

I sit, but all the rest of the guests stand, and clap Jenny. Whose tanned face, as you might expect, goes a deep red. I lean over; peck her cheek and whisper, "Sorry."

I only wish I could have publicly and openly thanked Phen but I know he wouldn't have welcomed that. Besides he already knows how grateful I am for his gifts and friendship.

'That is very nice Jake, and thank you for not blocking those thoughts from me.'

The following day, we meet up at "The Forge", and I ask Joel and Winston how they are getting on with helping out at the building site for the self-build club house of the youth club/football team?

"Fine," answers Joel, "the weathers been kind and because we've had the help of a number of experts from among the kid's parents, it's nearly finished."

"Super, I'll look forward to the opening."

With February looming, my Restoration business now well established, and Jenny helping me out with its Admin; I can't help wondering, what's next for the intrepid five???

'And before you think to ask; Yes, that does include you Phen and Phen, now that we are having some down time, there are some things I've been meaning to ask you.'

'Intriguing,' thinks Phen.

'Phen, even though you don't sleep as we do; you do rest, and sometimes go into some sort of trance.

'True, I do need to recharge from time to time, especially with some of the things you get us involved in.'

'I'm sorry about that Phen.'

'Do not be, I am enjoying our association very much.'

'Me too Phen, but that's not the only thing that puzzles me. You have passed to me these wonderful powers; which sustain me beyond my wildest dreams but what sustains you? For instance, you don't drink or eat as I do?

'I get my nutrients from your intake. The nutrients I extract from your foods are only a small percentage of your consumption but of only the purest kind. This means every single food and drink extract of yours I use, is used entirely. So, unlike you, I have no waste products to get rid of.'

'It's no wonder I'm hungry all the time. I was assuming it was because of all the energy I was using up, flying around etc.

'Your assumption is largely correct Jake. As I said, my consumption is only a small percentage of your intake, but PLEASE! DO CONSUME LESS JUNK.'

'I'll try Phen but I can't promise. God! This is how a woman must feel when she becomes pregnant. That thought Phen, it so happens, leads me nicely on to another thing I would like to know. How does your species reproduce?'

'We do not. As you know, our normal life span is about two hundred of your years. When that point is reached, we simply regenerate. Therefore, none of the intelligence, talent and knowledge that is built up over a life span is wasted. On the rare occasions that one of my species is killed, we do have an ancient gene bank we can call upon to replace that life. I am afraid, Jake, that I am one of those rare occasions. I have only had one re-generation. There are untold numbers of my species that are far more advanced than I. I would be considered a petulant youth on my planet.'

'I see, Phen. No worries though mate; I probably wouldn't get on so well with one of your more advanced people. God knows, I find it hard enough keeping up with you. Anyway, am I right in saying, because your population never increases or decreases, there is no need for you to acquire other planets?'

'Exactly, correct Jake.' Almost our entire reason for living is to acquire, more and more, of the three things already mentioned. Knowledge, intelligence and skills, but Jake what I am learning through you, and through my petulant insistence on paying your planet a visit, is that my species are in danger of becoming too insular.'

'How come?' I ask.

'Well, by being content to keep this vast build-up of knowledge etcetera; strictly within the bounds of our own planets.'

'So, you Phen, as an individual, do think your people should invade other planets, in order to spread these skills beyond your own borders?'

'Not exactly, arriving here in vast numbers would do no good at all. Besides you know we are totally against violence. It is not possible to persuade the people of your or any other planet, to alter their ways by force. It can only be done in the way we are doing it, by persuading them that there is a better alternative. For example, John & Ken.'

'But surely Phen, what you are doing here with me could be done on a much larger scale?'

'Possibly Jake, but my elders, so to speak, would not agree to such a thing, and I have to admit, I agree with them. It would not do to have more than one person going around with super powers. They are content to only add my experiences here with you to their bank of knowledge. From my point of view, if that helps in some small way to make them less insular; so much the better.'

'So, what you're doing Phen, is using me to achieve YOUR goals?'

'No Jake! Definitely not! I am merely providing you with the powers to assist you in achieving YOUR goals, and in being the person I know you to be; which of course, is why I chose you in the first place!'

I give an internal smile and nod of understanding, then think, 'You don't fool me Pal. I think you like being the only one of your people here.'

-The End-

Till the next time.

[Look out for more of Jake and Phen's escapades, in book two.]

Printed in Poland
by Amazon Fulfillment
Poland Sp. z o.o., Wrocław